Praise for the Immortals Series
by Alyson Noël

"Alyson Noël surpassed all my expectations. Not only is *Blue Moon* an amazing sequel; it sets the bar for the rest of this series very, very high! When I reached the last page of this one, all I could say was 'wow!'"
—*Teens Read Too*

"Noël's novel is absolutely amazing! Fans of her Immortals series will not be disappointed—Ever and Damen's love is challenged like never before, and the story ends with a big, satisfying twist that will have readers begging for more. This long-awaited installment is incredible."
—*Romantic Times* (Top Pick)

"It is the mark of a daring writer to defy expectations, and Alyson Noël does that to the power of ten in *Blue Moon*. I guarantee you will have no idea what's coming in the second book of the series while Alyson Noël surprises you with a big, fat twist and leaves you wanting more, more, more."
—*The Book Chick*

"A mesmerizing tale of teenage angst, love, and sacrifice with plenty of crossover appeal . . . The startling but satisfying ending shows that Noël knows how to keep her audience hooked. Ever's supernatural struggles are a captivating metaphor for teenage fears about love, relationships, and growing up."
—*Publishers Weekly* (starred review)

"*Blue Moon* was incredible. If you thought *Evermore* was full of suspense and unknowns, just wait until you read *Blue Moon*. . . . The plot was insane, and I mean that in a good way. Noël took this novel in a direction I was never expecting, resulting in an emotional rollercoaster ride that I never wanted to end. Fabulous."
—*The Story Siren*

"Beautiful main characters, tense budding romance, a dark secret, mysterious immortals—what more could you ask from this modern gothic romance?" —*Justine Magazine*

"When I got a copy of *Evermore*, I sat down to read it, intending to only read a chapter or two. Instead, I blazed through the first hundred pages before I knew it . . . and then I didn't want to put the book down. Except I couldn't keep my eyes open any longer. So I picked it up the next morning and finished it. Now I can't wait till July for the second book, to see what happens next." —*Blog Critics Magazine*

"Get ready for a wild ride that is filled with twisting paths and mystery, love and fantasy. . . . The writing style, story, and characters are a bit like Meyer's and Marr's popular books, but written with a new twist and voice. And after reading the book, you too will probably want your own Damen, even if it means making the ultimate sacrifice." —5 / 5 stars! *The Book Queen*

"Readers who enjoy the works of P. C. Cast and Stephenie Meyer will love this outstanding paranormal teen-lit thriller." —*Midwest Book Review*

"I found myself unwilling to put the book down, even though I had to at some points, because I wanted to know what was going to happen. . . . Ever was so real and her emotions were so believable that it was a little creepy. It's like Alyson Noël is actually a grieving, lovestruck teenager. She got Ever completely perfect. And by perfect, I mean delightfully flawed and deep." —*The Frenetic Reader*

"*Evermore* is a wonderful book that I believe would be a lovely addition to any library. . . . Definitely a book that fans of Stephenie Meyer and Melissa Marr should add to their collections. Definitely engaging and will catch your attention the minute you open to the first page!" —*Mind of a Bibliophile*

"Alyson Noël creates a great picture of each and every character in the book. I am a fan of the Twlight series and I recommend this book to those who like the series as well. It is a very quick read, with all the interesting twist and turns." —*Flamingnet Book Reviews*

"I loved this book. It really keeps your attention thoughout the story, because the puzzle gets pieced together bit by bit, but you don't know exactly what happened until the end. The only thing that disappoints me is that the second book won't be published for a while. I would definitely recommend this to my friends." —*Portsmouth Teen Book Review*

"This is the first installment of the Immortals series. Ms. Noël pens a well-detailed story that makes it easy for the reader to visualize both the characters and the world around them. *Evermore* has a familiar theme that attracts readers, but inside this book you'll find that the author has added some unique details that sets it apart."
—*Darque Reviews*

"*Evermore*'s suspense, eerie mystery, and strange magic were interestingly entertaining. . . . I found Ever to be a character I could really respect. . . . Recommended." —*The Bookworm*

"*Evermore* was a great way to lighten my reading load this winter and provided me with a creative, magical story that I really enjoyed. This is the first in a series for Noël and I think she may have a hit on her hands. . . . *Evermore* has good and evil, likable characters, vivid descriptions, and a good story." —*Planet Books*

"I fell into it easily, and loved the world Noël created. . . . The fact that Ever had psychic powers was truly interesting. They flowed neatly through the book and I felt Ever's pain. Trust me, this book was really good. I couldn't put it down. Alyson Noël created an amazing new world, and after this book I am so curious to see where it heads because honestly, I have no idea." —*Reading Keeps You Sane*

"Ever is an easy character to like. I really felt for her because of all she lost and what she struggled with daily. . . . *Evermore* was a really fast, engaging read with some great characters. It is the first in a series, so I'm eager to see if we will learn more about Ever, Damen, and friends in the next one . . . it's sure to be a great read." —*Ninja Reviews*

"The writing here is clear, the story well-defined, and narrator Ever has an engaging voice that teens should enjoy." —*January Magazine*

"*Evermore* is a fresh and original work that . . . branches out and explores new ground. Definitely recommended." —*Cool Moms Rule!*

"I totally LOVE Alyson Noël's *Evermore*. . . . Noël has delivered a deliciously fresh new series that will be the next new thing that has every teen and even adults everywhere hooked and waiting for more. . . . This is a keeper and a book that you have to go out and buy right now because if you don't you will be missing out. People will be asking if you have been living under a rock if you don't give *Evermore* a try, and that is just not acceptable." —*Talk About My Favorite Authors*

Also by Alyson Noël

alyson noël

Night Star

🦁 st. martin's griffin ⚏ new york

NIGHT STAR. Copyright © 2010 by Alyson Noël, L.L.C. All rights reserved. Printed in the United States of America. For information, address St. Martin's Press, 175 Fifth Avenue, New York, N.Y. 10010.

www.stmartins.com

ISBN 978-0-312-59098-7

First Edition: November 2010

10   9   8   7   6   5   4   3   2   1

For Bill Contardi—

Best. Agent. Ever.

acknowledgments

Once again, big, sparkly, major thanks are owed to the St. Martin's team: Matthew Shear, Rose Hilliard, Anne Marie Tallberg, Brittany Kleinfelter, Katy Hershberger, Angela Goddard, and everyone else who contributes so much!

Also, huge thanks to the Brandt & Hochman team: Gail Hochman, Bill Contardi, & Marianne Merola, for all that you do!

And, to my foreign publishers—thank you for all your hard work on the Immortals' behalf!

I'm also incredibly grateful for the love and support of my family and friends (you know who you are!), with a special shout out to Jim & Stacia—those once a month dinners provide the *perfect* diversion!

And, as always, much gratitude goes to Sandy, because I really, truly couldn't do it without him!

But, most of all, I want to thank my readers—you guys are THE ABSOLUTE BEST!

When it is darkest, men see the stars.

—Ralph Waldo Emerson

Night Star

one

"You'll never beat me. You'll never win this one, Ever. It's impossible. You can't do it. So why waste your time?"

I narrow my gaze and peer into her face—taking in her small, pale features, her dark cloud of hair, the absence of light in her hate-filled gaze.

My teeth clenched tightly, voice low and measured, I say, "Don't be so sure. You're running a serious risk of overestimating yourself. In fact, you *are* overestimating yourself. I'm one hundred percent sure of it."

She scoffs. Loudly, derisively, the sound of it echoing throughout the large empty room, bouncing off the plank wood floors to the bare white walls, meant to scare, or at the very least intimidate and throw me off my game.

But it won't work.

Can't work.

I'm too focused for that.

All of my energy concentrated down to one single point, until everything else fades away and it's just me, my readied fist, and Haven's third chakra—also known as the solar plexus chakra—the home of anger, fear, hate, and the tendency toward putting too much emphasis on power, recognition, and revenge.

My gaze narrowed on its location like a bull's-eye, right smack dab in the center of her leather-clad torso.

Knowing that one quick, well-directed jab is all it'll take to reduce her to nothing more than a sad bit of history.

A cautionary tale of power gone wrong.

Gone.

In an instant.

Leaving nothing behind but a pair of black stiletto boots and a small pile of dust—the only real reminder that she was ever here.

Even though I never wanted it to get to this point, even though I tried to work it out, tried to reason with her, to convince her to come to her senses so we could move toward some kind of understanding—cut some kind of deal—in the end, she refused to give up.

Refused to give in.

Refused to let go of her misguided quest for revenge.

Leaving me with no choice but to kill or be killed.

Leaving me with no doubt of how this one ends.

"You're too weak." She circles. Moving slowly, carefully, her gaze never once leaving mine. The stiletto heels of her boots assaulting the floor as she says, "You're no match for me. Never were, never will be." She stops and places her hands on her hips, head cocked to the side, allowing a stream of glossy dark waves to fall over her shoulder and hang well past her waist. "You could've let me die months ago. You already had your chance. But you chose to give me the elixir instead. And now you regret it? Because you don't approve of what I've become?" She pauses long enough to roll her eyes. "Well too bad. You have only yourself to blame. You're the one who made me this way. I mean, what kind of creator kills her own creation, anyway?"

"I may have made you an immortal, but you took it from there," I say, the words firm, deliberate, ground out between clenched teeth, despite Damen having coached me to stay quiet, stay focused, to make it swift and clean, and not unnecessarily engage her in any way.

Save your regrets for later, he said.

But the fact that we've found ourselves here means there is no *later* where Haven's concerned. And despite what it's come to, I'm still determined to get to her, to reach her, before it's too late.

"We don't have to do this." My gaze locks on hers, hoping to convince. "We can stop right here, right now. This doesn't have to go any further than it already has."

"Ha, you wish!" she sings, gleefully mocking. "I can see it in your eyes. You *can't* do it. No matter how much you think I deserve it, no matter how much you try to convince yourself of that, you're too soft. So what makes you think it'll be any different this time around?"

Because now you're dangerous—and not just to yourself, but to everyone else as well. This time is different, entirely different. As you're about to see . . .

Curling my fingers so tightly my knuckles instantly blanch, I steal a second to center myself, find my balance, and replenish my light—just as Ava taught me to do—while keeping my hand low and steady, my gaze fixed on hers, my mind cleared of all extraneous thoughts, face cleared of all extraneous feelings—as Damen recently coached.

The key is to give nothing away, he claimed, *to move quickly, with purpose. To get the deed done before she has the chance to ever see it coming—won't even realize what hit her 'til it's way past too late.*

Until her body has disintegrated and her soul's moved on to that bleak, dreary place.

Refusing her even the slightest opportunity to make a move or fight back.

A lesson learned on a long-ago battlefield that I never thought would apply to my life.

But even though Damen warned me against it, I can't keep from apologizing. Can't stop the words *forgive me* from coursing from my mind to hers. Seeing her respond in the flash of pity that tempers her gaze before it's quickly diminished by the usual mix of hate and disdain.

Her fist rising—aiming for me—but it's too late. Mine's already in motion, moving forward, in full swing. Slamming right into her solar plexus, sending her reeling—spinning—shattering—headed straight into the infinite abyss.

The Shadowland.

The eternal home for lost souls.

Aware of my own sudden intake of breath as I watch how quickly she disintegrates. Fragmenting so easily it's hard to imagine she was ever once solid form.

My gut churning, heart crashing, mouth so dry and parched no words will come. My body reacting as though what just happened before me—the act I just committed—wasn't just a game of make-believe, but the horrifying real deal.

"You did well. You were right on target, right on your mark," Damen says, crossing the room in a fraction of an instant, his warm, strong arms sliding around me as he pulls me close to his chest. His voice lilting softly in my ear as he adds, "Though you seriously might want to lose the *forgive me* part until after she's gone. Trust me, I know you feel bad, Ever, and I can't say I blame you, but it's like we've discussed, in a case like this, it's either *you* or *her*. Only one can survive. And if you don't mind, I prefer it to be *you*." He runs the tip of his finger down the length of my cheek, tucking a stray chunk of long blond hair behind my ear, before he adds, "You can't afford to give her any sign of what's to come. So please, save the apology for after, okay?"

I nod and pull away, still fighting to steady my breath. Glancing over my shoulder at the pile of black leather and lace on the floor. All that remains of the Haven I manifested, before I blink it away and erase every trace.

Stretching my neck from side to side, and shaking out each of my limbs in a move that could be taken as either letting off steam or preparing for more, Damen choosing to interpret it as the latter when he smiles and says, "So, another go then?"

But I just look at him and shake my head. I'm done for the day. Done with pretending to kill off the ghostly, soulless form of a former best friend.

It's our last day of summer, our last day of freedom, and there are much better ways for us to spend it.

Taking in the sweep of longish, wavy dark hair that spills across his forehead and falls into those amazing brown eyes, before drifting over the bridge of his nose, the angle of his cheekbones, to the swell of his lips, where I pause long enough to remember how wonderful they feel against mine.

"Let's go to the pavilion," I say, my eyes eagerly searching his before moving on to his simple black tee, the silk cord bearing the cluster of crystals that hides underneath, all the way down to his faded denim jeans and the brown, rubber flip-flops on his feet. "Let's go have *fun*," I reiterate, taking a moment to close my eyes and manifest a whole new costume change for myself. Swapping out the T-shirt, shorts, and sneakers I wore to train in, for a replica of one of the more beautiful, low-cut, corseted gowns I sometimes wore in my Parisian life.

And all it takes is one look at his clouded gaze to tell me it's as good as done. The lure of the pavilion is pretty much impossible to resist.

It's the only place where we can truly touch without the interference of the energy shield—where our skin can meet, and our DNA mingle, without any imminent danger to Damen's soul.

The only place where we can disappear into another world that holds none of the dangers of the one that we live in.

And even though I no longer resent the limitations of our life here, no longer pay it much notice now that I know it's a direct result of my making the *right* choice, the *only* choice, that my choosing to make Damen drink Roman's elixir is the only reason he's still with me today—the only thing that saved him from an eternity in the Shadowland—I'm happy to accept his touch in any form that it comes.

But still, now that I know there's a place where it gets so much better than this, I'm determined to get there, and now would be good.

"But what about practice? School starts tomorrow and I don't want you to get caught off guard," he says, obviously struggling to do what's noble and right even though it's clear that our trip to the pavilion is as good as done. "We have no idea what she's planned, so we have to prepare for the worst. Besides, we haven't even gotten to the Tai Chi yet, and I think we really need to. You'll be amazed at the way it helps to balance out your energy—recharging it in a way that—"

"You know what else is good at *recharging* my energy?" I smile, allowing him no time to answer before my lips meet his, willing him to just say the word so we can go to a place where I can kiss him for real.

The warmth of his gaze filling me with a glorious swarm of the tingle and heat only he can provide. Pulling away as he says, "Fine. You win. But then you always do, don't you?" He smiles, his gaze happily dancing with mine.

Grabbing hold of my hand and closing his eyes, as the two of us step through a shimmering veil of soft golden light.

two

We land in the middle of the field of tulips, surrounded by hundreds of thousands of gorgeous red blooms. Their soft red petals glinting in the ever-present, hazy glow, their long green stems swaying in the breeze Damen just manifested on his own.

The two of us lying on our backs as we gaze up at the sky, summoning a group of clouds overhead and shaping them into all manner of animals and objects simply by imagining it, before we clear it all away and head inside. Plopping side by side onto the large, white, *marshmallowy* couch, my body settling deep into the cushions as Damen reaches for the remote and snuggles beside me.

"So, where do we start?" he asks, brow lifted in a way that tells me he's just as eager to begin as I am.

I curl my feet underneath me and rest my head on my palm, gazing flirtatiously when I say, "Hmmm . . . that's a tough one. Tell me, what are my choices again?" My fingers creep under the hem of his shirt, knowing that soon, very soon, I can touch him for real.

"Well, there's your Parisian life, which, as it just so happens you're already dressed for." He nods, motioning toward the deep neckline of my dress, his gaze lingering at the plunging décolletage, before he meets my eyes again. "Then of course there's the Puritan life, which, I have to be honest, really wasn't one of my favorites . . ."

"Does it have anything to do with the clothing? All those dark, drab colors and high necklines?" I ask, remembering the ugly dresses I wore in those days, how uncomfortable they were, how the fabric scratched against my skin, and knowing it definitely isn't one of my favorites either. "Because if that's the case, then you must've really liked me in my London life as the spoiled daughter of a wealthy land baron with an amazing wardrobe full of sparkly, low-cut dresses and gowns, and piles and piles of amazing shoes." Knowing that's definitely one of my faves, if for no other reason than the sheer simplicity of my everyday existence back then, where, for the most part, all of the dramas I faced were ones I instigated all on my own.

He looks at me, eyes grazing over my face as his hand smooths my cheek—that insistent energy veil stubbornly vibrating between us, but only until we pick a scene.

"Well, if you must know, I have to say that I'm most partial to Amsterdam. Back when I was the artist, and you were the muse, and—"

"—and I spent most of my time partially nude, covered only by my long red hair and the slightest slip of silk." I shake my head and laugh, not the least bit surprised by his choice.

"But then I'm sure that's not the *real* reason, is it? I'm sure that's merely a coincidence, *right*? I mean, surely you were mostly interested in the artistic aspects of it more than anything else . . ."

I lean toward him, distracting him with a quick kiss to the cheek as I snatch the remote right out of his hand. Seeing the way his expression changes to one of mock outrage, as I enjoy myself with an impromptu game of keep-away.

"What're you doing?" he asks, concern moving in as he makes a more serious attempt to seize the remote right back.

But I won't give up. Nor will I give in. If for no other reason than the fact that every time we come here he's in control of this thing, and for once, I'd like to be the one who gets to surprise him.

I hold it up high above my head, switching it from one hand to the other, determined to keep it well out of reach. Breathing a little heavier from the effort as I look at him and say, "Well, seeing how it's so impossible for us to agree on a favorite, I figure I may as well just push a random button and see where we land . . ."

He looks at me, his face gone suddenly pale, his eyes grim. His whole expression, heck, his whole entire *demeanor* transformed in a way that's so stricken, so serious, and, to be honest, such a complete overreaction to what the situation warrants, I'm *this* close to handing over the goods when I suddenly change my mind and click it instead.

Mumbling something about his typical male need to control the remote, as the screen springs to life with an image of—

Well—something I've never seen before.

"Ever!" He gasps, voice low, steady, but there's no mistaking the urgency. "Ever, please, just give me the remote—I—"

He reaches for it again, but it's too late, I've already slipped it under the cushion.

Already secured it from him.

Already seen the images that play out before me.

It's—it's the antebellum South. And while I'm not exactly sure where, I can tell by the houses, the way they're constructed in a way I think is called Plantation Style—and by the way the atmosphere changes, the sky appearing hot, bright, and incredibly muggy in a way I've never seen or felt before in any of my other lives, that it's the Deep South. Like an "establishment shot" in a movie—a picture that clues you in to where you are in the story.

Then, just as quickly, we're inside that same house. Focusing on a close-up of a girl who stands before a window she's supposed to be cleaning—but is staring out of instead, her face soft and dreamy.

She's tall for her age, narrow shouldered and slim. With gleaming dark skin and long lanky limbs that seem to go on for miles before ending in a pair of skinny ankles that peek out from the hem of her plain, cotton dress. A garment that's so well worn it's obviously been mended again and again. But it's pressed and clean, just like the rest of her, and even though I can only view her in profile since she's turned to the side, I see that her long dark hair spirals the back of her head in a complicated series of knots and braids.

Though it's not until she turns, turns in a way where I can clearly see her face—that I look straight into those deep brown eyes and realize—

I'm looking at me!

I gasp—the sound of it echoing off the rounded white marble walls as I stare into a face so young and so beautiful, yet marred by an expression that's saddened way beyond her/my years. And a moment later, when a much older white man appears, the meaning of it all soon becomes clear.

He is the master. I am his slave. And there is no time for daydreaming here.

"Ever, *please*," Damen begs. "Just hand me the remote, *now*, before you see something you'll regret—something you'll never be able to erase from your mind."

But I don't hand it over.

I can't do that just yet.

I'm compelled to watch this strange man I don't recognize from any of my lives, take great pleasure in beating her—*me*—for the simple sin of dreaming of a better life.

I'm not there to hope, or dream, or anything of the sort. I'm not there to imagine faraway places, or a love that will save me.

There is no saving me.

No better place.

No love will come.

This is how I live—this is how I will die.

Freedom is not for my kind.

And the sooner I get used to it, the better, he tells me—repeating himself with every lash of his whip.

"How come you never told me?" I whisper, my voice low, almost inaudible. So struck by the images before me, watching as I withstand the kind of beating I could never have imagined until now. Absorbing each and every blow with barely a shudder, with a vow of absolute silence and dignity I'm determined to uphold.

"As you can see, it's not one of your romantic lives," Damen says, voice hoarse with regret. "Parts of it—like the part you see now—are extremely unpleasant, and I haven't had time to edit this one, or go over it in any way. That's the only reason I've kept it from you. But as soon as I do, I promise to let you see it. Believe it or not, there were happy moments. It wasn't always like this. But, Ever, *please,* do yourself a favor and turn it off before it gets any worse."

"It gets *worse?*" I turn, my eyes clouded with tears for the helpless girl before me—the girl I used to be.

But he just nods, retrieves the remote from under the cushion, and promptly shuts it off. Leaving the two of us sitting there, quietly shaken by the horrors we viewed only a moment before. Determined to break the lingering silence, I say, "And the rest of my lives—all of those scenes that we like to revisit—are they edited too?"

He looks at me, brows merged with concern. "Yes. I thought I explained that the first time we came here. I never wanted you to see anything as upsetting as that. There's no use reliving the trauma of things we can't change."

I shake my head and close my eyes, but it doesn't do anything to stop the brutal images that continue to play in my mind. "I guess I didn't realize it was *you* who edited it, I guess I thought *the place* somehow did it—like Summerland wouldn't allow anything bad to creep in—or—*something—*"

I drop the thread, choosing to let it just dangle instead. Remembering that dark, rainy, creepy part I once stumbled upon, and knowing that like the yin and the yang, every dark has its light, including Summerland it seems.

"I built this place, Ever. Made it especially for you—for *us.* Which means I'm the one who edits the scenes." He turns the remote back on, careful to choose a more pleasant view of the two of us sneaking away from a ball in full swing. A happy moment from the frivolous London life I'm so fond of—an obvious attempt to lighten the mood, to banish the dark we both just relived—but it doesn't quite work. Once seen, those horrifying images are not so easily removed.

"There are many reasons we don't remember our previous lives when we reincarnate—and what you just experienced is definitely one of them. Sometimes they're just too painful to deal with—too hard to get over. Memories are haunting things. I should know, I've been haunted by more than a few of my own. For over six hundred years."

But even though he motions toward the screen, motions toward a much happier version of me, it's no use. There's no immediate cure for what I now know.

Up until that moment, I was sure that my life as the lowly, Parisian servant was as bad as it got. *But an actual slave?* I shake my head. I'd never even imagined such a thing—never saw that one coming. And, to be honest, the brutality of it took my breath away.

"The point of reincarnation is to experience as many different lives as possible," Damen says, tuning in to my thoughts. "It's how we learn the most important lessons of love and compassion—by *literally* walking in each other's shoes—which, ultimately become our own."

"I thought you said the point was to balance out our karma." I frown, struggling to make sense of it all.

He nods, gaze patient and kind. "We develop our karma by the choices we make, by how quickly—or slowly—we learn what really matters in the world—how swiftly we can succumb to the *real* reason we're here."

"And what's that?" I ask, my mind still adrift. "The *real* reason, I mean?"

"To love each other." He shrugs. "No more, no less. It sounds simple enough, as though it should be rather easy to do. But one good look at our history, including the history you just saw, and I think it becomes clear what a difficult lesson that is for so many."

"So, you were trying to shield me from this?" I ask, my curiosity starting to niggle at me. Part of me wanting to see more, to see how she/I got through it—and part of me knowing that anyone who learned to withstand a beating like that, with such silence and dignity, had already lived through far too many of them.

"Despite what you saw, I want you to know that there were bright spots for sure. You were so beautiful, so radiant, and once I managed to get you away from all that—"

"Wait—you *rescued* me?" I gaze at him, eyes wide, as though I'm looking upon my very own Prince Charming. "You had me *freed*?"

"In a manner of speaking . . ." He nods, but his gaze wavers, his voice goes tight, and it's obvious he's more than ready to move away from all this.

"And, were we . . . *happy*?" I ask, needing to hear it from him. "I mean, really and truly happy?"

He nods. Giving me a quick lowering and rising of his head, but it's all that he gives.

"Until Drina killed me," I say, filling in the parts he's unwilling to share. It was always she who hastened my death, so why would a slave life be any different? Noting the way his face goes grim, and his hands begin to fidget, but still choosing to press ahead when I add, "So, tell me, how'd she do it this time? Did she push me in front of a carriage—throw me off a cliff—drown me in a lake—or did she try something totally new and different?"

He meets my gaze, obviously preferring not to answer, but

correctly assuming I won't give up until I hear it from him, he says, "All you need to know is that she never repeated herself." He sighs, face solemn and grave. "Probably because she enjoyed it too much, enjoyed thinking up inventive, new ways." He winces. "And I suppose she didn't want me to get suspicious. But listen, Ever, even though what you saw was unbelievably tragic, in the end, I loved you, and you loved me, and it was wonderful and glorious for as long as it lasted."

I look away, determined to absorb it, to take it all in. But it's a lot. Too much for right now, that's for sure.

"So, will you show me someday?" I face him again.

Seeing the promise in his gaze when he looks at me and says, "Yes, but first give me some time to edit it, okay?"

I nod, seeing the way his shoulders droop, the way his jaw loosens, and knowing that that was pretty much as hard for him as it was for me.

"But for now, what do you say no more surprises? Why don't we go somewhere happier—better—*funner*, if you will?"

I sit there for a moment, feeling so alone with my thoughts it's as though he's not there.

Soon roused by the sound of his voice at my ear, saying, "Hey look, they're getting to the good part—what do you say we become them?"

My gaze switches to the screen, where a very different version of me smiles radiantly. My glossy, dark hair sparkling with a collection of pins and jewels made specifically to match my beautiful, hand-sewn, emerald green dress. Seeing the way I hold myself with such confidence—so sure of my beauty, my privilege, my right to dream all I want, to *obtain* all I want, to *claim* anyone I want—including this dark, handsome stranger I've only just met.

The one who makes the whole string of suitors I left back inside seem dreadfully dull in comparison.

A version of *me* that's so opposite to the one I just saw a moment ago it hardly makes sense. And even though I'm determined to revisit that other *me* again soon, for now it can wait.

We came here to have a last bit of summer fun, and I'm going to make sure that we do.

Our hands clasped together, we rise from the couch and head for the screen, not stopping until we merge and meld, and become one with the scene.

My Parisian dress instantly replaced by an emerald green gown made especially for me, my lips nipping at the hard edge of Damen's jaw, flirting, teasing with the tip of my tongue, before spinning on my heel, lifting my skirts, and leading him deeper and deeper into the darkest part of the garden, to a place where no one can find us—not my father, not the servants, not my suitors, not my friends . . .

Wanting nothing more than to kiss this dark and handsome stranger, who always seems to appear out of nowhere, who always seems to know what I'm thinking, who thrilled me with his tingle and heat from the very first look.

The very first moment he peered into my soul.

three

"Shouldn't you be thinking about leaving for school soon?"

I twist the top from my bottle of elixir and glance toward the kitchen table where Sabine sits. Seeing the way her shoulder-length blond hair is tucked snugly behind her ear, the way her perfectly coordinated makeup is flawlessly applied, the way her suit is pressed and clean and immaculately put together without an odd crease or stray wrinkle in sight—and I can't help but wonder what it's like to be her. What it's like to live in a world where everything is so orderly, so obedient, so methodical, so tidily arranged.

Where every problem has a logical solution, every question an academic explanation, and every dilemma can be summed up in a simple verdict of *innocent* or *guilty*.

A world where everything is black and white and all shades of gray are promptly whisked away.

It's been so long since I've lived in that world, and now after all that I've seen, there's no way I'll ever reside there again.

She continues to stare, face stern, mouth grim, about to repeat herself when I say, "Damen's driving me today. He should be here soon."

Noting the way her whole body stiffens at the mere mention of his name. She insists on blaming him for my sudden fall from grace even though he was nowhere near the store that day.

She nods, her gaze slowly moving over me. Scrutinizing, carefully taking note of every last detail, starting from my head and working all the way down to my toes, before heading back up and starting again. In search of bad omens, flashing lights, hazard signs, anything warning of trouble ahead. The kind of telltale symptoms her child-rearing books have all warned her about, but getting little more than an image of a lightly tanned, blond haired, blue eyed girl in a white summer dress and no shoes.

"I hope we won't have any more trouble this year." She brings her mug to her lips and peers at me from over the top.

"And just what kind of *trouble* would you be referring to?" I ask, hating the way the sarcasm creeps so easily into my voice, but still more than a little tired of her always putting me on the defensive.

"I think you know." Her words are clipped, her forehead creased, as I take a deep breath and try not to roll my eyes in a way she can see.

Torn between feeling completely heartbroken that it's actually come to this—the long list of daily recriminations that can never be erased—and feeling completely infuriated by her refusal to accept me at my word—accept what I say as the truth, that this is who I really, truly am, for better or worse.

But still just shrugging when I say, "Well, then you'll be

happy to know that I don't drink anymore. I gave all that up not long after the suspension. Mostly because it wasn't working out for me all that well, and even though you probably don't want to hear this, probably won't even believe it, it was dulling my *gifts* in the very worst way."

She bristles. Physically *bristles* at my use of the word *gift*. Having already pegged me as a sad, pathetic, attention-starved phony, who's obviously crying out for help—she's really come to hate my use of the word more than anything. Hates that I refuse to back down, that I refuse to succumb to her side.

"Besides," I say, tapping my bottle against the counter, my gaze narrowed on hers, "I've no doubt you've already convinced Munoz to spy on me and submit a full report at the end of each day." Regretting the words the moment they're out, because while it may be true of Sabine, it's really not fair to Munoz. He's been nothing but nice and supportive toward me, and has never once made me feel bad about being the way I am. If anything, he's seemed intrigued, fascinated, and surprisingly informed. Too bad he can't seem to convince his girlfriend of that.

But still, if she's so unwilling to accept me for me, then why should I be so quick to accept the fact that she's in love with my old history teacher?

Except that I should.

And not only because two wrongs pretty much never make a right, but because, despite what she may think and despite what I may say, at the end of the day, all I really want is for her to be happy.

Well, that, and for her to move past all of this so that we can get back to how we once lived.

"Listen," I say, before she has a chance to react, knowing

I need to defuse the situation from getting any worse than it already has. Before it has a chance to escalate into one of the many screaming matches we've had since she caught me giving her friend a psychic reading under the alias of Avalon. "I didn't mean that. Really. I'm sorry." I nod. "So, can we just please call a truce here? One where you accept me, I accept you, and everyone lives happily ever after, in joy and peace and harmony and all that?"

I look at her, my gaze practically begging for her to give in, but she just shakes her head and mumbles under her breath. Something about me needing to come straight home from school from now until she decides otherwise.

But even though I love her—even though I'm grateful for all that she's done—there will be no restrictions, no groundings, nothing of the sort. Because the fact is, it's not like I *need* to live here. It's not like I *need* to put up with this stuff. I have options—*lots and lots* of options. And she has no idea just how far I go to make it seem like I don't.

Pretending to eat when I no longer need to, pretending to study when it's no longer necessary, pretending to be just like any other normal seventeen-year-old girl who's dependent on the adults in her life for food and shelter and money and pretty much her entire well-being—when I'm not even close to being that girl. I'm about as far from that as one could possibly get. And it's my job to make sure she never discovers any more than she already has.

"How about this," I say, swishing my elixir around and around, watching as it sparks and glows as it runs up and down the sides. "I'll make a concerted effort to stay out of trouble and out of your way—if you'll agree to do the same. *Deal?*"

She looks at me, brows merged, obviously trying to

determine if I'm being sincere or making some kind of threat. Lips pursed for a moment, long enough to gather her words before she says, "Ever—I—I'm just *so worried* about you." She shakes her head and runs her finger along the rim of her mug. "Whether you want to admit it or not, you are *deeply, deeply* troubled, and I'm at my wit's end on how to handle you, how to reach you, how to help you—"

I slam the lid back on my bottle, my last ounce of goodwill dissolving like *that*. Gaze narrowed on her when I say, "Yeah, well, maybe this'll help. One—if you really want to help me as much as you say you do, you could start by *not* calling me crazy." I shake my head and slip my sandals onto my feet, sensing Damen pulling into the drive, and not a moment too soon. "And two"—I toss my bag onto my shoulder and meet her glare with one of my own—"you could also stop referring to me as an *attention-starved, deeply troubled, needy fraud*—or some variation thereof." I nod. "Those two things alone would be a very good start toward *helping me*, Sabine."

Giving her no time to react before I storm out of the kitchen and out of the house, slamming the door much harder than I intended, but still just shrugging it off as I head for Damen's car.

Sliding onto the soft leather seat and squinting at him when he says, "So, this is what it's come to."

I follow the tip of his pointing finger all the way to the window where Sabine stands. Not bothering to peek through the blinds or even the crack where the drapes meet. Not trying to hide the fact that she's watching me—watching *us*. She just continues to stand there, mouth set, face stern, one hand on each hip, as she takes us both in.

I sigh, purposely avoiding her gaze in favor of his. "Just be glad I spared you the interrogation you would've gotten had you come in." I shake my head. "Trust me, there's a reason I told you to wait out here," I add, still drinking him in.

"She still at it?"

I nod and roll my eyes.

"You sure I can't talk to her? Maybe it'll help."

"Forget it." I shake my head, wishing he'd just back up the car already and get me out of this place. "There's no reasoning with her—she's completely *un*reasonable and, trust me, your trying to talk to her will only make it worse."

"Worse than the evil eye she just shot me from her perch at the window?" He glances between the rearview mirror and me as he backs down the drive, his lip curling in a way that's a little more playful than I'd like.

This is serious.

I'm serious.

And even though it may not be all that serious to him, it's still a pretty big deal to me.

But when I look at him again, I decide to let it go and cut him some slack. Reminding myself how the sheer breadth of his years, the expanse of his six centuries' worth of living, has left him more or less unfazed by the smaller, everyday dramas that always seem to take up so much space.

As far as Damen sees it, pretty much everything other than *me* slips into the "not worth the bother" category. To the point where it seems like the only thing he really cares about these days, the only thing he really focuses on, even more than finding an antidote so that we can finally be together after four hundred years of waiting, is protecting my soul from the

Shadowland. As far as he's concerned, everything else just pales in comparison.

And even though I really do get the big *pictureness* of it all, I can't stop caring about the "smaller" stuff as well.

And, unfortunately for Damen, the best way for me to make sense of it and sort it all out in my head, is to discuss it over and over again.

Believe me, you were spared, and spared big time. Had you insisted on coming in, it would've been way worse than that. The words coursing from my mind to his as I gaze out the windshield before me, amazed to see how unbelievably bright, hot, and sunny the day already is, even though it's only a few minutes past eight in the morning. And I can't help but wonder if I'll ever get used to this—if I'll ever stop comparing my new life in Laguna Beach, California, to the one I left behind in Eugene, Oregon.

If I'll ever be able to stop looking back.

My thoughts returning to the subject when Damen squeezes my knee and says, "Don't worry, she'll come around."

But even though his voice is confident, his expression tells otherwise. His words were based way more on hope than conviction—his desire to ease my mind easily trumps his desire for truth. Because the fact is, if Sabine hasn't come around by now, then it's highly doubtful she ever will, or at least not anytime soon.

"You know what bugs me the most?" I say, knowing he does, he's heard it before, but continuing anyway. "It's, like, no matter what I tell her, no matter how many times I try to *prove* it to her by reading her mind, and revealing all kinds of odd little nuggets about her past, present, and future that I couldn't possibly know if I *wasn't* psychic—it doesn't make a dent. In fact, it seems like it does just the opposite. Just convinces her to dig her heels in even deeper, absolutely *refusing* to consider any of my arguments, or anything else I have to say on the matter. She completely refuses to crack open her mind just the tiniest bit. Instead, she just shoots me that grim, judgmental look of hers, totally convinced that I'm faking, making the whole thing up in some big, pathetic bid for attention. Like I've totally and completely lost my mind." I shake my head and tuck my long blond hair back behind my ears, as my cheeks warm and flush. This is the part that really gets me going, leaves me all red faced and agitated every single time. "Even after I asked her why on earth I'd waste so much time and effort working that hard to keep my abilities a secret if I was only interested in the attention they'd get me—even after I begged her to listen to her own stupid argument so she could see how it doesn't make even the slightest bit of sense—she *still* refused to budge. I mean, she actually accused me of *fraud!*" I close my eyes and frown, remembering the moment so clearly it's as though it's happening right here before me.

Sabine barging into my room the morning after Roman died, the morning after I'd lost all hope of ever truly being with Damen, of ever getting the antidote. Not even giving me a chance to fully wake up, wash my face, brush my teeth, and prepare myself in some way.

Confronting me in a blaze of self-righteous fury, her blue eyes narrowed on mine, as she said, "Ever, don't you think you owe me an explanation for last night?"

I shake my head and clear the image from my mind. My gaze meeting Damen's when I say, "Because according to her, there is *no such thing as psychic powers, extrasensory perception, or anything else of the sort.* According to her, *no one* can see into the future. It's just a bogus claim made by a bunch of money-grubbing, unscrupulous, charlatan *frauds* like *me*! And I've been willfully engaging in *fraud* from the moment I took money for my first psychic reading. And, in case you didn't know, there are legal ramifications for that sort of thing, which, of course, she then took the pleasure of listing for me." I look at Damen, as wide-eyed and agitated as the first time I told the story. "So last night, when she had the nerve to bring it up *yet again*, I asked her if she could recommend a good attorney, seeing that I was headed for such big trouble and all." I roll my eyes, remembering how badly *that* went over.

My fingers nervously picking at the short hem of my white cotton dress as I balance my open bottle of elixir on my knee. Telling myself to calm down, to just let it go, we've been over this a gazillion times already and it only serves to make me more wound up than before.

Gazing out the window as Damen slows to a stop, allowing an older woman carrying a surfboard in one hand and a dog leash with a yellow Lab attached in the other, to make their way past. The dog reminding me so much of my old dog, Buttercup, with his wagging tail, shiny yellow coat, happy brown eyes, and cute pink nose, I actually do a double take, as that old, familiar pang curls its way through my gut—a constant reminder of all that I've lost.

"Did you remind her that she's the one who introduced you to Ava, which inadvertently led you to the job at Mystics and Moonbeams?" Damen says, bringing me back to the present as his foot switches from the brake to the gas.

I nod, peering into my side-view mirror, watching the

dog's reflection shrink smaller and smaller. "I mentioned it last night, and you know what she said?"

I look at him, allowing the scene to stream from my mind to his. Sabine at the kitchen counter, a pile of vegetables waiting to be washed and diced before her—me in my running gear determined to get out of the house without a hassle for a change—both of our tasks coming to a screeching, slamming halt when she decided to go for round fifteen in the never-ending battle of her versus me.

"She said it was a joke. A *party thing*. Meant for entertainment purposes only. That it was never meant to be taken seriously." I roll my eyes and shake my head.

About to say something more, not even close to the finish, when he looks at me and says, "Ever, if I've learned nothing else in my six hundred years of living, it's that people hate change almost as much as they hate for their beliefs to be challenged. Seriously. Just look at what happened to my poor friend, Galileo. He was completely ostracized for having the audacity to support Copernicus's theory that the earth wasn't the center of the universe. To the point where he was tried, found suspect of heresy, forced to recant, and then spent the rest of his life under house arrest, when, of course, as we all know, he was *right all along*. So, when you think about it, compared to that, I'd say you're getting off pretty easy." He laughs, giving me a look that practically begs me to lighten up and laugh too, but I'm just not there yet. Someday I may find this funny, but that day exists in a far-away future I cannot yet see.

"Believe me," I say, placing my hand over his, aware of the energy veil dancing between us. "She tried the whole house arrest angle, but no way was I going for it. I mean, it's really unfair how I'm supposed to just automatically accept her and the black-and-white world she chooses to live in, and yet, she won't even give me a chance to explain myself. Won't even consider my side of things. She just automatically pegs me as some crazy, needy, overly emotional teen because I just so happen to have abilities that don't fit into her close-minded views. And sometimes it makes me so mad I just—" I pause, pressing my lips tightly together, unsure if I should actually allow myself to really voice it out loud.

Damen looks at me, waiting.

"*Sometimes-I-just-can't-wait-for-this-year-to-be-over-so-that-we-can-graduate-and-go-somewhere-far-away-where-we-can-live-our-own-lives-and-be-done-with-all-this.*" I exhale the words so quickly they all run together so that one is practically indistinguishable from the next. "I mean, I feel bad for saying it, especially after all that she's done, but still, the fact is she doesn't even know the half of what I can do. All she knows is that I have psychic abilities—that's *it*! Can you even imagine how she'd react if I told her the *real* truth? That I'm an immortal with physical powers she can't even begin to fathom? Like the power of instant manifestation, and, oh yeah, let's not forget about that brief bout of time travel I engaged in recently, not to mention how I like to spend my free time in this charming little out-of-the-way alternate dimension called Summerland where my immortal boyfriend and I make out in our various past-life guises! Can you imagine how *that* would go over?"

Damen looks at me, eyes glinting in a way that instantly fills me with a swarm of tingle and heat, smiling as he says, "What do you say we don't find out, *okay?*"

He stops at the light and pulls me near. His lips grazing

my forehead, my cheek, down the length of my neck, until finally, finally, melding with mine.

Moving away just seconds before the light turns green, and glancing at me when he says, "You sure you want to go through with this?"

The warmth of his deep, dark gaze holding the look for just a tad longer than necessary. Allowing me plenty of time to say *no*, that I'm not at all ready, not even close, so he can turn the car around and head somewhere else. Somewhere nicer, friendlier, *warmer*—like a far-away beach or maybe even a Summerland retreat—a small part of him hoping I'll consent to just that.

He's over the whole high school scene. Has been for centuries. I'm the only reason he's here. The only reason he stays. And now that we're together, blissfully reunited after several painful centuries of being ripped apart over and over again, he just doesn't see the point to all this. Views it as some sort of useless charade.

And even though I don't always see the point either, since it's pretty hard to actually learn anything when the knowledge comes as easily as reading our teacher's minds or placing our hands on the cover of a book and intuiting the contents inside, I'm still determined to hang in there and see it all the way through.

Mostly because it's pretty much the only part of my totally bizarre life that's even the slightest bit normal. And no matter how bored Damen may get, no matter how often he begs me to just blow it all off so we can go start our lives instead, I won't do it. Can't do it. For some strange reason, I just really want us to graduate.

I want to hold that diploma in my hand and toss my cap in the air.

And today we're taking the first step toward that end.

I smile and nod and urge him to continue, seeing a flash of unease cloud his face, and returning the look with a new-found confidence and strength. Straightening my shoulders and scraping my hair into a ponytail that sits low on my neck, smoothing the wrinkles from my dress and preparing for the battle ahead.

Even though I'm not sure what's coming or exactly what to expect, even though I can't see into my own future as easily as I can everyone else's, if there's one thing I know for sure, it's that Haven still blames me for Roman's death.

Still blames me for *everything* that's gone wrong in her life.

And has every intention of making good on her promise to ruin me.

"Trust me, I'm *more* than ready." I gaze out the side window, scanning the crowd for my former best friend, knowing it's just a matter of time before she'll make the first move, and hoping I'll have a chance to turn it around before we both do something we'll no doubt regret.

four

It isn't until lunch that we see her.

Everyone sees her.

She's impossible to miss.

Like an unexpected swirl of icy blue frost—like an intricate icicle edged in sharp curves—she's as enticing, exotic, and startling as a surprise wintry chill on a hot summer day.

A large group of students swarm all around her—the very same people who looked past her before.

But there's no missing her now.

No missing her unearthly beauty, her irresistible lure.

She's not the same Haven she used to be. She's entirely different. Transformed.

Where she used to fade, she now glistens.

Where once she repelled, she attracts.

And what I used to think of as her standard black leather and lace, rock 'n' roll gypsy look, has been swapped for a sort of languorous, mesmerizing, slightly morbid glamour. Like an arctic version of a dark, mournful bride, she's dressed in a long body-skimming gown with a deep V in front, long floaty sleeves, and layer upon layer of soft, silky blue fabric that drags behind her, sweeping the ground, while her neck practically sags with the weight of jewels she's layered upon it—a combination of glossy Tahitian pearls, glittery cabochon sapphires, large roughly cut chunks of turquoise, and highly polished clusters of aquamarine, with long, jet black hair that hangs in glossy, loose waves trailing all the way down to her waist. The platinum streak that once marked her bangs now dyed the same deep shade of cobalt that graces her nails, lines her eyes, and glistens in the jewel that marks the space just above and between her finely arched brows.

A look the old Haven could've never pulled off; she would've been laughed out of school before the first bell could ring—but not anymore.

I mumble under my breath, as Damen reaches for me. His fingers grasping mine in what's meant to be a reassuring squeeze, but we're just as entranced as everyone else in this school. Unable to tear our eyes away from the sheen of her ultra pale skin, the way it gleams in a sea of black and blue. Resulting in an oddly fragile, ethereal look—like a freshly made bruise—completely belying the determination within.

"The amulet," Damen whispers, gaze briefly meeting mine, before returning to her. "She's not wearing it, it's . . . *gone.*"

My eyes instantly locate her neck, searching through the complicated tangle of dark, shining jewelry, only to see that he's right. The amulet we gave her, the one that was meant to keep her safe from harm, safe from *me*, is no longer there. And I know it's no accident, nothing of the kind. It's a message meant for me. One that's intended to scream loud and clear:

I don't need you. I've outgrown you. I've transcended you completely.

Having risen to a pinnacle of power of her very own making, she's now in a place where she no longer fears me.

Despite the fact that her aura is no longer visible, hasn't been since the night I had her drink from the elixir that turned her immortal like me, it's not like she needs one for me to *sense* what she's thinking.

To *know* how she's feeling.

Her grief over Roman, combined with her rage toward me, is what spawned this whole thing. She's completely guided, completely *redefined*, by an overwhelming sense of anger and loss, and is now seeking revenge on every single person who's ever once done her wrong.

Beginning with me.

Damen stops in his tracks and pulls me close to his side, allowing me one last chance to cry uncle and bail on this scene, but I won't. *Can't.* While I'm fully committed to letting her make the first move, the second she does I'll have absolutely no problem reminding her just who's in charge around here. It's what I've been training for. And while she may feel confident and sure of herself now, I happen to know something she doesn't:

She may feel strong, empowered, and completely invincible— but her powers can't even begin to touch mine.

Damen shoots me a worried glance, aware of the pierce of her gaze, little arrows of hate aimed straight at me. But I just shrug and keep moving, leading him toward our usual table, the one she surely thinks is beneath her, knowing that the hateful looks are just the beginning, something we'd better get used to if we've any hope of surviving the year.

"You okay?" He leans toward me, concern in his eyes, hand on my knee.

I nod, gaze never once leaving hers, knowing that if she's anything like Roman, she'll drag this thing out like a cat with a mouse, take her sweet time before she moves in for the kill.

"Because I want you to know that I'm *here*. I'll always be *here*. Even though we don't have any classes together, thanks to *you* I might add"—he shakes his head—"I want you to know that I'm not going anywhere. I won't cut, sneak out, play truant, or anything of the sort. I'll go to every last boring class on this godforsaken schedule of mine. Which means if you need me, all you have to do is call and I'll—"

"*Be there.*" I meet his gaze, but only for a moment before it returns to *her*. Watching as she revels in her position as the new queen of the A list, presiding over a table that just a few months before she wasn't even allowed to walk past, much less sit at. And I can only assume that Stacia and Honor decided to exercise their new senior year privilege of going off campus for lunch, since they would never allow this to happen if they were around, which only makes me wonder how they'll react when they return to find Haven has taken their place.

"Listen," I say, twisting the top from my elixir and taking a sip. "We've been over this, and I'm fine. I can handle it. I can handle her. *Really.*" I turn toward him, giving him a look that shows just how much I mean it. "We have an *eternity* together—just you and me and infinity." I smile. "So it's not like we need to sit next to each other in physics too, *right?*" My heart practically skipping when I see the way his eyes brighten, his mood lightens, and he smiles too. "You have no reason to worry about me. Between my meditations with Ava and my training with you—I'm like a new and improved, more powerful me! And I can handle Haven, believe me, I've no doubt about that."

He glances between us, his face a mask of apprehension, obviously struggling between his own nagging doubt and his desire to believe. Despite my continued assurances, his fears for my safety, his belief that he alone is to blame for setting this whole thing in motion the day he decided to *turn* me, is what keeps him from fully taking that leap.

"Okay, but one last thing—" He tilts my chin until I'm eye level with him. "Just remember that she's angry, powerful, *and* reckless—a dangerous combination if there ever was one."

I nod, not missing a beat when I reply, "Well, that may be true, but don't *you* forget that I'm *centered*, more *powerful*, and have way more *control* than she ever will. Which means she can't hurt me. No matter how badly she may want to—no matter how hard she tries—she won't win this one. Not to mention, I have something she doesn't—"

He looks at me, eyes narrowed, not anticipating this sudden change in the script we've rehearsed so many times.

"*You.* I have *you.* Always and forever, *right?* Or at least that's what you said last night when you were trying to ravish me in the English countryside . . ."

Oh, so it was me *trying to ravish* you? *You sure about that?* He laughs, closing his eyes as he presses his lips to mine, at first softly, gently, then with more urgency. Kissing me in a way that causes my entire body to ignite with the kind of tingle and heat only he can provide, only to pull away just as quickly, knowing we can't risk losing our focus this way.

These things can wait. Haven cannot.

I've barely had a chance to cool down and pull myself together again, when Miles steps out of the crowd, away from her table, and heads in our direction. Stopping just a few feet away, taking a moment for a quick spin around, allowing for the full, three-hundred-and-sixty-degree view of himself, before nailing the stop in a modelesque pose, complete with steely gaze, pouty mouth, and a hand perched on each hip.

"Notice anything different?" His eyes dart between us. "Because excuse me for saying so, but Haven's *not* the only one who had a transformational summer, you know?" He drops the pose and moves closer. "So in case you didn't hear me before, allow me to repeat myself. '*Notice. Anything. Different?*' He pronounces the words slowly, deliberately, taking time to enunciate each and every one.

And when I look at him—when *we* look at him—it's as though everything comes to a screeching, slamming halt. All breathing, blinking, and heartbeating is instantly replaced by sheer, awkward, open-mouthed gaping. Reducing us to nothing more than two frozen immortals, sitting side by side, wondering if we're gazing upon a third.

"So, come on, tell me . . . whaddya think?" Miles sings, doing another quick spin before landing yet another pose he's determined to hold 'til one of us speaks. "Holt didn't even recognize me."

What do I think? I think the word different *doesn't even begin to describe it.* My eyes dart toward Damen, before settling back on Miles again. *Heck, even* radically altered *or* completely transformed *barely cuts it!* I shake my head.

The brown hair he's worn cropped for as long as I've known him is now longer, wavier, almost like Damen's. And the baby fat that once padded his cheeks, making him look a good two years younger, has now vanished completely, paving the way for things like cheekbones, a square jawline, and a more defined nose. Even his clothes, which pretty much consist of the usual jeans, shoes, and shirt he always wore, somehow look entirely altered—different—nothing like before.

Like a caterpillar that decided to ditch his ratty old cocoon so he could show off his new and improved butterfly wings.

And just as I'm thinking the worst—sure that Haven got to him long before I could—I see it. *We* see it. His brilliant orange aura glowing all around him—the only thing that allows us to relax and get our breathing back on track.

Still taking a moment to process it all, unsure of even where to begin, I'm relieved when Damen says, "Looks like *Firenze* was good to you. *Very* good to you, in fact." He directs a smile toward Miles, while giving me a reassuring squeeze of his hand.

Miles laughs, his face lifting in a way that softens all those new edges. But then, just as quickly, it's gone, his aura wavering and flaring as he focuses on Damen, and that's all it takes for me to *remember*.

I guess I've been so caught up in my drama with Haven and Sabine I'd forgotten all about Damen and the portraits Miles uncovered of Drina and him.

Portraits that were painted centuries ago.

Portraits that bear no easy answers—no logical explanations of any kind.

And even though I vowed never to do it unless absolutely necessary, I think this is definitely one of those moments that constitutes an emergency. So while Damen's engaging him in small talk about *Firenze*, I quietly take a moment to peer into Miles's mind. Needing to see what he thinks, what he suspects, and surprised to see he's not at all focused on any of the things that I feared. Instead, he's focused on *me*.

"I'm disappointed," he says, interrupting Damen in favor of addressing me.

I cock my head to the side, having slipped out of his mind seconds before I had a chance to grasp just what he's truly trying to get at.

"I came home new and improved, as you can see." He runs his hand down the length of his body like a game-show model displaying the grand prize. "And I was pretty much planning for this to be my best year yet. But now I learn that my friends are *still* fighting, *still* not speaking to each other, and *still* forcing me to choose between them, even though I specifically warned them to get it settled before I returned, because no way will I play this game. No way will I be forced to play Meryl Streep in *Sophie's Choice*. I just won't. In fact—"

"Is that what she said?" I cut in, sensing that this particular monologue could go on 'til the final bell rings if I let it. "She said you had to *choose*?" Lowering my voice as a group of students file past.

"No, but then again, she didn't have to. I mean, I think it's pretty clear that if you're not talking to *her* and she's not talking to *you*, then I'm going to have to choose. Either that, or lunch just got even more awkward than it was last year." He shakes his head, his shiny brown locks waving softly from side to side. "And I will *not* tolerate that. I just won't. So, basically, you have between now and tomorrow to get it all figured out. Or I will be forced to brown bag it elsewhere. Oh, and just in case you're not taking me seriously, you should know that now that I have the keys to my mom's old car, you no longer have the carpool advantage. You and Haven are on equal footing as far as my affections are concerned. Which means you've no choice but to work it out, if you ever want to see me again, or—"

"Or *what?*" I try to keep my voice light, jokey, since I have no idea how to break it to him that if anything, knowing Haven, our problem will only have escalated by then.

"*Or* I'm going to find a whole *new* table and a whole *new* group of friends." He nods, glancing between Damen and me, wanting us to know he has every intention of making good on the threat.

"We'll see what we can do," Damen says, wanting just to move past it, past all of this.

"No promises," I add, eager to tone it down, keep it realistic, and not play into any sense of false hope he might have.

Assuming we're in the clear the moment the bell rings, Damen grabs my hand and starts to lead me toward class. Stopping when Miles taps his shoulder and says, "And *you*—" He pauses, long enough to carefully look him over from his head to his feet. "You and I will talk later. You've got some serious explaining to do."

five

I guess I'd been so focused on Haven I hadn't even thought about my other nemeses—namely Stacia Miller and her faithful sidekick Honor.

But by the time I slip into sixth-period physics, the door closing behind me the second the final bell rings, the sound of their muffled laughs and snickers is pretty much all the reminder I need.

I head straight for the middle, smiling to myself as I catch a glimpse of Stacia's shocked face as I claim the empty seat nearest them. I mean, why force them to strain their necks to get a good look when I can just as easily pick a desk that provides for a much better, far more clear, totally unobstructed view of their favorite object of torment—*me*.

But Stacia's the only one who seems shocked by my choice. Honor just takes it in stride. Sitting up a little straighter as she lifts her brow and looks me over, her gaze so guarded, so conflicted it's nearly impossible to decipher.

Nearly.

Though I'm far less focused on her expression than the thoughts that stream through her head. Thoughts she purposely directs right at me, correctly assuming I'm listening when she thinks:

I know you can hear me. I know all about you. And I know that you know what I plan to do to Stacia. How I plan to make her pay for every crappy thing she's ever done to me or anyone else unfortunate enough to get in her way. What I don't know is if you're planning to help me or stop me. But just in case you're planning to stop me, you really need to rethink it. For one thing, she's been a total bitch to you from the start, and for another, well, even if you do try to stop me, you can't. No one can. Not you, not Jude, and especially not Stacia, so it's best to not even go there—

And even though she's looking right at me, eager for some kind of reaction, some kind of acknowledgment that I've received her message loud and clear, I've no intention of giving her the satisfaction. No intention of listening to any more than I already have.

Between her pathetic, revenge-driven manifesto, Stacia's usual mean-spirited inner commentary, Mr. Borden's silent lament how yet again, another year of his life will be wasted on a fresh supply of ungrateful, incurious students—an embarrassing collection of bad haircuts and worse clothing, completely indistinguishable from those who came and went before—between all of that and everyone else's private dramas and angst—the din is too great.

Too depressing.

And totally depleting.

So I tune it all out in favor of a little cross-campus telepathy with Damen.

Sixth-period physics and so far so good, you? I think, preparing to raise my hand when my name is called for roll, used to being one of the first on the alphabetical list with a last name like Bloom.

Art. Great way to end the day—gives me something to look forward to. Wish the whole day could be one long art class. Oh, and Ms. Machado is thrilled to have me back. Told me so herself. Never before has she seen such talent, such a natural gift in someone so young. She even wants to set aside a time to speak to me about my future and which art schools I'm applying to.

What about me? Did she pass on a greeting to the most untalented, ungifted student she's ever seen? Or has she purposely blocked me from memory?

Don't be so hard on yourself—your replica of van Gogh was incredibly unique.

If by unique *you mean gawd awful, then yep, so true! Just make sure you tell her that I won't be back for round two. I need to keep my confidence up, to stay strong both mentally and physically, which means I can't take the risk of what another semester of horribly gloppy stick figures will do to my psyche. So, what's your first project? Another Picasso—your own rendition of van Gogh?*

He scoffs. *Impressionism is so last year. I thought I'd go really ambitious and maybe do a mural of some sort. Re-create the Sistine Chapel. You know, cover the walls and the ceiling and really spruce up the classroom a bit—what do you think?*

I think that's a great way to keep that low profile you're always going on about! I laugh, unaware that I actually laughed out loud until Stacia Miller peers at me, rolls her eyes, and sings, "*Looo—ser!*" under her breath.

And I immediately sign off. Knowing that if Mr. Borden's frowning face is any indication, I've just unwittingly put myself on his watch list. Having been pegged within the first

five minutes on the first day of class as one of the more particularly ungrateful troublemakers.

"Something funny, Miss—" He bows his head to peer at
the seating chart he's in the process of making. "—*Bloom*?
Something you'd like to share with the rest of the class?"

I steal a quick intake of breath and shake my head. Avoiding
Stacia's baleful glare, the amused quirk of Honor's brow, and
the bored sighs from the rest of my classmates who've grown
all too used to the always embarrassing display that is me.

Opening my new textbook, and reaching into my bag for
some paper and a pen only to find it chock full of tulips instead. Like a love letter from Damen, those red, waxy petals
serving as a reminder to hang in there, promising that no
matter what happens, our undying love is the real deal—the
only thing that matters in the midst of everything else.

I trace my finger along the stem, taking a moment to send
him a silent *thanks*, before manifesting the supplies that I
need. Closing my bag, confident that nobody saw, until I catch
Honor studying me closely, intently, just like she did that day
on the beach.

A deeply knowing kind of stare that leaves me wondering
just how much she knows about me.

And I'm just about to delve further, to peer into her mind
and get to the bottom of it, when she turns away, Mr. Borden
calls on me to read, and I slip into the role of ambitious student trying to get my bearings on my very first day.

"Hey, Ever, wait up!"

The sound comes from behind me, but I just keep going,
following my first instinct to ignore it.

But when she calls out again, I decide to stop and turn. Not the least bit surprised to find Honor running to catch up, though it's always odd to see her on her own without Stacia. Like she's suddenly missing an arm or a leg or some other essential part of herself.

"She's in the bathroom," she says, her brown eyes searching my face, answering the question she finds in my gaze. "Either reapplying her makeup, purging the fruit smoothie she slurped down at lunch, or thinking up new ways to blackmail the cheerleading squad—or heck, who knows, maybe all three." She shrugs, cradling a stack of books in her arms, calmly looking me over from my long blond hair to my pink polished toes.

"Which makes me wonder why you even bother?" I ask, doing the same. Taking in her long dark hair with the recent addition of red streaks, her black denim leggings, knee-high flat black boots, and the sheer knit cardigan that clings to the tank top beneath. "I mean, if you hate her so much, why go to all the planning and bother? Why not just let it go and move on with your life?"

"So you *can* read my mind." She smiles, keeping her voice so soft and low, it's almost as though she's speaking to herself instead of me. "Maybe someday you'll teach me how to do that."

"Doubtful." I sigh, veering *this* close to peering into her mind to see what this is really about, then reminding myself that it's wrong, that I need to be patient and let it unfold on its own.

"Then maybe Jude will." She lifts a brow, gazing at me as though it's a test—or maybe even some kind of thinly veiled threat.

But I just press my lips together and peer toward my locker, eager to dump all of the books I've already "read" and make my way toward Damen, who's waiting for me in his car. "Don't count on it," I say, preferring not to think about Jude in any way, shape, or form. Other than the odd text message here and there, just to check in and make sure he's still okay, still alive, and that Haven still hasn't gotten to him, we haven't really spoken since the night he killed Roman.

Since the night I was put in the awkward position of having no choice but to protect the one person I'm so angry with, I'm tempted to kill him myself.

"Last I checked, that wasn't really one of his *gifts*," I add, shifting my bag to my other shoulder and shooting her a look that says: *I'm not sure what your point is here, but if in fact you have one, then you really need to get to it!*

Prompting her to shrug and look away, focusing on nothing in particular, just grazing the hall as she says, "Don't you ever want to see her *pay* for all the crap that she's done?" She turns, regarding me seriously. "I mean, considering all the hell she's put you through, what with the suspension, the YouTube video—*Damen*—" She pauses dramatically, hoping for some kind of reaction, but she can pause all she wants, I won't be reacting anytime soon. "Anyway," she continues, the words hurried, having read my expression and knowing I'm *this* close to leaving. "I guess I'm just surprised you're not jumping on board. If anything, I thought you'd be first in line—well, maybe the second, you know, right behind me."

I take a deep breath, wanting more than anything to get out of here and on with the better part of my day, but still taking a moment to say, "Yeah, well, here's the thing, Honor, if you're gonna choose to look at it that way, then you also gotta admit that you've been pretty awful to me too." She shifts awkwardly, the movement slight but enough to convince me to continue. "In fact, you played a major part in my getting suspended, as you well know, and let's not forget that it was also you who stood right alongside her in Victoria's Secret the day she shot the video of me that ended up all over the Internet. And even if it wasn't your idea, even if all you did was stand by and observe, well, in the scheme of things, it's pretty much all the same thing. It doesn't make you any less guilty. Instead, it makes you *complicit*. Because not trying to stop a bully, and choosing to hang with a bully, pretty much makes you an *accessory* to everything that bully does in your presence. And yet, you don't see me harassing you or obsessing on getting revenge, do you? And you know why?" I pause, sensing her interest is way closer to waning than peaking, but forging ahead anyway. "Because it's *not worth it*. It's not worth my time or effort. That's what karma's for— to balance it all out in the end. Seriously, you really need to rethink this whole plan of yours. It's totally misguided and a total waste of your time. Because the fact is, it's not like you're all that innocent yourself, and these things have a way of boomeranging right back in ways you'll never see coming." I nod, unwilling to add that I happen to know this through my own, very recent, personal experience.

She looks at me, her eyes partially obscured by her bangs as she slowly shakes her head. "*Karma?*" She laughs and rolls her eyes. "Well, I hate to break it to you, Ever, but now you're starting to sound *a lot* like Jude, what with all of his good *mojo* and bad *mojo* talk. But, seriously, maybe you should ask yourself this—when was the last time karma took notice of

Stacia?" She lifts a brow. "Because in case you haven't noticed, she just goes through life doing *whatever* she wants to
whomever she wants. And while you may be fine with all that,
and while you may be comfortable playing the victim to her
never-ending crap, I'm over it. I'm sick of her games. Did you
know that she totally tried to hook up with Craig for no
other reason than to hurt me? To show me who's queen and
who's a permanent number two."

I gaze at her, not saying a word, the hall emptying out all
around us as everyone scrambles to leave. Everyone but us,
that is.

But Honor just continues, taking no notice of the time or
the fact that we should be getting out of here too. Her voice
low and deep when she adds, "Too bad for her, it didn't work.
But still, what kind of *friend* does something like that?"

"Is that why you guys broke up?" I ask, not really caring
either way. I already know the truth about Craig, about his
true *preferences,* I'm just wondering if she knows it too.

"No, we broke up because he's gay." She shrugs. "And
there's really no future in that for me. But don't tell anyone—" She looks at me, face panicked, eager to protect him
and keep his secret, but I just wave it away. I have no interest
in gossip like that. "Anyway, the thing is, while I'm truly
sorry about being—*complicit,* or whatever it is that you called
it, that's all over now. I have no plans to get in your way,
Ever. As long as you stay out of mine."

I squint, wondering if that was some kind of thinly veiled
threat. Just about to inform her that I have way bigger fish to
fry, that refereeing her popularity showdown with Stacia is
of absolutely no interest to me—when I see Haven.

Standing at the end of the hall, gaze entwining with mine

until everything dims but the chill of her energy, the sharp stabbing pierce of her limitless hate, and the curl of her summoning finger.

And the next thing I know, I'm off. Honor's voice reduced to a vague and distant hum as I chase after the train of Haven's azure-blue gown. Floating, beckoning, as she disappears around a corner, and I race to keep up.

six

I stand before the door, eyes closed, taking a moment to engage in one of the fast and simple mini-meditations Ava taught me in order to empower myself. Imagining a radiant white light coursing through my body and seeping through all of my cells, as my fingers anxiously seek the amulet I wear at my neck. The collection of crystals meant to keep me from harm and guard all of my chakras, especially my fifth—the center for the lack of discernment and a misuse of information—my one major weakness that, if targeted, will doom me to the infinite abyss.

Stealing a second to tune in to Damen, to let him know there's a good chance it's started, while also reminding him of his promise to stay put unless I specifically call out for his help.

Then I take a deep breath and push my way in, moving across the ugly pink tiled floor, stopping just shy of the row of white sinks that jut out from the wall. My posture relaxed, arms loose by my sides, watching as Haven kicks open the door of every last stall, making sure we're alone, before she turns, places her hands on her hips, cocks her head to the side, and shoots me an appraising look that does nothing to mar her newly enhanced face.

"And so begins senior year." She smirks, the sapphire marking the space just above and between her brows, catching the fluorescent light and glinting at me as she smiles in a way that doesn't quite reach her eyes. "How are you finding it so far? Your teachers—your classes—is it everything you dreamed it would be?"

I shrug, refusing to give her anything more, refusing to get caught up in her game. This is the kind of useless wordplay Roman loved to engage in, and if I didn't play it with him, I certainly won't indulge her.

She continues to study me, not the least bit daunted by my silence. If anything, it only encourages her. "Well, as for me, it's turning out even better than planned. I'm sure you've already noticed how popular I am. In fact, I can't decide whether to try out for cheerleader, run for class president, or both. What do you think?" She pauses, allowing plenty of time for me to weigh in, but when I don't, she just shrugs and continues. "I mean, let's face it, not to be all full of myself but there's really no doubt I can do anything I want now. Surely you've noticed the way people look at me, the way they follow me around. It's like—" Her eyes light up, her cheeks flush bright pink, and she wraps her arms around her middle, hugging herself in a burst of conceit. "It's like I'm a rock star or something—they just can't get enough of me!"

I sigh, loud enough for her to hear. Meeting her overconfident gaze with a look of complete and total boredom when I say, "Trust me, I've noticed." Instantly wiping the triumphant smile from her face when I add, "Too bad it's not real. I mean, you *are* aware of that, right? You're *making* it happen. You're deliberately luring them to you, robbing them of choice, of their own free will, just like Roman used to do. It's *not* the real deal."

She laughs, dismissing my words with a wave of her hand, walking in slow, deliberate circles, before she stops just before me and says, "Sounds like someone's been snacking on the sour grapes." She curls her lip and shakes her head. "Seriously. I mean, what's your deal, Ever? Feeling a little *jealous* because I finally made it to table A while you're still a big dork who's permanently stuck in loserville?"

I roll my eyes, remembering my old life in Eugene, Oregon, back when I was a walking, talking, popular cliché. And even though I used to miss it, missed the seeming simplicity of it—the rules of conformity that seemed so easy to follow at the time—I wouldn't go back to it for anything. It's not even the slightest bit tempting these days.

"Hardly." I gaze at her, my eyes narrowed. "Though I am surprised to see how much you've embraced it. I mean, considering how much you used to mock them and all. But I guess you only did that to hide the fact that you secretly wanted to be one of them. You pretended not to care when they snubbed you, when, apparently, you really did." I shake my head, shooting her a look of pity, which, if the look in her eyes is any indication, has only enraged her even more. "But I doubt that's why you summoned me here," I add, eager to get back on point. "So why don't you just go ahead and spill it? What is it that you're just dying to tell me that can't wait or can't take place somewhere other than this gawd-awful bathroom?"

I gaze at her patiently, waiting for her to begin, while silently repeating the promises I made to myself:

I will not start the fight.

I will not take the first swing, throw the first punch, or anything of the sort.

I will exhaust all other possibilities before it even has a chance to come to that.

I will not end her life unless my life or another's is threatened.

I will leave it to her to make the first move.

But when she does, well, from that point on, I'm no longer responsible for what happens to her . . .

She rolls her eyes and heaves an exasperated sigh, looking at me as though the view pains her when she says, "Oh, and now you're worried about getting caught loitering in the bathroom on your first day of school?" She clucks her tongue against the inside of her cheek as she lifts her hand to admire the stack of silver and blue rings she wears on each finger. "Why you insist on trying to act so *normal*—so ridiculously *ordinary*—is beyond me. I mean, seriously, you truly are the sorriest excuse for an immortal I've ever seen. Roman was right—both you and Damen are a complete waste of space." She exhales, forcing a gust of air from her lungs that sends a bitter chill through the room. "It's like, what could you possibly expect to get out of that? A gold star—a nicely framed certificate stating that yes, you are indeed the ultimate teacher's pet?"

She sticks out her tongue and crosses her eyes in a way that reminds me of the old Haven, the one who used to be my friend, but just as quickly it's gone when she says, "And even more importantly, why would you even care? Because in case you haven't noticed, the school rules are pretty much useless for people like us. We can do *whatever* the hell we want, *whenever* the hell we want, and *no one* can stop us. So not only do you need to lighten up and fugging unclench *as usual*—but you also need to put your sucking-up talents to much better use. Because if you're determined to get on any-one's good side, it should be *mine*." She quirks her brow, and stares right into my eyes. "I mean, you've already ruined Damen—ever since he hooked up with you he's like, destina-tion boring town." She takes a moment to grin at the remark. "Still, I am thinking of transferring into his fifth-period AP English class, and I'll probably even sit next to him if I do. Does that bother you?"

I shrug, busying myself with my nails, even though they're clean, smooth, unpolished, and so short there's not much to see. But I won't give in to her badgering, and I certainly won't give her the satisfaction she seeks.

But it's not like she cares, she'd much rather hear the sound of her own voice anyway, so she just forges ahead when she says, "I mean, on the one hand, he really has lost that exciting bad boy edge I loved so much—but on the other, I'm willing to bet he's still got a good bit of it somewhere buried down deep. Really, *really* deep." Her gaze gone spar-kly and bright as it lands on me. "Because when something's that *ingrained*, when something stretches all the way back through the centuries, well, it's hard to shake it completely, if you know what I mean."

Not only do I have no idea what she means, but no way of peeking into her mind to see for myself, since her shield is far too powerful for that. All I can do is just stand there and pre-tend not to care. Act as though her words aren't causing the slightest bit of curiosity or interest, even though I'm ashamed to admit that they are.

She knows something. That much is clear. This isn't just posturing on her part. She's onto something about Damen—about his past—and she's practically begging me to make her reveal it.

Which is exactly why I can't.

"I mean, as you've probably already guessed, Roman told me some pretty sordid stuff. Some of which you probably already know so there's no use going over it again, but then, just the other day, I was going through some of his belongings when I came across this whole stack of diaries." She pauses, allowing plenty of time for her words to sink in. "I mean, you should've seen it—it was like—*stacks and stacks* of them—entire boxes full. Turns out, Roman documented *everything*. Kept hundreds, hell, maybe even *thousands* of journals—I totally lost count. But anyway, from what I can tell, they stretch all the way back through the centuries. He wasn't just collecting antiques and artifacts—he was collecting history. *His* history. *The immortals'* history. There are photos, painted portraits, cards, letters—the works. Unlike Damen, Roman kept in touch. He didn't just move on with his life and leave the other orphans to fend for themselves, he looked after them. And after a hundred and fifty years passed and the elixir began to wear off, he made a new one—a *better* one. Then he tracked them all down and had them drink from it again. And he kept it up, through all those years, never once letting anyone down. Never once leaving anyone to flounder—or wither—or *die,* like Damen did. I mean, he may have had his issues with you guys, but then there's no doubt that he had good reason—you were his only enemies. The only ones who saw him as this horrible, evil immortal who deserved what he got. To everyone else, he was a hero.

He cared about them, offered them a better—*eternal*—life. Unlike the two of you, he believed in sharing the riches— and he did so freely—with those he deemed worthy."

I narrow my gaze even further, nearing the end of my patience and needing her to know it. "So why didn't he share it freely with *you*, then?" My gaze burns on hers. "Why the big game—why trick *me* into doing it?"

But Haven waves it away. "We've been over that, he was just having a little fun. I was never in any danger. He totally would've brought me back if he had to." She rolls her eyes and shakes her head, clearly annoyed by the interruption. *"Anyway,"* she says, putting major emphasis on the word, "about the diaries and photos and stuff—let's just say that some of it would be of *great* interest to you—" She pauses, obviously hoping I'll take the opportunity to beg to hear more.

But it's not gonna happen. Even though her words instantly remind me of something that both Roman *and* Jude alluded to when they hinted about some sordid secret in Damen's past—even though I can't help but think of yesterday in the pavilion when I stumbled upon the life Damen so desperately tried to keep hidden from me—I can't ask for more. Can't let her know that it's working—that I care—that her words have crept right under my skin. Can't let her win this one.

So, instead, I just lift my shoulders and sigh as though I'm bored beyond belief and couldn't care less if she says another word.

Which causes her to frown and say, "Whatever. It's not like you can fool me with all of your sighing and shoulder shrugging. I *know* you want to know, and I can't say I blame you. Damen's got secrets. Big, juicy, dark, and dirty secrets." She turns toward the mirror, leaning toward it as she fluffs her hair and admires herself, entranced by the sight of her own reflection. "But—I'm perfectly fine with saving all that for another day. I mean, it's not like I don't get your point—the past is the past and all that. Until the day it comes back to bite you in the ass anyway. But, whatever. I mean, he's just so tall, dark, and dreamy, who cares what atrocities he's committed over the course of the last several hundred years, *right*?" She quirks a brow and looks at me, tilting her head to the side and allowing her glossy dark waves to spill down the front of her dress. Moving toward me, slowly, deliberately, twirling a lock of hair between her fingers, doing her best to put me on edge.

"The only thing you should be concerned about right now is *your* future. Since, as we both know, it may not be *quite* as long as you originally anticipated. I mean, surely you no longer believe I'll let you hang around for *infinity*. Heck, you'll be lucky if I let you make it to the end of the semester." She stops just shy of me, her gaze taunting, gleaming, dangling the words before me like an apple before Eve—practically begging me to taste.

But I just swallow hard, making sure to keep my voice firm and steady when I say, "Damen and I have no secrets. And I know full well what Damen's heart is like—and it's good. So unless you have something more to say, I'm outta here—"

I make for the door, having every intention of leaving, of ending it before it can go any further, but before I can even reach it, she's there.

Arms crossed, face grim, eyes like slits when she says, "You're not going anywhere, Ever. I'm not even close to being done with you yet."

seven

I stare into her eyes, her face, knowing I have only a handful of seconds to make the choice between pushing right past her, getting myself outside, and allowing us both some much needed time to cool off—or staying right here and trying to reason with her, or at the very least, allow her to think that she "won" this one.

My silence providing all the encouragement she needs to pick up right where she left off. "You honestly mean to tell me that you and Damen have no secrets?" Her tone a perfect match for the sneer on her face. "Seriously? *None at all?*" She throws her head back and laughs, exposing a milky white neck littered with jewels, and the faint and flashing trace of a colorful Ouroboros tattoo. Reminding me of the one Roman had, and Drina before him, only Haven's is far smaller than theirs and easily hidden by her long mane of hair. Her confidence blown completely out of proportion, mistaking my stillness for apprehension and fear, when she says, *"Please."* She flutters her lashes. "Don't kid yourself, and don't even try to kid *me*. Six hundred years is an awfully long time, Ever. So long it's impossible for either of us to imagine. Though it is more than enough time to rack up a few dirty skeletons for the old metaphorical closet, *right?*"

She smiles, her eyes crazy, her energy so frenetic, so intense, so tightly wound, my only goal is to keep her in check. Keep her from starting something she'll surely regret.

"None of that concerns me," I say, careful to keep my voice low and steady. "Our past may shape us, but it doesn't define us. So there's really no point in lingering there any longer than necessary."

Trying not to wince when she scrunches her brow and veers toward me, her face so close to mine I can feel the blast of her chilled breath on my cheek, can hear the chime of her swaying jeweled earrings, the long strands of stones chafing against each other.

"True." Her eyes move over me. "But then again, some things *never* change. Some—*appetites*—just get bigger and bigger, if you know what I mean."

I move back toward the sinks, leaning my hip against one as I glance at her and sigh. Wanting her to know just how boring I find this, but she's not the least bit affected. She couldn't care less. This is her stage, I am her audience, and this particular show is far from over yet.

"I mean, doesn't it ever worry you?" She moves toward me, closing the distance between us in a handful of steps. "That you'll never be able to *truly* satisfy him in the way that *he*, well, that any guy for that matter, really and truly *needs?*"

I start to look away—*want* to look away—but something won't let me. *She* won't let me. Somehow she's locking my gaze.

"Doesn't it ever worry you that he'll get bored with all the abstinence and angst until he has no choice but to sneak off somewhere for a little . . . er, *relief,* shall we say?"

I breathe, just look at her and breathe. Concentrating on the light residing within me, and doing my best not to panic at this sudden loss of control.

"Because if I were you, I'd be worried. *Very* worried. What you're asking of him, well, it's just . . . *unnatural,* now isn't it?" She rubs her hands up and down her arms, shuddering as though it's too awful, too unimaginable, as though it somehow affects *her* more than me. "Still, I wish you all the best on that, for as long as it lasts anyway."

She releases me from her grip but continues to study me. Amused by the way I just involuntarily shook, the way I try not to let on just how much she's disturbed me.

Her lip pulling up at the side as she looks me over and says, "What's the matter, Ever? You look a little . . . *upset.*"

I concentrate on taking slow, deep breaths, once again weighing the choice between bolting and allowing her to carry this even further. Choosing to stay and hoping to put some sense back into her when I think: *Seriously, this is it? You summoned me into the bathroom so you can express your concerns about Damen and my sex life?* I sigh and shake my head as though I'm far too lazy to even summon the strength to say it out loud.

More like, lack-of-sex life. She laughs, meeting my gaze and rolling her eyes. "Trust me, Ever, as you well know, I've got much bigger things planned. And thanks to you, I have both the time and the power to see them through!" She cocks her head to the side and looks me over. "Remember what I said last time I saw you—the night you killed Roman?"

I start to refuse it but just as quickly force myself to stop.

There's no point in repeating it yet again. There's no changing her mind. Despite Jude's full-on confession, she still chooses to hold me equally responsible for that particular mess and there's nothing I can do about it.

"Just because you didn't deliver the blow doesn't make you any less *complicit*. Doesn't make you any less of an *accessory*." She smiles, allowing for a flash of blinding white teeth, as she revisits her door-kicking routine. Her words punctuated with a series of loud, crashing *slams* and *bangs* and *cracks* as she says, "Isn't that what you told your good friend Honor just a moment ago? Because the fact is, you were *right there* when he barged in and you did nothing to stop it. You just sat there and let it happen without making a single move to save him. And that makes you both *complicit* and an *accessory*. To use your own argument against you."

She stops and turns, her gaze meeting mine, waiting for the words to sink in, wanting me to know that she's not just keeping tabs on my conversations, but just might be capable of far more than that.

I lift my hands before me, palms facing her in a gesture of peace, hoping to defuse this before it's too late. "We don't have to do this." I regard her carefully. "*You* don't have to do this. There's no reason we can't just—*coexist*. No reason why you need to go through with this—"

But I can't even finish before her voice overrides mine, eyes darkening, face hardening, as she says, "Don't even bother. You won't change my mind."

She means every word of it. I can see it in her eyes. Still, the stakes are too serious, leaving me with no choice but to try. "Okay, fine. So you're determined to make good on your threat, and you think I can't stop you. Whatever. That remains to be seen. But before you do something you'll no doubt regret, you need to know that you're wasting your time. In case you don't get it, I happen to feel just as badly about what happened to Roman as you do. And while I know that's hard to believe, it's true. But even though I can't take it back, even though I was too late and too slow to stop Jude, I never meant for it to happen. I never *wanted* it to happen. In the end, I had a much better understanding of just who Roman really was, what made him tick, why he did the things he did. And because of it, I *forgave* him. That's why I went to see him, so I could explain to him once and for all that I was done fighting, that I wanted us to call a truce. And I'd just convinced him of it, we'd just agreed to work together, when Jude came in, misread the whole thing—and—well, you know the rest. But, Haven, I *never* saw it coming. If I had, I definitely would've stopped him. I never would've let it go down like that. By the time I realized what was happening it was too late to do anything to stop it. It was a tragic misunderstanding, but that's all it was. It wasn't sinister, it wasn't premeditated, it wasn't anything like you assume." I nod, not entirely convinced of that myself but still desperate to convince her.

Whether or not Jude really did misread the situation and was only trying to protect me—or if he had a much darker agenda in mind, stopping me from obtaining the antidote so that he could finally have a shot at me after hundreds of years of rejection, is something I've been mulling over and over since the night it all happened. And I still haven't reached a conclusion.

"He assumed I was in danger, in over my head, and ruled by dark magick. He acted purely on instinct, nothing more, nothing less. Seriously, you can direct all the anger you want at me, but please leave Jude out of it, okay?"

But even though I try my best to convince her, my words have no effect. They just roll right off her like rain down a windowpane, leaving a faint trace behind but refusing to penetrate in any real way.

"You want to protect Jude—that's your problem." She shrugs, as though he's as disposable as last year's boy band. "But I think you should know, there's only one way for you to accomplish that, and that's by making him drink. Otherwise, it's not a fair fight. He'll never survive it. He'll never survive *me*." She turns to the doors again, kicking one after another in such quick succession it's like a blur of speed and sound, while I shake my head and watch.

I have no intention of turning Jude or anyone else for that matter. But even if I can't convince her to leave him alone, there's still one last thing I can say. Something I'm sure she doesn't know, something that'll probably anger her even more, but still, she needs to hear it. Needs to know just what her so-called beloved Roman had planned.

"Here's the thing," I say, my gaze calm, even, wanting her to know I'm not the least bit impressed or intimidated by her door-kicking display. "The only reason I didn't tell you this before is because I didn't see the need, and I didn't want to hurt you any more than you already had been. But the fact is, Roman was planning to leave." My gaze bores into hers, seeing her flinch ever so slightly, but still enough for me to catch, enough to convince me to continue full speed. "He was headed back to London—*jolly old England* as he called it. Said this town was too slow, not enough action, and that there was no way he would miss it—*or anything in it.*"

She swallows hard and pushes her bangs out of her eyes. Two of her usual giveaways, proving she's not so new and improved after all, that a good bit of all the old insecurities and doubts have managed to survive. But still putting forth a show of false bravado, she says, "Nice try, Ever. Pathetic, but certainly worth a shot, right? Desperate people do desperate things, isn't that what they say? I figure if anyone should know for sure, it's *you*."

I lift my shoulders and clasp my hands before me as though we're just two good friends enjoying a nice friendly chat. "You can deny it all you want, but it still doesn't change the truth. He told me that night, told me all about it. He was feeling hemmed in, suffocated, said he needed to get away from it all. Go someplace bigger, more exciting—someplace where he could be free from the store, Misa, Rafe, Marco, oh, and of course, *you*."

She plants her hands on her hips, struggling to appear strong, tough, completely impenetrable, but her body tells otherwise, betraying her with the slightest bit of tremble.

"Oh, okay, sure." She scowls, drumming her hips with her thumbs and rolling her eyes dramatically. "So I'm just supposed to believe that Roman would choose to confess all of that to *you*, and yet totally fail to mention it to me, the person he was sleeping with? I mean, seriously Ever, this is totally pathetic and ridiculous—even for you."

But I just shrug, sure that it's working, that my words are getting to her. Looking her over, studying her closely, knowing I may be overstating it, embellishing a few bits here and there, but the gist is the same. He was planning to ditch her, and yet she's hell-bent on destroying Jude and me in his name.

"He knew you'd make a big scene if he told you, and you know how he hated that kind of thing. No one's saying he didn't like you, Haven, heck, I'm sure he liked you just fine. If nothing else, you were a pleasant enough way to pass the time. But make no mistake, Roman *didn't* love you. He *never* loved you. You even said so yourself. You remember when you said how in every relationship there's always one who loves more than the other—isn't that what you claimed? And then you even went on to admit that in your case it was you. That you loved Roman and he didn't love you. But it's not like it's your fault or anything. So don't take it too hard, or beat yourself up. Because the thing is, Roman was completely incapable of loving *anyone,* having never experienced it for himself. The closest he ever came to it were his feelings for Drina. But even still, that wasn't love. It was more like obsession. She was pretty much all he could think about. Remember his *dark drags* as you used to call them? The times when he'd lock himself in his room for hours on end? You know what he was doing? He was trying to reconnect with her soul, so he wouldn't feel so alone in the world. She's the only other person he ever really cared about in all of his six hundred years. Which, I'm sorry to say, pretty much reduces you to little more than yet another notch on his belt."

She's quiet, so quiet I start to feel bad, wondering if I've taken it too far, yet still driving the point when I say, "You're vowing revenge for the loss of a guy who was planning to ditch you at the first opportunity."

She glares, eyes narrowed to where I can just barely see them, brows merging together as the sapphire that marks her forehead emits a dark, eerie glow. And the next thing I know, all the faucets are gushing, the soap dispensers are pumping, the toilets are flushing, the hand dryers are blasting, while reams of toilet paper go sailing through the room and bouncing off the walls.

And even though it's clear that she's making it happen,

there's no way of telling whether it was intended or was the result of the out-of-control anger I've triggered.

But either way, it doesn't deter me. Now that I know that it's working, I have no choice but to continue.

I move along the row of sinks, calmly shutting each of the taps as I say, "It just doesn't make any sense—this whole revenge thing. Your big romance with Roman was nothing more than—well, as he would put it, *a couple of mediocre shags, mate.*" I look at her, indulging a small smile at my spot-on British accent. "So why waste your time on avenging a past that never really was, when you've got the future of your making all stretched out right before you?"

But I've barely had a chance to finish before she's on me.

Right on me.

Slamming me all the way across the room and into the pink tiled wall. Bashing my head against it so hard the awful dull *thud* of it echoes throughout the room, as a trail of warm blood drips its way from the gash where it cracked all the way down to my dress.

I stagger, lurch forward, only to fall back again. Reeling from side to side, struggling to regain my focus, my balance, but I'm so shaken, so woozy, so unsteady, I can't fight the fingers that push into my shoulders and pin me in place.

Her face hovering just inches from mine when she says, "Make no mistake, Ever, I'm not vowing revenge just *for* Roman—I'm vowing revenge *against* you." Her eyes bore into me, shooting me a look so hateful I can't help but turn away and close mine against it. Aware of the bite of her chilled breath on my cheek, her lips at the edge of my ear, as she takes a moment to rest against me and savor her victory.

The fixtures settling, the toilets calming, the dryers halting, as piles of soap seep slowly across the floor and into the grout, her voice a gruff, raspy whisper just inches away. "You've ripped away everything that's ever meant anything to me. You're also the one who made me this way. So if anyone's to blame here, it's *you*. *You* made me what I am. And now *you* decide that *you* don't like what you see and *you're* determined to stop me?" She leans back to better observe me, allowing her fingers to creep dangerously close to the amulet that hangs from my neck. "Well, too bad." She laughs, flicking the stones with her fingers and setting my whole body on edge. "You *chose* to feed me the elixir, you *chose* to turn me, you *chose* to make me exactly what I am, and now there's no going back."

She dares me to deny it, dares me with her gaze. But I can't meet it. I'm too busy willing the dizziness to end, too busy begging for the healing to begin. Struggling for each and every breath, the words ground out between gritted teeth. "You're not just delusional, but you're *wrong.*" I fill my lungs with air and surround myself with white light, knowing I need all the help I can get. This is not going at all as I'd planned.

Having mistaken her small stature for a lack of strength— having misjudged the power of hate, along with the live wire that strums inside her, fueling her with a seemingly endless supply of rage.

Careful to keep my face neutral, my tone steady, not wanting to alert her to my newly alarmed state. "I may have made you immortal—but what you do with that is entirely up to you." The words reminding me of the scene I manifested just yesterday, except this scene is nothing like the victorious one I'd rehearsed.

Then, just like *that*, I feel it. I'm back. My wound healed.

My strength returned. One look in her eyes tells me she senses it too.

And just like *that*, it's over.

She's already pushed me away.

Already made for the door.

Glancing over her shoulder to say, "Hey, Ever—before you go lecturing me on *forgiveness*, maybe you should do a little digging around. There's a ton of stuff you don't know about Damen—stuff he'd never choose to confide on his own. Seriously. You should look into it."

I don't respond. I should, I know, but the words just won't come.

My gaze is locked with hers when she adds, *"Forgiveness,* Ever. Think about it. So easy to preach—so difficult to practice. Maybe you should ask yourself if *you're* truly capable of it? Can you really forgive the sins of Damen's past? That's what I wanna know—and that's the only reason I let you live now. The only reason I'll let you hang around just a little bit longer. If nothing else, it'll be interesting to watch. But make no mistake, the moment you start to bore me or annoy me, well, you know the drill—"

And the next thing I know, she's gone.

Though her words continue to reverberate all around me.

Teasing.

Taunting.

Refusing to dissipate as I busy myself with washing the blood from my hair and manifesting a new dress to wear.

Readying myself to see Damen, who's no doubt still waiting for me.

Desperate to bury the evidence of what just went down, along with my own nagging doubts.

eight

"You sure you're okay with this?" I turn toward Damen, more than willing to let him join me if he wants but still hoping to handle this one on my own. Things between him and Jude are always so weird, and even though I totally get the reason behind it, I still prefer to lessen the tension whenever I can.

He nods, and one look in his eyes makes it clear that he is. His trust in me is complete, just as mine is in him.

"Do you want me to wait or come back later?" he asks, more than willing to do either one of those things.

But I just shake my head and gaze toward the store. "I don't even know how long it'll take. I have no idea what to expect." I scrunch my nose and lift my shoulders before dropping them again. "All I know is I can't avoid him any longer. Haven's serious about going after him, she's not about to back down. Trust me, she made that abundantly clear." I swallow hard and look away. Still shaken from the scene in the bathroom, still reeling from the force of her power and strength, not to mention her ability to surprise me, overwhelm me, and control me in a way I hadn't seen coming, and certainly hadn't rehearsed for. But when I look at Damen again, I know I'm doing the right thing by playing it down. He's freaked enough as it is, there's no need to make it any worse.

"I just—" I pause, searching for just the right words. Knowing how uncomfortable it must make him, the thought of me being alone with Jude, and wanting to make it clear that not only is it strictly business, but that I can totally handle myself where he's concerned. "I just need to convince him of the seriousness of all this. I also have to try to help him find a few ways to protect himself, even though, short of hiring an immortal bodyguard, I'm not even sure what good it'll do. But anyway, that's my goal, and I have no idea if he'll even agree to cooperate, much less listen to me. He could take me up on it, or he could kick me out within the first fifteen seconds and warn me never to return. Nothing would surprise me at this point."

Damen nods, his tone more knowing than jealous when he says, "Oh, I doubt he'll kick you out . . ."

He looks at me, leaving the thought unfinished, causing me to nervously fiddle with the hem of my dress. "Anyway." I clear my throat, desperate to move away from all that. "The point is, I can always just manifest a car or something when I need a way home. I'll just have to remember to ditch it as soon as I turn onto my street—don't want to give Sabine yet another reason to freak." I sigh, trying to imagine how I'd ever go about explaining something like *that*—my ability to manifest large, expensive, inanimate objects, then make them disappear at will. Looking at Damen when I add, "But here's the thing—"

He meets my gaze.

"As much as I appreciate this, and as much as I like being

with you . . . you don't have to do this. You don't have to chauffeur me to and from school every day or anywhere else for that matter. I'm fine. Really. And I'll continue to be fine. I can totally handle this. So . . ." I pause, hoping my words sound more convincing than they feel. "So please, don't waste any more energy worrying about me, okay?"

He smooths the leather-wrapped steering wheel with his thumbs, going back and forth, forth and back, the movement deliberate, rhythmic, then he says, "I can do everything on your list except *that*." He turns, allowing his gaze to bore into mine, looking at me in a way that makes my heart race, my cheeks flush, as my skin begins to tingle and heat. "I can stop chauffeuring you if that's what you want, but I could never stop worrying about you. I'm afraid that's just something you're destined to live with." He leans toward me, cupping his hands around the sides of my face, his touch so soothing, so calming, his voice low and deep. "So, tonight? Shall we visit our favorite Summerland haunt?"

I press my lips to his, softly, briefly, before pulling away. "I wish. But I think it's probably better if I take the night off from all that. You know, stay home, pretend to eat dinner, pretend to do my homework, and pretend to be completely normal in every conceivable way so that Sabine can start to relax, find another focus, and get on with her life—which will allow me to finally get on with mine."

He hesitates, still not convinced of his inability to fix this despite what I've said. "And would you like me to come over and pretend to be your perfectly normal boyfriend?" He arches his brow. "I can do a pretty good imitation of that. I've played the part many times, had over four hundred years of experience so far."

I smile, leaning in to kiss him again, longer, deeper this time. Lingering for as long as I can, before pulling away with a sigh. The words hurried, breathless, I say, "Believe me, I'd like nothing more. But Sabine wouldn't. So for now, I think it's probably better if you stay away for a while. At least until things calm down and have a chance to sort themselves out. For some strange reason, she's chosen to focus on *you* as the number one suspect to blame for my downfall."

"Maybe because *I am*." He looks at me, tracing his finger down the length of my cheek. "Maybe she's on to something without even realizing it. Ever, when you boil it right down to its very essence, to its very origins, I *am* the one who caused the change in you."

I sigh and look away, we've had this discussion before, and I'm still not quite willing to see it his way. "You—the near-death experience—" I take a deep breath and turn to him again. "Who's to say for absolute sure? Besides, it's not like it matters, it is what it is and there's no going back."

He frowns, clearly not willing to take my side but willing to drop it for now. "Okay," he says, almost as though talking to himself. "Maybe I'll stop by Ava's then. The twins started school today and I'm eager to see how it went."

I balk, trying to imagine Romy and Rayne navigating their way through junior high. Everything they know about modern American teenage life they learned either from my ghostly little sister Riley or reality shows on MTV—not the best sources, for sure.

"Well, hopefully for them it was way more uneventful than ours." I smile, sliding out of the car and closing the door between us, leaning through the open window when I add, "At any rate, tell them I said hi. Even Rayne. Or, should I say, *especially Rayne."* I laugh, knowing how much she dislikes me, and hoping that someday I'll be able to mend that—but knowing that day is still a long way away.

Watching as he speeds away from the curb, leaving me with a smile that lingers, circling all around me like a hug, before I enter the store on my own, surprised to find it dark and empty, with no one around.

I stand there and squint, allowing a moment for my eyes to adjust, before making my way toward the back. Freezing right there in the office doorway when I find him completely slumped over with his head on his desk.

And the second I see him I can't help but think: *Oh crap—I'm too late!*

I mean, just because Haven said she'd spare me for the time being, doesn't mean she'd extend the same courtesy to Jude.

Though just after I think it, I catch a reassuring glimpse of his aura and immediately relax.

Only living things have auras.

Dead things and immortals do not.

But when I notice the color, the blotchy, dull, brownish-gray haze that surrounds him, I can't help but think: *Oh, crap*, all over again.

As far as colors go, his is pretty much at the bottom of the aura rainbow; only black, the color of imminent death, could be worse.

"Jude?" I whisper, my voice so soft and low it's almost inaudible. *"Jude—are you okay?"*

He lifts his head so suddenly, so startled by my presence, he knocks over his coffee. Causing a milky brown trail to race across his desk, just about to spill over the side and onto the floor when he stops it with the long, slightly frayed sleeve of his white T-shirt—allowing the liquid to spread into the fabric, leaving a sizable stain.

A stain that reminds me of—

"Ever, I—" He runs his fingers over his tangle of golden-brown dreadlocks, blinking a few times until he's able to fully focus. "I didn't hear you come in—you startled me—and—" He sighs, gazing down at the desk and mopping up the rest of the spill with his sleeve. Then, noticing my speechless, wide-eyed gaping, he says, "Trust me, *this* is nothing. I can either wash it, toss it, or take it to Summerland and cure it." He shrugs. "A stained T-shirt is the least of my worries right now . . ."

I lower myself onto the seat just across from him, still shaken by the stain and the new idea it just spawned. Hardly able to believe I was so caught up with training and Haven and all the drama she's created that I hadn't even thought of it until now.

"What's happened?" I ask, forcing myself away from those thoughts and back onto him, though vowing to return to them as soon as I can.

Sensing that something terrible has happened and assuming it's more threats from Haven, when he says, "Lina's gone." The words simple, stark, though the meaning is clear.

I look at him, eyes wide, mouth open, but unable to speak and unsure what to say if I could.

"Her van crashed in Guatemala, on the way to the airport. She didn't make it."

"Are you . . . *sure?*" I ask, immediately regretting the words. It was a dumb thing to say, when it's so obvious that he is. But that's what bad news does—it creates unreasonable denial and doubt, prompting a search for hope in places where there clearly is none.

"Yeah, I'm sure." He wipes his eyes with his dry sleeve, gaze clouded with the memory of when he first heard. "I *saw* her." His eyes meet mine. "We had a pact, you know? We promised each other that whoever went first would stop by and tell the other. And the second she appeared before me—" He pauses, his voice tired, hoarse, prompting him to clear his throat and begin again. "Well, the way she just *glowed*, the way she looked so . . . *radiant* . . . there was no mistaking it. I knew she'd moved on."

"Did she say anything?" I ask, wondering if she decided to cross the bridge or stay behind in Summerland, since, unlike me, Jude can communicate with spirit in all of its forms.

He nods, his face beginning to lift ever so slightly. "She told me she was *home*. That's what she called it, *home*. Said there was so much to see, so much to explain, and that it's even better than the Summerland I told her about. And then, before she left, she said she'd be waiting for me when it was my turn—but not to hurry over anytime soon."

He laughs when he says it—well, as much as one can laugh when they're consumed by grief. And I swallow hard and gaze down at my knees, tugging on the hem of my dress, straightening the seam until it fully covers them. Remembering the first time I saw Riley in my hospital room, and how it seemed so dreamy and unreal I pretty much convinced myself that I'd somehow imagined it. But then it happened again—and again—and it kept on happening until I was able to convince her to cross the bridge to the other side—which, unfortunately, made her disappear from me forever. Making Jude my only connection to her.

I peer at him again, taking in his bleary aura, hollow gaze, and shaken face—so different from the cute, sexy, laid-back surfer boy I first met. And I can't help but wonder how long it'll take for him to return to that, or if he even can. There's no quick fix for grief. No shortcuts, no easy answers, no way to erase it. Only time can do that, and even then, just barely. If I've learned nothing else, I've learned that.

"Then, about an hour later," he continues, voice so low I have to lean forward to catch it, "I got the call that confirmed it." He shrugs and leans back in his seat, gazing at me.

"I'm so sorry," I say, knowing firsthand just how small those words are in the face of something so big. "Is there anything I can do?" Doubting there is, but extending the offer anyway.

He shrugs, busying himself with his sleeve, his long dark fingers rolling the wet fabric away from his skin. "Make no mistake, Ever, my grief is for me, *not* Lina. She's fine . . . *happy* even. You should've seen her—it was like she was headed off on her most exciting adventure yet." He leans back in his seat, smoothing his tangle of hair, gathering it all together and holding it briefly, before releasing it again and allowing it to spill down his back. "I'm really going to miss her. Everything just feels so empty without her. She was more a parent to me than my birth parents were. She took me in, fed me, dressed me, but most importantly, she treated me with respect. She taught me that my abilities were nothing to be ashamed of, nothing I should try so hard to deny. She convinced me that what I had was a *gift*—not a curse—and that I shouldn't let other people's narrow minds and fears determine how I live, what I do, or how I perceive myself in the world. She actually made me believe that in no way, shape, or form did their uninformed opinions make me a freak." He looks away, taking in the overflowing bookshelves, the collection of paintings on the wall, before returning to me. "Do you have any idea just how big a deal that was?"

He meets my gaze, holding it for so long I can't help but look away. His words instantly reminding me of Sabine, and how she took the exact opposite approach of Lina when she chose to blame me.

"You were lucky to know her," I say, my throat going all hot and tight, until it threatens to close up completely. I know all too well how he's feeling. My own family's death is never far from my mind. But I can't let myself go there—there's another crisis on the horizon and I need to focus all of my energy on containing it.

"But if you were serious about helping out—" He pauses, waiting for my assurance before continuing on. "Well, I'm wondering if you wouldn't mind watching the store. I mean, I know you don't really want to work here anymore, and believe me, I know how angry you've been with me lately, and trust me, I don't think for a minute that any of that will change because of this, but—"

I swallow hard. Swallow my words, knowing I have no real choice but to wait for him to continue. I came here not just to talk about Haven and all the ways he could go about protecting himself from her, but also to try to determine just what his intentions were the night he killed Roman.

What was he thinking?

What's the real reason he did what he did?

But now, after all this, there is no way that conversation is going to happen anytime soon.

"—there's just . . ." He shakes his head and breaks the gaze, squinting far into the distance when he says, "There's just so much to take care of—the house, the store, the funeral arrangements . . ." He takes a deep breath, takes a moment to compose himself. "And I guess I'm just a little over-whelmed at the moment. And since you already know how everything works around here, it would be a huge help if you could stay and close up. But if not, no worries. I can probably try Ava, or even Honor I guess, but since you're already here, and since you already offered—I just figured—"

Honor. His friend-slash-trainee Honor. Yet another topic we'll have to discuss at some point.

"Not a problem." I nod, eager to assure him. "I'm ready and willing to stay and work for as long as you need." Know-ing that if Sabine somehow finds out, it will *not* go over well, not in the least. But then again, it's really none of her business. And if she chooses to make it her business, well, she can't really fault me for helping a friend in his time of deep need.

Friend?

I look at Jude again, my eyes grazing over him, studying him carefully. No longer sure if the word still applies, or if it ever really did. We shared a past. We share a present. That's all I really know at this point.

He sighs and shuts his eyes, his fingers moving over the lids, past the spliced brow, before dropping to the desk and gripping the sides as he stands. Taking a moment to dig deep into the front pocket of his jeans, fingers fishing around until he finds the bulky ring of keys he tosses toward me.

"Do you mind locking up?" He makes his way around the desk as I rise to my feet, the two of us suddenly finding our-selves face-to-face, sharing an awkwardly close proximity.

Close enough for me to take in the depths of those blue-green eyes—to feel the lull and sway of the wave of calm his mere presence brings.

Close enough to prompt me to take a step back, an act that causes a flash of pain to flit across his gaze.

Waving my hand at the keys when I say, "I don't actually need those, you know."

He looks me over for a moment, then nods and pockets them again.

The silence lingering between us for so long, I'm desperate to break it when I say, "Listen, Jude, I—"

But when his eyes meet mine, his amazing aqua gaze reduced to a bottomless sea of loss, I know I can't even give him the summarized version of what he needs to know. He's far too consumed by his grief to care about Haven or the threats she promises to keep—far too depressed to even think about the best ways of defending himself.

"Just . . . just take all the time you need. That's all I wanted to say," I mumble, watching the way he moves, carefully, cautiously, allowing for a wide berth between us, working to avoid any sort of accidental physical contact with me.

But I know it's more for my benefit than his. His feelings for me haven't changed, that much is clear.

"Oh and Jude—" I call, noting how quickly he stops, though he refuses to turn. "Be careful out there . . . *please*?"

He nods, his only reply.

"Because later, when things have settled a bit, and you have some time, we really need to—"

Not even giving me a chance to finish before he's already making his way down the hall.

Discarding the words with a wave of his hand, as he moves through the dark store and into the daylight, disappearing into the warmth of the sun.

nine

By seven o'clock, the last sale has been rung, the front door locked, and I'm in the back room with my feet propped up on the desk, peering at my cell phone long enough to see that Sabine has left no less than nine messages, all of them demanding to know where I am, when I'll return, and what possible explanation I could have for flaunting her rules in such a deliberately blatant way.

And even though it makes me feel bad, I don't return the call. I just turn off my phone, stash it back in my bag, and blow it all off in favor of Summerland.

Stepping through that shimmering veil of soft, golden light and landing right on the front steps of the Great Halls of Learning. Hoping that, once again, it'll come through in a pinch and provide the answers I seek.

I stand before the door, breath caught in my throat, as I gaze upon the glorious, ever-changing façade of all the world's most beautiful and wondrous places. Watching as the Taj Mahal morphs into the Parthenon, which turns into the Lotus Temple, which becomes the great pyramids of Giza, and so on, until the doors swing open and I'm swept inside. Taking a moment to gaze all around, wondering if I'll run into Ava or Jude now that they both know how to get here, but not recognizing anyone, I settle onto one of the long wooden benches, slipping in amongst the monks and rabbis and priests, and various other seekers, before closing my eyes and focusing on the answers I need.

My mind rewinding to the exact moment when Jude's spilled coffee ran across his desk, just about to race over the side and down to the floor, when he stopped it with his sleeve. Allowing the liquid to seep into the fabric, to blend with the fibers, until it caused a big stain, much like the anti-dote stained Roman's white shirt.

Leaving behind a big blotch of green.

An imprint of sorts.

A combination of chemicals—a kind of recipe if you will—permanently embedded into those soft, cotton fibers.

Chemicals that if properly broken down will lead me to the formula for the antidote that I need—the only thing that will allow Damen and me to truly touch each other again.

While I once thought that all hope of claiming the cure died along with Roman—now I know better—now I know it lives on.

What I'd originally thought was lost forever—survives in the stain on his shirt.

The shirt Haven snatched right out of my hands.

The shirt I have no choice but to snatch right back if Damen and I are ever going to enjoy any kind of normal life together.

I take a deep breath, replacing the image of Jude's stained

T-shirt with Roman's white linen one, as my mind asks the question:

Where is it?

Soon followed by:

And how do I go about getting it?

But no matter how long I wait—no matter how many times I inquire—no answers come.

The stubborn silence ultimately growing into a message of its own.

An undeniable refusal to help.

Just because the Halls welcomed me, doesn't mean they're willing to assist. This isn't the first time they've denied me the answers I seek.

And I've finally come to realize it means one of two things: Either I'm delving into something that is none of my business, which really doesn't make any sense in this case since it's obviously very much my business, or I'm delving into something I'm not meant to know at this time or possibly any other, which, unfortunately, makes plenty of sense.

Something is always conspiring against us.

Something is always keeping us apart.

Whether it's Drina always killing me, Roman always tricking me, or Jude either intentionally or unintentionally sabotaging me—something is always standing in the way of Damen's and my ultimate happiness.

And I can't help but wonder if there's some kind of reason behind it.

The universe is not nearly as chaotic as it seems.

There's a definite reason for everything.

But when the Great Halls decide to shut you out, no amount of clever rephrasing can change that.

This one is on me.

It's my job to find the shirt. My job to determine if Haven even realizes what it is that she's keeping from me.

Is she holding it for sentimental reasons, because it's the last thing Roman wore on the night he died?

Does she keep it as a visual reminder that helps fuel her rage against Jude and me?

Or does she know about the stain and the promise it holds?

Has she known all along what I'm just discovering now?

All I know for sure is that without the aid of Summerland, I've got no choice but to head back to the earth plane to see what I can learn there.

And I'm just about to make the portal again, when I sense him.

Damen.

He's here.

Somewhere close by.

So, instead, I close my eyes and make one last request, asking for Summerland to lead me to him.

ten

The next thing I know, I'm making my way through the field of blazing red tulips, following the pull of Damen's energy all the way to the front door of the pavilion.

I pause just outside it, unsure if I should really go in. At first, thinking it odd that he'd come here without me, then figuring it's just his way of being near me when I'm busy elsewhere, I poke my head inside, barely making out the top of his head peeking up from the couch. Just about to call out, let him know that I'm here and share what I've learned about the shirt, when I see it.

The screen.

And the horrible scene that's projected upon it.

It's my Southern life.

My slave life.

Back when I was helpless and abused, but not without hope.

And on this particular day there seems to be an abundance of hope—at least, all things considered anyway. Because even though it takes me a moment to catch up to what's truly going on, one thing is clear—I'm being sold. Removed from my horribly abusive master so I can go work for a much younger man with dark wavy hair, a long, lean build, and heavily lashed eyes that I recognize immediately.

Damen.

He bought me. Rescued me. Just like he said!

And yet—if that's the case, then why do I look so sad? Why is my bottom lip quivering, my dark eyes tearing, on the day when my one true love, my soul mate, my knight in shining armor has come to save me from a life of drudgery?

Why do I look so unhappy, with shaking limbs and a gaze filled with fear—continually glancing over my shoulder while dragging my feet—so clearly reluctant to join him?

And even though I know it's wrong to spy, that I should speak up and let Damen know that I'm here, I don't. I don't say a word. I just remain right where I am. Quiet and still. Allowing only the shallowest breath, knowing this is *it*. The big thing he's been hiding all along—the same thing Roman and Jude hinted at, and Haven taunted me with. And if I want to get to the bottom of it, see the scene as real and raw as the day it all happened, I can't alert him to my presence. Though his inability to sense me proves just how engrossed he really is.

And it's not long before I see it—the real reason behind all the sadness. The real reason why I reacted the way I did.

I'm being pulled away from my family. From everyone I've ever loved. From the only circle of support I've ever known in the world.

This kind and wealthy white man may think he's saving me, committing some kind of noble, good deed, but one look at my face is all it takes to see that he's doing so at the expense of my only source of happiness.

My mother sobs in the background, as my father stands tall and silent beside her. His gaze is grief-stricken, troubled, though urging us all to stay strong. And even though I cling to them, hanging on with all that I've got, determined to seal the impression of their scent, their touch, their very being, it's not long before I'm pulled away from it all.

Damen grasping my arm as he pulls me toward him and away from my mother—my pregnant mother who anxiously embraces her large, swollen belly that shelters my unborn sister—pulls me away from my father, my family—away from the boy just behind them who reaches for me—the tips of our fingers just barely meeting, the touch cool and fleeting, before I'm yanked far out of his reach. Though my gaze refuses to leave him, my eyes remain steadfast, drinking him in, until the image is seared onto my brain—this lanky, black boy with the piercing brown eyes that instantly reveal who he is.

My friend—my confidant—my intended—the one I know in this life as Jude.

"Quiet now," Damen whispers, his lips at my ear, as my family is told to turn away and get back to work. "Hush now, please. Everything's going to be okay. I promise to keep you safe. As long as you're with me, no one can ever hurt you again. But first you have to trust me, okay?"

But I won't trust him. Can't trust him. If he really cared about me, if he's really as rich and powerful as he claims, then why can't he buy us all? Why can't he keep us together?

Why does he take only me?

But before I can see any more, Damen cuts the scene. Just cuts it right off. Instantly erasing it as though it never did exist.

And in that moment I know that this is what he means by *editing.*

He's not just sparing me from viewing uncomfortable scenes like my own gruesome deaths—he's sparing *himself*—the image he's worked so hard to craft—unwilling to allow me to witness his more shameful acts.

Like the one I just saw.

The one that may be erased but is forever sealed in my brain.

And I don't even realize I've gasped, don't even realize I've made any sound at all, until he leaps from the couch, his eyes wide, face frantic, when he finds me standing right there behind him.

"Ever!" he cries, voice choked with panic. "How long have you been there?"

But I don't answer. My expression alone is answer enough.

His gaze darts between me and the screen, as he rakes through his glossy, dark hair, the words rough, unsteady, when he drops his hands to his sides and says, "It's not what you think. I swear, it's—it's not at all what it appeared to be."

"Then why'd you cut it?" My gaze harsh, unforgiving, unwilling to bend even the tiniest bit. "Why'd you erase it, if not to hide it from me?"

"There's more to the story—much, much more and I—"

"You don't trust me?" I cut in, unwilling to hear his denials. Not when we both just watched the same, horrible thing. "After all that we've been through, after all that I've *shared* with you—you're still hiding things from me?" I fight to steady my breath as I press my hand flat against my belly, feeling more than a little sickened by this. "So tell me, Damen, just how far does this go—this *editing* of yours? What else could you possibly be hiding from me?" Remembering what Haven alluded to in the bathroom today and warning myself not to fall into her trap, not to let her divide and conquer us. Then dropping the thought just as quickly. I saw what I saw. The evidence played out before me clear as day.

"First you wait until the very last minute to tell me the truth about you and me and Jude—and now—*now this*?" I shake my head, still reeling from the vision of who I was and who he might still possibly be. "Is this some sort of sick game you're playing? Is this how you get your kicks? Tell me, Damen, just how many times, in how many lives, have you pulled me away from my family and friends?" He looks at me, face ashen, but I'm on a roll and there's no stopping me now. "I mean, there's the time we just saw, and there's this life, the one I'm in now . . ." I pause, knowing that's not exactly fair. I'm the one who lingered in the field of my own free will. I'm the one who was so entranced by the magick of Summerland I chose to stay back while the rest of my family moved on. But still, had he not fed me the elixir, maybe I would've eventually found them—maybe we'd all be together right now. And I'm so upset by my thoughts, by the images that refuse to stop playing in my head, that I can't decide which is better—for me to have died and joined up with my family—or for me to have lived so I can deal with all this.

I turn, legs shaking, heart crashing, needing to get out, get some air, no longer able to breathe in this room.

Damen's voice calling out from behind me, begging me to stop, to slow down, claiming that it can all be explained.

But I refuse to stop.

Refuse to slow down in any way.

I just keep on running.

Just keep on going until I've found my way home again.

eleven

"What the hell, Ever? You drop out of school and forget to tell me?"

I glance up from the register where I'm busy ringing up a sale, only to find Miles lurking behind my squinty-eyed, not-one-bit-amused customer.

Taking a moment to shoot him my very best *not now* look, as I charge her credit card and wrap her books and meditation CDs in some purple tissue paper, before I slide them into a matching bag and send her on her way.

"Nice one." I nod, the words competing with the bell clanking hard against the door as she leaves. "I'm sure we won't be seeing her again anytime soon."

Miles waves it away, dismissing the thought with a shrug as he says, "Whatever. Trust me, I've got *much* more important things to discuss than Jude's bank statement."

"Yeah? Like what?" I shove the receipt into the purple box where we store them, aware of Miles's gaze weighing heavily, waiting for me to acknowledge it so he can get on with the real reason for his visit.

"Well, like *you*, for instance." He watches me settle onto the stool, crossing my arms before me. Careful to keep my gaze neutral, expressionless, as though I'm not at all anxious or worried, as though I'm just patiently waiting for him to continue. "I mean, for one thing, except for the very first day, I've yet to see you at school. Which means you haven't been *going* to school, because as it just so happens, I've been looking for you. Waiting outside your classes, next to your locker, at the lunch table, but—*nothing, niente,* you *so* haven't been there."

I shrug, unwilling to confirm or deny—at least not just yet anyway. First I need to see just how strong a case he plans to build against me.

"And even though I'm sure you'll probably try to claim that you have your reasons, that your extended absence— your *super-sized summer* if you will—are pretty much none of my business, I just want you to know that you're wrong. It *is* my business. In fact, it is *very much* my business. Because, as your friend, as one of your *very best* friends, I'm here to tell you that your no-show silent treatment is affecting not just me but *all of us.* Even the people you don't consider your friends—believe it or not—it's affecting them too."

I shrug. Unsure what to say, but knowing it's not really time for that anyway. Miles loves nothing more than an extended monologue, and from the signs of it, this one is nowhere near coming to a close.

"You know, people like *me*—and *Damen*—and, well, maybe not so much Haven anymore, but still, never mind that, we'll get to it later. What I'm trying to say is that it's like you're just—" He pauses, thumbs hooked in the front tabs of his jeans as he gazes all around, searching for just the right word. Finally returning to me when he says, "It's like you're just totally ignoring us. Like you've *dismissed* us. Like you've *ceased* to even care about us—"

"Miles—" I start, pressing my lips together as I try to think of the best way to continue. "Listen, I get what you're saying. Really I do. And believe me, I totally get why you might see it that way, but trust me, there's *a lot* more to it than you might think. *Way* more than you could ever even begin to imagine. I mean, seriously, if I was to tell you the real truth behind all of this—" I close my eyes and shake my head, knowing that half the time I'm hardly able to believe it myself. "Anyway, I can't really get into it, but just trust me when I say that if you knew even a fraction of what was *really* going on, well, you'd definitely be thanking me for keeping you out of it." I pause, allowing enough time for my words to sink in, hoping he'll see just how serious I am. "And while I'm really sorry that you feel like I'm ignoring you, and that I don't care about you, it's not *at all* true. Seriously, not even a bit. You're pretty much the only real friend I have left at this point. And I really want to make it up to you, and I promise I will. Soon. *For sure.* But right now I'm just . . . I'm just a little . . . preoccupied, that's all."

"And what about Damen? You gonna make it up to him too?"

I look at him, not even trying to bury my shock. I mean, I cannot believe he's seriously choosing to confront me with that.

"Please don't assume you know more than you do," I say,

my voice a little harsher than I intended. "There's a lot more to it. Stuff you don't understand. Nothing is anywhere near as simple as it may seem on the surface, and believe me, this goes way beyond that—the roots are pretty dang deep."

He gazes down at the ground, digging the toe of his shoe into the carpeted floor, taking a moment to collect his thoughts, decide just the right way to confront me, before he lifts his head, looks me right in the eye, and says, "And would one of those *things* that I can't possibly understand have anything to do with the fact that you're—?"

Our eyes meet, leaving me frozen, unable to breathe. The word speeding toward me, crashing straight into my energy field before it can even leave his lips.

And there's nothing I can do about it, no way to rewind or stop him from saying:

"Immortal?"

His gaze locks on mine, and no matter how much I may want to, I can't look away.

My skin is prickled with cold when he adds, "Or is it the fact that you're *psychic*? Gifted with all manner of *mental* and *physical* powers. Or maybe it's the fact that you'll stay young and beautiful *forever. Never* aging, *never* dying, just like your sidekick Damen, who's been around for six hundred years and counting and who only just recently decided to turn you like him?" His eyes narrow, as his gaze sweeps my face. "Tell me, Ever, am I on the *right track*? Are these the *things* you were referring to?"

"How did—" I start.

But the words are drowned out by his voice when he says, "Oh, and let's not forget about *Drina,* who, as it turns out, was also *immortal*. And then, of course, there was Roman as well. Not to mention Marco, Misa, and Rafe—the three somewhat annoying tagalongs Haven's chosen to hang with for whatever unknown reason. And, I can't believe I almost forgot to mention the most recent addition to the gang of the eternally beautiful—our dear friend Haven herself. Or, should I say, *my* dear friend, your newfound immortal enemy—even though you're the one who chose to make her like you? Is this the kind of stuff I couldn't possibly begin to understand?"

I swallow hard, stunned into silence and unable to think of anything better to do than sit there and stare. And even though I mostly feel horrified to have it all laid out before me like that—the accumulated facts of my very strange life revealed in a way so neutral, so ordinary, it hardly seems real, even to me—there's also a small part of me that's relieved.

I've been carrying this secret for so long, I can't help but feel lighter, brighter, as though I've finally been freed of a burden that was far too heavy to bear on my own.

But Miles isn't finished. He's only just begun. So I shake my head and refocus on his words, struggling to keep up when he says, "And the ironic thing is, if you really stop and think about it, if you really stop and ponder it in a *methodical, logical* way, well then, I think it's pretty clear that *I'm* the one who should be avoiding *you*."

I squint, not quite following how he arrived at that conclusion but knowing he's about to explain.

"I mean, imagine how it feels to find out that the friends I thought I knew *so* well, the same friends I felt confident sharing *everything* with, are not only *not at all* what they appear to be, but that they're also, *every single one of them*, members of a super-exclusive, super-secret club. A club where, it's pretty

dang obvious that everyone is welcome. Everyone *but me*."
He stops, shaking his head as he moves toward the front of
the store, gazing out the display windows at the sun-dappled
street just beyond. His voice bearing the burden of his words
when he says, "I gotta tell ya, Ever, it *hurts*. Make no mistake.
It really and truly hurts me to the core. I mean, the way I see
it, which is the only way anyone *could* see it, but still, the way
I see it, it's like you don't want me to be immortal too. It's
like you don't want to know me, or even be my friend, for
anything even close to resembling eternity."

He turns, turns until he's facing me, and one look at his
face is all it takes to know that this is even worse than I
thought. And I know I have to say something quick, something to temper all this, but before I can even open my
mouth, he's back for round two, forcing me to sit back and
wait for my turn.

"And you know what really kills me the most? You know
who saw fit to finally fill me in on all this?" He pauses as
though waiting for me to respond, but I won't, the question
was obviously rhetorical. This is his show, his script, and I
have no intention of stealing his scene. "The one and only
person out of your entire super-secret gang of the eternally
beautiful—the only one out of all of you who was willing to
sit down and level with me, without pulling any punches or
trying to pass off any kind of bull—the one and only person
who was willing to look me in the eye and reveal all was
surprisingly enough—"

And before he can finish—before he can utter the word I
already know.

Damen.

Remembering the moment Miles e-mailed the portraits

he'd uncovered in Florence—the portraits Roman was determined he'd find.

The way Damen's fingers trembled as I passed him the phone, the way his lids narrowed, his jaw tightened, the way he so valiantly accepted the sudden unearthing of his centuries-old secret.

The way he vowed to come clean with Miles, to stop hiding, stop lying, to finally tell the truth and get it all out in the open.

But never once believing he'd actually go through with it.

"Damen." Miles confirms, nodding emphatically, gaze never once leaving mine. "And when you consider the fact that I've known him for—*what?* Less than a year? Less time than I've known you anyway, that's for dang sure, and certainly *far* less time than I've known Haven. And yet *he's* the one who told me. Despite the fact that I talk to him far, *far* less than I talk to either of you—he's the one who chose to be straight with me. Even though he's always been the quiet keep-to-himself type—*and now I know why*—but anyway, even though we've never really bonded, so to speak, he's still the only one who treated me like a *true friend*. Like someone he could trust and confide in. He just sat me down and spilled it—told me the truth about you, about him, about—about everything—*all of it!*"

"Miles—" I start, my voice hesitant, unsure what to say, unsure if he's really ready to listen to me anyway.

But when he stops long enough to gaze at me, head cocked to the side, brow raised in a challenge, I know that he is. Yet before I can even begin to go there, before I can start up with the whole laundry list of reasons for why I purposely kept him in the dark—all the very good and valid reasons for why he should be *glad* he was kept in the dark—I need to see for myself.

Need to see what Damen told him.

The exact words he used.

And, even more important, why he decided to divulge everything *now*, when surely some of it could've waited 'til later—much later, in fact.

Closing my eyes for a moment, allowing my mind to merge with his. Knowing I'm reneging on my promise to never spy on my friends' innermost thoughts or memories unless absolutely imperative, and forging ahead anyway, desperate to see just what went down that day.

The words *forgive me* filling the space that divides us, blossoming, growing, 'til I can practically see the letters taking shape.

Hoping he can sense the words too, and will soon find a way to pardon what I'm about to do.

twelve

I reach over the counter quickly. So quickly Miles has no way to stop me. No idea what's about to happen until it's too late. Slamming his wrist hard onto the glass, harder than I intended, I secure my hand over his in a way that presses his palm flat against it, rendering him completely helpless. Vaguely aware of his struggle, the way he squirms and wriggles and tries to break free.

But it's no use.

His fight barely registers. It's less than a blip on my screen.

When it comes to brute strength, there's no matching me.

And when he finally realizes that, he heaves a deep sigh and settles in, opening his mind, and surrendering to what he knows I'm about to do.

I slip inside his head, fluidly, easily, taking a moment to get my bearings and have a brief look around, before I discard all extraneous thoughts and swoop in on the exact scene I came here to see.

Seeing Miles climb into Damen's car, at first relaxed and happy, anticipating a nice off-campus lunch, only to grab hold of his seat in a death grip—his eyes wide, face a mask of fright, as Damen speeds out of the school parking lot and onto the street.

And to be honest, I'm not sure what surprises me more—the fact of what Damen's about to do—or that he's still keeping his promise of going to school and attending all of his classes even though I've clearly reneged on mine.

"*No worries,*" *Damen says, glancing at Miles, his face creasing into a smile.* "*You're perfectly safe. I can almost guarantee that.*"

"*Almost?*" *Miles flinches, shoulders scrunching, eyes squinching, as Damen maneuvers in and out of a long string of cars traveling well below his unnaturally high speed. Cautiously venturing a quick glimpse at him as he says,* "*Well, at least I know where you get it— you drive as crazy as everyone else in Italy!*" *He shakes his head and winces again.*

Causing Damen to laugh even harder.

The mere sound of it causing my heart to swell in a way I can barely contain.

I *miss* him.

There's just no denying it.

Seeing him like this—with the sun bouncing off his dark glossy hair, as his strong, capable hands grip the wheel—well, it just makes it clear how empty my life feels without him.

But then, just as quickly, I stop—reminding myself of all the reasons why I did what I did. There's still so much left to uncover about our former lives together, stuff I need to know before we can go any further.

I blink it away, determined to move past all that as I continue to watch.

Seeing Damen brake at the Shake Shack, where he buys Miles a coffee shake with crushed Oreo cookies inside, before leading him toward one of those blue painted benches, the exact same one where he and I once sat. Taking a moment to gaze down at a beautiful beach filled with colorful umbrellas that look like giant polka dots pinned into the sand, at a lineup of surfers waiting for the next big wave, to a flock of seagulls circling overhead, before turning his attention to Miles, who slurps his shake quietly and waits for Damen to begin.

"I'm an immortal," he says, looking right at him.

Just throws the first pitch without a warm-up, without a batter in place. Just tosses the ball right out there, face patient, still, allowing plenty of time for Miles to step up and take a swing.

Miles sputters, spitting the straw from his mouth and brushing his sleeve across his lips as he gapes at Damen and says, "Scusa?"

Damen laughs, and I'm not sure if it's the result of Miles's attempt to speak Italian or Miles's dramatic attempt to draw it all out and pretend as though he didn't actually hear what he so clearly did. Still, Damen continues to hold his gaze as he says, "Your ears did not deceive you. It's exactly as I said. I'm an immortal. I've roamed this earth for just over six hundred years, and up until recently, Drina and Roman did too."

Miles gapes, his coffee shake all but forgotten as his gaze moves over Damen, attempting to make sense of it, attempting to take it all in.

"Forgive me for being so blunt—and trust me when I say that I didn't put it out there like that to enjoy a little shock value at your expense. It's just that, if nothing else, I've come to learn that news like this—news of the unexpected kind—is best told quickly and bluntly. I've definitely paid the price of holding back." He pauses, his gaze suddenly saddened, faraway.

And I know he's referring to me—the time he waited so long to tell me the truth behind my own existence—and how he's made the same mistake once again, by not coming clean about our shared history.

"And I'll admit, part of me just assumed you'd already figured it out. What with Roman making sure you'd find the portraits and all. You must've drawn some sort of conclusion about them."

Miles shakes his head, blinks his eyes a bunch of times, and abandons his shake to the table. Looking at Damen with an expression that's one hundred and eighty degrees past confused when he says, "But—" his voice so hoarse, he clears his throat and starts again. "I mean, I guess—well, I guess I don't get it." He squints, slowly taking him in. "For starters, you're not all pasty white and weird looking. In fact, you're pretty much the opposite, and ever since I've known you, you've been rockin' a tan. Not to mention, in case you haven't noticed, it's daylight. Like, ninety-five degrees' worth of daylight. So, excuse me for saying so, but in light of all that, what you just said really doesn't make any sense."

Damen tilts his head, wearing an expression that's far more confused than Miles's. Taking a moment to add it all up, before he throws his head back, allowing great peals of laughter to spill forth, until he finally slows down enough to shake his head and say, "I'm not a mythical immortal, Miles, I'm a real immortal. The kind without the burden of fangs, sun-avoiding, or that gawd-awful blood-sucking." He shakes his head again, musing under his breath at the idea of it, remembering how I once assumed the same thing. "Basically, it's just me and my trusty bottle of elixir here—" He holds up his drink, swinging it back and forth as Miles watches, transfixed by the sight of it. The way that much sought-after substance, the one mankind has searched for forever, the one Damen's parents were murdered for, glows and glints in the bright afternoon sun. *"Believe me, this is really all it takes to keep me going for, well, for eternity."*

They sit in silence. Miles scrutinizing Damen, looking for give-aways, nervous tics, self-aggrandizement, gaping holes in the story, or any other telltale sign of a person who's lying, while Damen just waits. Allowing Miles all the time he needs to get accustomed to the idea, to settle in with it, to warm up to a new possibility he never really considered before.

And when Miles's mouth begins to open, about to ask how, *Damen just nods, answering the unspoken question when he says, "My father was an alchemist back in a time when it was not so uncommon to experiment with such things."*

"And what time was that, exactly?" Miles asks, having found his voice again, obviously not believing it really could've been as long as Damen claims.

"Six hundred and some odd years ago—give or take." Damen shrugs, casting it off as though the beginnings hold very little mean-ing to him.

But I know differently.

I know just how much he prizes that time with his family, the memories they shared before they were so cruelly stolen.

I also know just how painful it is for him to admit it. How he prefers to shrug it off, to pretend he can barely remember it.

"It was during the Italian Renaissance," he adds, not missing a beat.

Their gaze continues to hold, and even though he doesn't show it, bears absolutely no visible signs of it whatsoever—I know it kills Damen to have to admit it.

His most well guarded secret, the one he'd managed to hold on to for six solid centuries, now spilling out like water from a busted pipe.

Miles nods, nods without flinching. Forfeiting his milkshake to a curious seagull, pushing it away as he says, "I'm not even sure what to say at this point, except maybe—thank you."

Their gaze meets.

"Thank you for not lying. For not trying to cover it up and pretend that those portraits were some kind of distant relative or weird kind of coincidence. Thank you for telling the truth. As unbelievable and strange as it may be . . ."

"You *knew*?"

I let go of his hand, moving so quickly it takes a moment for him to realize he's no longer held hostage by me.

He flinches and pulls away, flexing his fingers as he twists his wrist back and forth, doing whatever it takes to get the blood flow back to normal again.

"Jeez, Ever, *intrude much?*" He shakes his head and paces the store. Angrily slaloming through the bookshelves, the angel displays, the CD racks, before starting the course all over again. Needing a moment to forgive me, to blow off a good bit of steam, before he's ready to even look at me again. Tapping his thumb over the spines of a long row of books as he finally sighs and says, "I mean, it's one thing to *know* you're capable of reading minds, it's quite another to have you *actually* get in there and probe around *without my consent*." The words followed by a string of others he mumbles under his breath.

"I'm sorry," I say, knowing I owe him much more than that, but still, it's a start. "Really. I . . . I took a vow to never do that. And for the most part, I've kept it. But sometimes . . . well, sometimes the situation's so urgent it can't be ignored."

"So you've done it before? Is that what you're saying?" He turns, his eyes narrowed, mouth grim, fingers fidgeting at his side. Assuming the worst, that I've made myself at home in his brain on more occasions than I can count. And even though it's nothing quite as bad as all that, and even though I'd really prefer not to have to cop to any of it, I also know that if I have any hope of regaining his trust, I have to start here.

I take a deep breath, keeping my gaze level on his. "Yes. A few times in the past, I have dropped in completely unannounced and without your consent, and I'm really and truly sorry about that. I know what an invasion that must feel like to you."

He rolls his eyes and shows me his back. Mumbling in a way intended to make me cringe—and it does.

Though it's not like I blame him. Not in the least. I've invaded his privacy, there's no doubt about that. I just hope he can learn to forgive me.

"So basically, what you're telling me is, *I have no secrets.*" He faces me again, gaze pouring over me. "No private thoughts, nothing that you haven't had a super-exclusive sneak peek at." He glares. "And just how long has this been going on, Ever? Since the day we first met, I assume?"

I shake my head, determined for him to believe me. "No. Really, none of that's true. I mean, yes, I've read your mind before, I've already admitted to that, but I've only done it a few times, and even then it was only when I thought you might know something that would—" I take a deep breath, seeing his narrowed gaze, his clenched jaw, a sure sign that this is not going over as well as I'd hoped. Still, he deserves an explanation, no matter how mad it makes him, so I clear my throat and forge ahead when I add, "Seriously, the only times I've ever looked inside your head was to see if you were on to the truth about Damen and me—that's *it*. I swear. I haven't bothered with anything else. I'm not nearly as un-ethical as you think. Besides, just so you know, I used to hear *everyone's* thoughts—hundreds—sometimes *thousands* of thoughts jumping out all around me. It was deafening, and disheartening, and I hated every single second of it. That's why I wore the hoodies and the iPod all the time. It wasn't just *tragic fashion sense*, you know." I pause and look at him, seeing the way his back and shoulders stiffen. "It was the only way I could think of to block it all out. I mean, it may have looked ridiculous to you, but it served its purpose. It wasn't until Ava taught me how to shield myself and tune it all out that I was able to move on. So yeah, in a way, you're right. From the day I first met you I could hear everything that coursed through your brain—just like I heard every-thing that coursed through *everyone's* brain. But it wasn't because I wanted to hear it, but because *I had no choice* but to hear it. But as for the rest, your business is your business, Miles. Seriously, I've completely avoided eavesdropping on your secrets. You have to believe me on that."

My gaze follows him, watching as he continues to roam the store, back turned, face hidden in a way I can't read. Though his aura is brightening, lightening, a sure sign he's coming around.

"I'm sorry," he says, finally turning to me.

I squint, wondering what on earth he has to be sorry for in light of all this.

But he just shakes his head and says, "The things I used to think about you—well, not really *you*, it was mostly about your choice of clothes—but *still*." He cringes. "I can't believe you were privy to that."

I shrug. More than willing to let it go. It's ancient history as far as I'm concerned.

"I mean, after all that, you were still willing to hang around me, still willing to drive me to school every day, still willing to be my friend—" He lifts his shoulders and sighs.

"Never mind that." I smile hopefully. "All I want to know is: Are you still willing to be mine?"

He nods. Nods and moves toward me, hands splayed out on the counter when he says, "In case you're wondering, it was actually Haven who first told me."

I sigh, having figured as much.

"Well, no, backtrack, because she only *kind of* told me." He stops, points at a ring just under the glass that I promptly hand to him to try on. "Basically, she called me over to her house—" He pauses, brows merged as he lifts his hand to admire the ring before slipping it off and pointing to another. "You know she moved out, right?"

I shake my head. I didn't actually know that, but again, I guess I should've assumed.

"She's living at Roman's now. Not sure how long that'll last, but she's talking about getting herself legally emancipated so I guess she's pretty serious about it. Anyway, long story short, she basically invited me over, poured me a big goblet full of elixir, and tried to make me take a swig without telling me what it was."

I shake my head. I can't believe how irresponsible that is. Well, coming from Haven I can believe it, but still, that is *not* good.

"And when I waved it away, she got all dramatic and looked at me and said—" He clears his throat, preparing for just the right raspy-voiced Haven inflection, and completely nailing it when he says, "'Miles, if someone were to offer you eternal beauty, eternal strength, amazing physical and mental powers . . . would you accept?'" He rolls his eyes. "And then she looked at me, that blue sapphire she's somehow embedded into her forehead practically blinding me, and totally gaping in outrage when I said, 'Uh, no thanks.'"

I smile, trying to imagine the scene for myself.

"So then, of course, she assumed I didn't quite understand just what she was getting at, and she tried to explain it again, with more detail this time. But I still said *no*. So then she started to get really upset and told me pretty much everything that Damen did—about the elixir, about how he turned you, about how you turned her. And then she threw in some stuff that Damen *didn't* tell me, about how *you* ended up killing both Drina *and* Roman—"

"I didn't kill—" *Roman*. I start to say that *I didn't kill Roman*. That Jude is responsible for that. But just as quickly I wave it away. Miles already knows more than he should. It's not my place to add any more.

"Anyway"—he shrugs as though he's speaking about purely normal and rational things—"then, when she tried to get me to drink again, I again said no. And then when she started to get mad, and I mean really worked up, like a two-year-old having a meltdown kind of mad, I said: 'Uh, hel-*lo*, here's the thing: If this stuff really worked, then Drina and Roman would still be here, right? And since they're not, well, I guess that means they weren't really all that immortal after all, were they?'" He stops and looks at me, his gaze boring into mine. "So then she said that as soon as she's done away with *you*, that little issue will be fixed for good. That I just need to trust her, that her elixir is *way* better than yours and all I needed to do was take a couple sips and eternal health, eternal well-being, eternal beauty, and eternal life would be mine, for, well, *eternity.*"

I swallow hard, my gaze fixed on his aura, now beaming a bright shade of yellow. The only assurance I have that he didn't take the bait—or at least not yet anyway.

"And, I gotta tell ya, she was so convincing in her sales pitch, I told her I'd have to think it over." He shrugs. "Told her I'd do a little research of my own and get back to her in a week or so."

I balk, so many words rushing forth at once I have no idea where to start.

But he just bursts into a deep, belly-clutching laugh, shaking his head as he looks at me. "Relax. I'm totally joking. I mean, jeez, what do you take me for—some kind of vain, superficial idiot?" He rolls his eyes, then catches himself when he adds, "Sorry, I meant no offense. But the point is, I told her *no.* A flat-out, unequivocal *no.* And she told me that the offer still stands, that if I change my mind at any time, the fountain of youth will be mine."

I gaze at him, seeing him in a whole new light. Amazed that he would actually turn down an offer like that. I mean, Jude always claims he wouldn't choose immortality, but then he's never actually been offered a drink, so who's to say what he'd choose if it really came down to it? And Ava, well, Ava came really, really close to making the leap, but in the end, she dumped it out. But still, I can't think of many other people besides Miles and Ava who would turn down an offer like that.

He looks at me, brow raised in mock offense when he says, "What? Why are you so surprised? Is it because you figured someone like me—someone who's both *gay* and an *actor* would surely just jump at the chance?" He narrows his gaze and shakes his head. "That's stereotyping, Ever. You should be ashamed of yourself for even thinking it." He shoots me a look of absolute scorn that leaves me feeling so bad I rush to defend myself. But before I can start, he's waved it away. Smiling triumphantly when he says, "Ha! And *that* is what you call acting!" He laughs, his whole face lighting up, eyes shining with glee. "Or at least that very last part was acting—the part about the stereotyping. Everything else was totally true. See how much my craft is improving?"

He rakes his fingers through his hair, secures his elbows on the counter, and leans toward me. "Here's the thing—the only thing I want in the world, the only dream that I have, is to be an *actor*." His gaze bores into mine. "A real, dedicated-to-the-craft *thespian*. That's my only goal. My soul's ambition. I have no interest in being some big, phony, glossed-up movie star. A walking *People* magazine cover. I'm not in it for the parties, or scandals, or multiple rehab stints—I'm in it for the *art*. I want to bring stories to life, to fully embody a variety of characters. I can't tell you what it feels like to lose myself in a role, it's . . . it's *amazing*. And it's something I want to experience again and again. But I want to play all kinds of roles—not just the young and beautiful ones. And in order to learn and grow and better myself, I need to experience *life*. I need to experience it *fully*, in *all* its stages—youth, middle age, old age—I want it *all*. You can't possibly *act* life if you don't allow yourself to *experience* it." He pauses for a moment, allowing his eyes to search my face. "That fear of death you've managed to do away with? I want it. Heck, I *need* it. It's one of the most basic, primal, driving forces we have—so why would I even consider ridding myself of that? The experiences I allow myself to have will only feed my craft in the end—but only if I remain mortal. *Not* if I purposely turn myself into some frozen-in-time, ultra-glamorous *himbo* who never ever changes, no matter how many centuries pass."

My gaze meets his and I don't know whether to be relieved or offended, but in the big scheme of things, I settle on relieved.

"Sorry." He shrugs. "Seriously, no offense. I'm just trying to explain my side of things. Not to mention the fact that I happen to *like* eating. In fact, I like it so much that I can't even imagine going on a permanent liquid diet. Also, I *like* seeing the changes each passing year makes, the impressions they leave behind. *And*, believe it or not, I don't want my scars to disappear either. I like them. They're part of *me*— part of *my* history. And someday, if I'm lucky enough to live to be an old man—one who'll probably be impotent, senile, fat, *and* bald, while you all stay exactly the same—well, then I'll be content with my memories. I mean, providing they're not all lost due to Alzheimer's or something. But seriously, before you go defending yourself—" He lifts his hand from the counter and flashes his palm, sensing I'm about to butt in. "Before you go telling me how Damen's racked up enough memories for us all and how he's perfectly well-rounded and happy, here's the *real* point I'm trying to make: What I want, *more than anything*, is to reach the end of my life with a solid before-and-after picture to reflect back on. To show I did the absolute best that I could with what I was given and that my life was well-lived."

I stare at him, trying to find my voice, mumble some kind

of reply, but I can't. My throat's gone hot and tight, closed up completely. And before I can stop it, before I can switch my gaze to something other than him—the tears begin.

Falling freely down my face and gaining in intensity to the point where I can no longer stop it, can no longer curb the sobbing, the shoulder shaking, and the deep pit of despair that makes my gut curl.

Aware of Miles hurrying around the counter and gathering me into his arms, smoothing my hair and doing his best to calm me, as he whispers sweet things into my ear.

But I know better.

I know the sentiments aren't at all true.

It really *won't* be okay.

At least not in the way that he claims.

I may have eternal youth and beauty—I may have the *gift* of living forever—but I'll never again have the kind of wonderful, lovely normalness that Miles just described.

thirteen

By late Saturday afternoon, there's just no avoiding them. Sabine is in the kitchen chopping up a pile of vegetables for a Greek salad, while Munoz stands beside her, molding ground turkey into generously sized patties.

"Hey, Ever." He looks up, smiling briefly. "You planning to join us? There's plenty more where this came from."

I glance at Sabine, seeing the way her shoulders stiffen, the way her knife hits the board just a little bit harder as she pummels a tomato, and I know she's still a long way from forgiving me, from accepting me, and I just can't deal with it now.

"No, um, actually, I'm about to head out," I say, barely meeting his gaze, hoping to avoid a stop and chat, since I'm far too eager to make my way out of here.

Making for the entry, just about free, when he finishes with the patties, looks at me, and says, "You mind getting the door?"

I pause, knowing this isn't just about getting the door. This is about him wanting to talk to me somewhere quiet and private, where his girlfriend can't overhear. But knowing there's no good way to get out of it, I follow him outside and over to the grill where he wrestles with the hood, spins the dials, and goes about some serious burger prep.

So engrossed in the task, I'm just about to leave, figuring I completely misread him when he says, "So, how's school going this year? I haven't seen you around much—if at all." He steals a quick glance at me, before he's back at it again, shaking some kind of secret spice blend onto the meat as I stand there and try to come up with a reply.

Figuring there's no use lying to someone who can just as easily check the attendance records, I lift my shoulders and say, "Well, that's probably because I've pretty much skipped every day but the first. In fact, other than that, I haven't gone at all."

"Ah." He nods, placing the spice jar on the granite counter before he turns and allows his eyes to graze over me. "Bad case of senioritis, I guess."

I scratch my arm, even though it doesn't itch, and try not to squirm any more than I already have. Averting my gaze to the window where Sabine stands watch, the very sight of her making me yearn for escape.

"Usually doesn't start until the last semester, that's when it all falls apart. But it looks like you caught the bug early. Is there anything I can do to help?"

Yeah, you can tell your girlfriend not to judge me—you can tell Haven not to try to kill me—you can tell Honor not to threaten me—and you can uncover the long-buried truth about Damen and me—oh, and in your free time, if you could get your hands on a certain stained white shirt and send it over to the crime lab for analysis—that would be great!

Though, of course, I don't say any of that, instead, I just

shrug and sigh louder, hoping he'll hear it and tune in to the not-so-silent message it contains.

But if he does, he chooses to ignore it. "You know, just in case you think you're alone in all this—you're really not."

I squint, not sure what he's getting at.

"I've talked to her, you know. Shared some of the research I've run across on people who've had near-death experiences."

Despite my wanting to leave, I place my hands on my hips and lean slightly toward him. "And how do you just *run across* that type of research?" I ask. "I mean, seriously. Isn't that the kind of thing you have to go looking for on your own?"

He focuses on the meat, transferring it from the plate to the grill. His voice low, matter of fact, when he explains, "I saw a piece on TV once, and I found it quite fascinating. So fascinating I bought a book on the subject, which led to more books on the subject, and . . . *so on.*" He presses his spatula to the burger, causing the juices to riot and sizzle. "But you—you're the first one I've met who's actually experienced such a thing. Have you ever thought of taking part in one of those research groups? I hear they're always looking for new subjects."

"*No,*" I say, barely giving him a chance to finish the question. My answer firm, final, sparing no time to really consider. The last thing I need is to take part in some schlocky case study.

But he just laughs, raising his mitt-covered hands in surrender, saying, "Don't shoot. Just asking is all."

He flips the burgers, one after the other, causing a popping, sizzling, barbeque soundtrack we both stand there and listen to.

Then, as soon as they're ready, he scrapes 'em right off and drops 'em back onto the plate, stopping long enough to look at me and say, "Listen, Ever, just give her some time to get comfortable with the idea. It's not easy having your whole belief system challenged, you know? But if you'll just ease up a little, she'll come around. Really she will. I promise to continue to work on her, if you'll promise to do your part too. And, before you know it, it'll all blow over. You'll see."

Is that your prediction? I want to ask, but thankfully choke back the words. He's only trying to help, and whether or not I believe him, whether or not Sabine will ever come around to my side, isn't really the point. He's just trying to connect, and the least I can do is allow it.

"But as far as school and your attendance is concerned—" He shoots me a stern look. "It's only a matter of time before she catches on. So, try not to make things any tougher on yourself than they already are, okay? Or at least think about it anyway. Besides, last time I checked, getting a high school diploma didn't hurt anyone. In fact, it can only help."

I mumble some sort of halfhearted reply, give a quick wave of my hand, and head for the gate. Having no idea if the conversation was actually over, but knowing my part of it is. Those kinds of things, the rules he referred to, no longer apply. The pomp and circumstance of a high school graduation is for other people.

Normal people.

Mortal people.

Not me.

Starting my car with my mind long before I've reached its spot on the drive, I pull out of the gate and onto the street, speeding toward the place where I told Jude we'd meet.

fourteen

The moment I pull into the parking lot I see him.

Waiting for me in his Jeep, thumbs tapping the steering wheel in time to the music that blares from his iPod, looking so peaceful, so content to be sitting alone there like that—I'm tempted to turn my car around and head back to where I came from.

But I don't.

This is far too important to miss.

Haven has no plans to renege on her threat, and for all I know this could be my one and only chance to convince him of the importance of this.

I pull up beside him and wave. Watching as he removes his earbuds, tosses them aside, and jumps out, leaning against the door, arms folded before him as he watches my approach.

"Hey." He nods, studying me carefully as I heave my bag over my shoulder and straighten the T-shirt I wear over my tank top. "You okay?" He tilts his head and squints, clearly confused as to why I summoned him here.

I nod and smile, thinking if anyone should be asking that question, it should be me asking him. "Yeah, I'm good." I stop just shy of him, unsure where to take it from here. Just because I asked him to meet me doesn't mean I took the time to memorize my long list of talking points. "Um, and you . . . *are you okay?*" My gaze moves over him, noting how he certainly looks better than the last time I saw him, the color's returned to his face, his gaze isn't nearly as empty and bleak, and one glance at his vibrant green aura is all it takes to know he's definitely on the mend.

He nods and lifts his shoulders, obviously waiting for me to make the next move, to tell him what this is really about. But when I don't, when I just continue to stand there before him, he takes a deep breath and says, "Seriously. I'm—I'm getting used to the idea of her being gone. I mean, I can't change it, so I may as well adapt to it, *right?*"

I mumble some sort of agreement, some standard-issue, easily forgettable reply. Then, knowing I've stalled long enough, that it's time to get to it, the real reason we're here, I take a deep breath and say, "And Haven? Have you seen or heard from her lately?"

He looks away, fingers working the slight sheen of stubble just beginning to show on his chin, his voice sounding tired, resigned, when he says, "Nope, not a word. Which, when you think about it, probably isn't a good sign. But then again, this whole thing is a little out of my league, so who knows?" He glances at me for a moment, eyes moving over my face before wandering again.

"But what if I were to tell you it wasn't?" I pause long enough for his gaze to find its way back to mine. "What if this whole thing wasn't *out of your league* at all?"

He grunts, mumbles something completely indecipher-able under his breath, then shakes his head and says, "You're joking, right?"

I hold my ground, hold the serious expression on my face. "Trust me, it's no joke. In fact—"

But before I can finish, before I can even get to the point, he cuts me right off, having already drawn his own conclu-sion as to what this is about and eager to stop me before I can go any further. "Listen, Ever—" He sighs, kicking his foot out before him as he buries his hands deep into the front pockets of his jeans. "While I appreciate your concern for my safety, I want to make it clear that I have absolutely no inten-tion of drinking the elixir and becoming immortal like you."

My eyes go wide as I fight to keep my jaw from dropping to my knees. I can't believe he actually thought I was offer-ing such a thing.

"I mean, I know I've said it before, and I don't mean to get all judgmental on you or anything, but that kind of unnaturally long lifespan . . . well, I have no interest in that sort of thing."

That makes two in as many days, I think, unable to keep myself from gaping.

"After going to Summerland, and after *seeing* Lina, well, I think you'd have to be pretty crazy to want to stay here. To choose an extra-long, extended stay in such an imperfect, hate-filled world when there's something so much better waiting 'round the bend—so to speak."

And even though his words hit me, hit me as hard as Miles's did, I don't cry. I'm done with all that. For better or worse, I am what I am and there's no going back. Though that doesn't mean I have any intention of convincing all the others to join me.

"Surely it's not that bad—*is it?*" I say, hoping to lighten the tone.

But he just lifts his shoulders, voice completely serious when he says, "No, I suppose you're right. It's not all hatred and hardship out there. Every now and then, if you're lucky, you can stumble upon the occasional pocket of happiness."

"Wow, that's a little *dark*, don't you think?" I force a laugh, though his words have left me more shaken than I care to admit.

But he just shrugs and squints, his eyes narrowing to where I can just barely see them. "Anyway, not trying to insult you, it's just not my thing, that's all. I have no interest in it."

I shrug too, ready to move on, out of this parking lot, and onto the real reason we're here.

"So . . ." He looks at me. "Is that it? Are we good here?"

"Sure, we're *good*. But we're a long ways from *done*." I motion for him to follow as I make for the gate. Taking a moment to close my eyes, and *see* the lock springing open in my mind, before calling over my shoulder to say, "Trust me, we haven't even begun yet."

I push the gate open, assuming he'll follow, and surprised when I glance back only to find him still standing on its other side.

"Ever, what's this really about? Why'd you want to meet here of all places? I thought you were through with school?"

I shake my head, taking a moment to gaze at a group of buildings I've managed to ditch all week and didn't miss even the slightest bit. "Turns out I'm not. Besides, this is the only place I could think of that would offer us the space and privacy we're gonna need."

His spliced brow jumps, clearly intrigued.

But I just roll my eyes and head for the gym, knowing he's right behind me this time.

"That door locked too?" His gaze moves over my arms, my legs, the back of my neck, pretty much anyplace where my skin is bared.

I nod, concentrating on the door, hearing the bolt slam back into place before I open it and say, "You first."

He heads inside, his rubber flip-flops squeaking against the polished wood floor as he makes his way to the middle of the room, where he stops, lifts his arms to his sides, throws his head back, inhales deeply, and says, "Yep, it's definitely got that universal high school gym stench I remember so well."

I smile, but only a little, before I'm back to business again.

I didn't come here to joke around or engage in useless small talk. I came here to save him. Or, more correctly, to teach him everything he needs to know so that he can save himself in case I'm not around to do it for him.

Because no matter how angry I may be with him, no matter how many doubts I may have about him, I still feel it's my duty to guard him from Haven.

"So, I figured we should just get right to it, no use wasting any more time than we already have."

He looks at me, face wearing the slightest sheen of sweat. Though it's unclear if it's due to the stuffy, hot air or the apprehension of wondering just what it is that he's gotten himself into, what might be expected of him.

I take a moment to settle in, dropping my bag in the corner, retying my shoe, and removing my T-shirt to reveal the white, finely ribbed tank top I wear underneath. Smoothing my hands over the front of it and adjusting the elastic waistband of my shorts, as I approach him and say, "Obviously you know about the chakras." I stand before him, studying him carefully but allowing him no time to react when I add, "I mean, since you so successfully killed Roman that way—"

"Ever, I—" He starts, but I won't permit it, won't allow the flow of excuses to begin. I've heard all that, and I'm not one bit swayed. Besides, I can't afford to be coerced into an argument that may change my mind about him—about *this*.

"Save it." I raise my hand between us. "That's another topic, for another day. For now, the only thing we're going to discuss is the fact that Haven has powers you can't even begin to imagine—" *That even I can't begin to imagine.* "Powers she's pretty drunk on at the moment, which makes her reckless and dangerous and someone you need to steer clear of at all costs. But if by chance you run into her for some reason, or, even worse, she decides to come after you, which, I'm sorry to say, is really the more likely scenario, well, either way, you need to be prepared. So, with all that in mind, with everything you know about her, which chakra would you choose to obliterate her?"

He looks at me, lip quirked to the side, and it's clear he's not taking this at all seriously, which is a grave mistake on his part.

"The sooner you answer, the sooner we'll get through this—" I sing, hands on my hips, fingers impatiently tapping against them.

"Third." He nods, flattening his palm just under his chest for emphasis. "Solar plexus, otherwise known as the revenge center, the home of deep-seated anger issues, and that sort of thing. So, are we good here? Did I pass? Can I collect my gold star and go home now?" He lifts his spliced brow.

"Okay, so now I want you to pretend that *I'm* Haven," I

say, completely ignoring the question along with the obvious plea in his gaze. "And I want you to come at me, to target me in the exact same way you'd target her."

"Ever, *please*," he begs. "This is ridiculous! I *can't* do it. Really. I mean, while I appreciate your concern and all, trust me, it means a lot to me, but this sort of forced reenact-ment—" He shakes his head, dreadlocks swinging from side to side. "It's—it's a little embarrassing. To say the least."

"*Embarrassing?*" My eyes practically bug out of my head. The male ego is pretty much unfathomable to me. "I'm just going to pretend you didn't even say that. I mean, she has the power to cause you all kinds of hurt before she decides to take mercy and finally finish you off, and you're worried about be-ing *embarrassed*? In front of *me*?" I shake my head again, wav-ing it away with both hands. "Listen, if you're worried about hurting me—forget it. You won't and you can't. It's com-pletely impossible. No matter how hard you try, you just can't get to me. So feel free to put that right out of your mind."

"Well, that's reassuring. Not to mention *emasculating*." He shakes his head and allows his shoulders to slump.

"Not trying to insult you." I shrug. "Just stating the facts, that's all. I'm stronger. I mean, I think you've already experi-enced plenty of evidence to support that. And, I hate to break it to you, but Haven's stronger too. And while there's noth-ing you can do to change either of those things, she does lack something I have."

He looks at me, only partially curious to learn what that is.

"She stopped wearing her amulet. She's got nothing pro-tecting her now. Whereas I never remove mine . . ." I pause, remembering all the times I did in the past and amending the statement when I add, "At least not anymore. Also, my solar plexus is *not* my weak chakra, not that I'm about to reveal which chakra is my weak one, but anyway, even if you've already figured it out by now, even if you decided you were so desperate to get out of here and on with your night that it just might be worth it to do me in, well, then you should know that you wouldn't be able to get anywhere near it before I'd stop you right in your tracks."

He rolls his eyes and sighs, raising his hands in defeat, realizing he really has no choice but to give in. Saying, "Okay. Fine. Whatever. Just tell me, what is it you want me to do? Am I supposed to charge you or something?"

"Sure, why not?" I shrug, figuring it's as good a place to start as any.

But he just looks at me and says, "Because here's the thing, that is a totally unrealistic situation. I would never just *charge* Haven or anyone else, not without first being provoked, and probably not even then. I just wouldn't do it. I'm a pacifist. You *know* that. It's not my style. So, I'm sorry to say it, but if you really want me to participate, then you'll have to come up with something a little better than that."

"Okay, fine." I nod, determined to not let him wriggle his way out of this. "But just so you know, I have no plans to charge Haven either. I have no plans to start anything or go after her in any way. Still, I don't think either one of us can ignore the fact that she's vowed to destroy us—she's made that abundantly clear. And make no mistake—she *can* destroy us, Jude. Especially *you*, since you're so unprepared. She can take you down *easily*—without even breaking a sweat! So, with that in mind, we both need to prepare ourselves for that event. Even though you've made it clear how you have no interest in being immortal, I'm also willing to bet you're not all that eager to die at Haven's hand. So, in light of all that, what do you say I charge you first? Would that make you feel better? Because that's probably how it'll go down anyway."

He shrugs. Shrugs *and* flips his hands.

A simple act that annoys me so much, I rush toward him at full force without warning him first.

Moving so fast that one second he's standing in the center of the gym, acting all causal and cool, and the next, I've knocked him clear across to the other side of the room, where I press him up hard against the padded wall, just like Haven did to me that day in the bathroom. And also like Haven, I'm not the least bit winded from the effort.

"*This* is what it'll be like," I say, my fingers gripping the front of his shirt, working the fabric so hard a piece of it tears off in my hand. Aware of his cool, shallow breath hitting my cheek, my face a mere razor's width from his, as I gaze into those surprised aqua-green eyes. "*This* is how fast it'll happen. You'll have no time to react."

He meets my gaze, the look deepening, his breath quickening, as a line of sweat drips down his brow, and his heart begins to race.

Though it's not the result of fear or even surprise—no, it's the result of something else entirely.

Something I immediately recognize.

It's the same look he gave me the night we nearly kissed in the Jacuzzi.

The same look he gave me the night he told me he loved me, that he's always loved me, through every single one of our lives, and that he's not about to give up on me anytime soon.

And even though I want to, even though my rational mind

is telling me to let go of his shirt, to turn around, and get myself as far from him as I possibly can—I can't do it.

Instead, I just grip tighter, press my body even closer, soothed by the wave of calm that emanates off his skin, as I dive headfirst into those deep ocean eyes of his.

The small voice in my head reminding me of all the reasons I should run—my long list of suspicions, all the unanswered questions—but my body ignores it. Choosing instead to respond to him just like the girl in my slave life.

Lifting my hand to his face, fingers shaking, aching, wanting nothing more than to meld with him.

To disappear in his skin.

My name escaping his lips, the sound like a moan. Like it pains him to say it. Like it pains him to feel me so close.

But I won't let him continue, won't let him speak. I just press my fingers to the gentle swell of his lips, discovering their warmth, the way they yield to my touch, and wondering what it would be like to press my mouth there instead.

Aware of the way his heart pounds against mine, the way it gains in intensity. And even though I try to fight it, even though I really and truly do make a full case against it, there's just something I have to see for myself. Something I need to know, once and for all, so I can finally kill the question that plagues me. And I'm hoping his kiss will reveal it in the same way Damen's once did.

Is there really a connection between us?

Is it the two of us that are supposed to be together, and Damen who purposely got in the way?

And knowing there's only one way to find out, I take a deep breath, close my eyes, and wait for the crush of his lips against mine.

fifteen

"Ever, *please*." His fingers caress the soft underside of my chin, urging me to open my eyes and look at him.

So I do. Reluctantly lifting my eyes to meet his. The startling blue-green of his gaze providing such stark contrast to the brown of his skin, the golden-bronze spray of dreadlocks that fall across his face, and his slightly crooked white teeth.

"I've wanted this for *so* long . . . for *so* many years, but first, before we do this, I need to know—"

I wait for the question—barely able to breathe.

Never expecting him to say the words: "Why *me*? Why *now*?"

I squint and lean back. That lure, that pull toward him that seemed so irresistible just a second ago, now starting to fade. Only a mere trace of it managing to hang on when I shake my head and say, "I don't even know what that means."

My fingers loosen their grip on his shirt, watching as a small square of fabric falls to the ground as I start to push away.

But he won't let me go. Grasping both of my hands, and holding them tightly in his, he says, "What I meant was, what *happened*? What is it that changed between Damen and you that made you even think to consider me?"

I take a deep breath, take in his hands, his fingers entwined around mine, his wrist resting against the crystal horseshoe bracelet Damen gave me that day at the track, and this time, when I'm ready to move, I do. My breath slowly returning to normal again, the spell of him waning more and more with every step I put between us.

Knowing he deserves an answer, that there's no way I can leave it like this, I take a deep breath and say, "I discovered something." I sneak a quick peek before I quickly look away. "Something about the past . . . something that—" I swallow hard and start again, voice surer, stronger when I add, "Something he's been hiding for a very long time."

Jude looks at me without a trace of surprise. He's alluded to Damen's secrets on more than one occasion. Of his inability to fight fair, especially when fighting for me. But then, in Damen's defense, he's freely admitted to all of that too. In fact, he felt so bad, so wracked with guilt, he actually chose to step aside for a while so I could make a clean choice for myself.

And I did.

I chose *him*.

For me it was never a contest. From the moment we met, he's all I could see.

But what if I've been wrong?

What if all this time—Jude was meant to be the one?

I mean, he's stood right there beside me in all of my lives— including the one I just recently learned about. And yet he's always the loser, always the one getting shot down. Always the one who ends up alone.

But what if it was never supposed to happen like that?

What if all this time, I've been so captivated, so swayed by Damen's magick I've made the wrong choice every time?

Why is it that we keep coming back to each other again and again? Is it so we'll have yet another chance at getting it right—to finally be together after all of this time?

I gaze at Jude standing before me—he's mesmerizing. Not in the same way that Roman was with his slick, golden glossiness—or even in the way of Damen's dark and sexy tingle and heat. No, Jude's more the cool and dreamy type— seemingly normal on the surface, but deep down inside, he's so much more.

"Ever—" He starts, his expression waging the battle between wanting to just grab me and kiss me, and wanting to show some restraint and try to talk to me first. "Ever, what did you *see*? What is it that was so bad it brought you to me?"

And the way he says it, so aware of his age-old position as the discarded one—well, my heart breaks on his behalf.

I turn away, taking in the bleachers, the scuffed wood floor, the basketball net with the hole in the side, allowing for whatever remains of his lure to wear off, so that logic and a long list of questions can stand in their place.

Deciding to be firm and up-front, just state the facts as they are and see where it leads, I turn to him and say, "A while back, you sort of—" I shake my head. "No, not *sort of*, you *definitely* alluded to knowing some kind of secret about our shared pasts. It was after you'd been to the Great Halls of Learning for the very first time and everything about you seemed different. And when I asked you what happened in there, you played it pretty vague. But later, you mentioned some stuff about Damen not playing fair in the past, and how all that was about to change because, as you put it: *knowledge is power, and, thanks to Summerland, you had that in spades*—or something to that effect, and anyway, I need to know what that meant."

I stand before him, silent and still, waiting for him to respond. Watching as he squinches his eyes together as he rubs the space between them, fingers digging in deep, before he drops his hands to his sides and takes me in.

"Where would you like me to start?" He shrugs, following it with a laugh that's much closer to harsh and gruff than anything resembling joy.

And I start to say, *anywhere, start anywhere you choose,* figuring it might be good to let him take the lead on this one, and allow him to reveal the things he thinks I should know. But then I think better. Despite the fact that I know Damen edited all of my lives, which means every last one of them holds some sort of secret he'd prefer I not know, well, there's only one life—one secret—I really need to know right now.

Only one in particular that brought me to this point—that made me want to kiss him to see where it led.

"The South." I look at him. "The antebellum South. What do you know about our lives back then—when you and I were both slaves?"

He blanches, like seriously blanches. The light draining from his eyes so fast I can hardly believe I just witnessed that. Mumbling something inaudible under his breath as his gaze darts all around, pausing on the school mascot painted on the wall, while his hands and feet begin a nervous, fidgety dance.

And seeing him react like that, well, I can't help but wonder if I just unwittingly revealed something he didn't yet
know.

But the thought vanishes just as quickly when he finally
turns to me and says, "So, you know." He takes a deep breath
and shakes his head. "I gotta tell ya, Ever, I'm pretty shocked
he'd even tell you about it. I have to say, no matter what I
may think of him—that was pretty damn gutsy on his part.
Or maybe just reckless, who knows?"

"He didn't tell me," I blurt, before I can stop. "Well, not exactly anyway. Let's just say I sort of . . . stumbled upon something he definitely didn't want me to see."

Jude nods, gaze narrowing, changing, as it slowly moves
over me. His voice grave and serious when he says, "Can't say
I blame him. It was definitely one of our very worst ones—if
not *the* worst." He shrugs. "Or at least that's the way it turned
out for me . . ."

sixteen

On Monday, I skip school again so I can go to Lina's memorial.

But it's just an excuse. I would've skipped anyway.

Despite Munoz's claim that a diploma can only help me ensure a bigger, better, brighter future for myself, well, I beg to differ.

Maybe it helps normal people by guaranteeing serious consideration from college admissions boards and prospective employers—but those things mean nothing to me. Even though just a week ago it was important to me too, now I finally see how misguided that was. How I've been avoiding the obvious fact that there's just no point in following the normal course of events when I have a life (and a future) that is anything but.

And it's time I stop pretending otherwise.

And, yeah, if I'm going to be perfectly honest, then I also have to admit that Damen plays a part in that decision as well—if not the most major part. Because the thing is, I'm just not ready to face him. Not yet. Maybe someday, maybe even soon, but at the moment, that day feels like a long way away.

Though to his credit, he seems to be totally on board with it. Allowing me plenty of time and space to figure things out on my own. The occasional manifested red tulip that appears out of nowhere is his only intrusion, serving as a gentle reminder of the love we once shared.

Still share.

I *think.*

I twist the cap on my bottle of water and gaze around the living room, looking for at least one familiar face in a very large crowd. According to Jude, Lina had no shortage of friends, and from what I can see it's true. What he failed to mention is just how diverse they all are. I mean, as much as I love living here, Laguna Beach isn't exactly known for being a melting pot, and yet every ethnicity you could think of is pretty much present and accounted for. And from the blend of accents that trill all around, it's clear that many of them traveled from great distances for the chance to say their good-byes.

I continue to stand there, awkwardly dangling the bottle of water by my side as I weigh my options of trying to find Jude to tell him I'm leaving, or hanging out just a little bit longer for appearances' sake, when Ava waves at me from the other side of the room, and as she makes her way toward me, I quickly calculate how long it's been since we last spoke. Wondering if she too belongs to the small group of people who feel abandoned by me.

"Ever." She smiles, leaning in for a brief, warm hug. Her heavily ringed fingers still clutching my arms, her large brown eyes carefully scanning mine, as she pulls away and says, "You're looking well." She laughs, the sound of it light and airy as she adds, "But then, you always do, don't you?"

I gaze down at the long purple dress I designed and manifested especially for this occasion, since Jude strictly prohibited the wearing of black. Claiming that Lina would hate to gaze upon a crowd of people all wearing the same, depressing color. She didn't want people to mourn her life—she wanted them to celebrate it instead. And since purple was her favorite color, we were asked to show up in some variation of it.

"So, is she here?" I ask, watching as Ava squints and tucks her wavy, auburn hair behind her ear, her whole face changing when she assumes the worst, assumes it's Haven I'm asking about. *"Lina,"* I say, before she has a chance to even go there. Haven's the last thing I want to talk about here. "I meant *Lina*. Have you seen her?" My eyes grazing over the citrine pendant she always wears, to the embellished purple cotton tunic, the skinny white jeans, and the cute gold sandals on her feet, before meeting her gaze once again. "You know I can't see the ones who've crossed over, I can only see the ones who still linger."

"Do you ever try to talk to them, convince them to move on?" She hitches her purple purse up high onto her shoulder.

I look at her like she's crazy, the thought never even occurred to me. It took me so long to learn how to ignore them, to tune them out completely, I can't even imagine engaging them now. Besides, I've got no shortage of my own problems to solve, the last thing I need to do is get involved with a bunch of misguided ghosts.

But Ava just laughs, gaze dancing around the room as she

says, "Trust me, Ever, they *all* manage to find their way to their own funerals. I've yet to see the spirit who could resist! The chance to see who shows up, who says what, who wears what, and who's truly mourning versus who's merely just faking it—it's pretty tempting stuff."

"Are you *truly* mourning?" I ask, not really meaning it in the way that it sounded, like she might be faking it or something. I mean, I'm mostly here to support Jude and to honor someone who was kind enough to help me at a time when I really needed it. But even though I know Lina was Ava's employer, I have no idea if it went any deeper, if they were actually friends.

"If you're asking if I'm mourning the loss of a kind, generous, compassionate, awakened soul"—she looks at me without blinking—"then the answer is *yes, of course, why wouldn't I be?* But if you're asking if my mourning's more for her than for me—then I'm afraid the answer is *no.* The majority of my sadness is purely selfish."

"That's exactly what Jude said," I mumble, my voice wistful, as I gaze around the room, searching for a glimpse of him.

Ava nods, tossing her mass of curls over her shoulders. "And when you lost your family, who did you mourn for the most?"

I look at her, surprised by the question. And even though I want to say that I mourned entirely for my parents and Buttercup and Riley's unrealized dream of being a teenager and turning thirteen—I can't do it. It's simply not true. Even though I felt their loss in a horrible, gut-wrenching, deep-down kind of way, I have to admit that the majority of my sadness was due to the fact that I was left behind while they all moved on—away from me.

"Anyway." Ava shrugs. "To go back to your original question, *yes*, I did see her. It was brief, only for a second really, but boy was it beautiful." She smiles, her face lifting, cheeks flushing, as her eyes shine at the memory. And I'm just about to ask for a little more elaboration when she says, "It was right when Jude got up to speak. You remember the way he faltered and started to break down? When his voice cracked and he had to pause for a moment before he could start up again?"

I nod. I remember it well. Remember the way my heart broke for him at that very moment.

"Well, that's when she appeared right behind him. Hovering just ever so slightly as she placed her hands on his shoulders, closed her eyes, and surrounded him with a beautiful bubble of love and light. And I tell you, not a second later he was back on track, able to finish his eulogy without a problem as she faded from sight."

I sigh, trying to imagine how that must've looked and wishing I could've seen it for myself. Gazing at Ava when I say, "Do you think he actually *felt* it—her presence? I mean, obviously he felt it since it helped him get through it, but, like, do you think he was *aware* of it? Do you think he knew it was *her* who helped him get through it?"

Ava shrugs, motioning past the glass doors toward the patch of grass where he stands, talking to a small group of Lina's friends. His long hair spilling down his back and over the sleeves of his purple tee that bears a picture of some vaguely familiar, multicolored Hindu deity on its front.

"Why don't you ask him yourself?" she says. "I hear you two are growing much closer these days."

I balk, my gaze immediately returning to her. Wondering

if she actually meant it in the way that I think, and wondering who could've possibly informed her of that.

"Well, obviously you've been skipping school in order to fill in at the store, even though I've made it perfectly clear, many times over, that I'm more than happy to do it. And then, there's the fact that Damen's been looking pretty despondent these days—or at least that's what I've gotten from the few glimpses I've had of him, though the twins have certainly confirmed it. They see him much more than I do, you know. What with him constantly whisking them off to the movies, or go-cart racing, or shopping at Fashion Island, or the water rides at Disneyland—just about every local Orange County attraction you can think of has been covered—at least twice. And as much as they love it, and as kind and generous as it is of him to do it, you really don't have to dig all that deep to realize what's really behind his sudden burst of altruism." She pauses, looking right at me. "Clearly he's looking for a distraction. Desperately trying to stay busy so he won't obsess over *you*, and the fact that you're no longer there for him like you once were."

My shoulders droop, all of me droops, thinking how the old me would've gotten very angry by now, would've already launched some ridiculous argument to defend myself or, at the very least, cut her off before she'd had a chance to say all of that.

But I'm no longer that person. Not to mention there's no denying the fact that everything she just said is true.

I've made Damen sad.

And lonely.

And in need of distractions.

And there's just no denying it.

Though it's also not as simple as that. There's a lot more to it, and I doubt she's even vaguely aware of that fact.

Still, like she said, I *have* grown closer to Jude. Though not in a romantic way like she assumes.

While there's no doubt that there's definitely some kind of undeniable *pull* that seems to eternally link us—ironically, this time around, Jude's the one who's applying the brakes. Making it more than clear that he has no interest whatsoever in gaining only a temporary part of me.

He wants me for reals.

He wants me for good.

Wants to be sure I've made a clean break from Damen and all that we share.

Wants me to take a sure step toward him without a single glance back at what I once had.

Claims he can't risk that kind of heartbreak again.

That just because it's happened multiple times through the centuries doesn't make it any easier this time around.

And since I just can't give him that yet—despite what he told me about our past life in the South, confirming my very worst suspicions that Damen bought me, removed me from my family, and turned his back on them forever so that he could have me to himself—I'm still not ready to go there.

Even after he revealed the rest of it—that shortly after Damen took me away, he, along with the rest of my family, perished in a terrible fire they never would've been in if only Damen had bothered to save them. Resulting in a string of tragic deaths there's just no logical excuse for.

I mean, once his immense wealth and formidable power is taken into account, well, an act like that, an act so cold, so calculating, and so callous that ended in such tragedy—is completely inexcusable on his part.

And yet, I'm still not ready to give up on him.

Though I'm not ready to see him yet either.

But even though I'm not about to share any of that with Ava, I still just shake my head and say, "There's a lot more to it than that." I purposely hold her gaze.

She nods and reaches toward me, her hand grasping mine in a gentle squeeze. "I've no doubt about that, Ever. No doubt at all." She pauses, making sure she has my full attention when she adds, "Just make sure you don't do anything rash. Take the time to dig deep, to really think it through. And when in doubt, well, you know my favorite remedy—"

"Meditation," I mumble, laughing and rolling my eyes, grateful for the burst of light she always seems to provide even in the darkest of times. Pulling her back to me when she starts to move away. Not ready to part with her just yet, my gaze practically pleading with hers when I say, "Ava, do you know something?" I grip her arm tightly, finding myself suddenly desperate for her guidance, for a few enlightened words. "Do you know something about this? About Damen, Jude, and me? About who I'm supposed to choose?"

She looks at me, her gaze soft and caring, but still she just shakes her head slowly. A lock of auburn hair falling over her forehead and into her eyes, obscuring them briefly before she pushes it away and says, "I'm afraid that's your journey, Ever. Yours and yours alone. Only you can discover which path to take. I'm only here as your friend."

seventeen

"Thanks for all your help." Jude tosses a damp dish towel over his shoulder and leans against the ancient refrigerator that's nothing like Damen's or Sabine's—not stainless, not the size of a walk-in closet—just old and green, with a fondness for making loud, strange, gurgling noises. His thumbs hitched in his empty belt loops, legs casually crossed at the ankle, watching as I load the last of the cups and glasses into the dishwasher, before closing the door and pressing the *start* button.

I reach up, removing the elastic band from my hair, allowing the waves to spill down my back, stopping just shy of my waist, while trying to ignore Jude's intense stare. The way his eyes narrow, drinking me in, hungrily following the trail of my hands as I smooth them over the front of my dress and lift a fallen strap. His gaze lingering for so long, I know I have to break it, find a way to distract him.

"It was a nice memorial." I meet his eyes briefly before looking away. Busying myself with tidying up the tiled counters, the white porcelain sink. "I think she would've liked it."

He smiles, wads up the towel and drops it on the counter, then heads into the den and sinks onto the old brown couch, just assuming I'll follow, which, after a moment, I do.

"Actually, she *did* like it." He kicks off his flip-flops, settles his feet onto the cushions.

"So, you saw her?" I drop onto the chair just opposite him, before propping my bare feet onto the old wooden door he uses as a coffee table.

He turns, slowly looking me over, spliced brow raised in surprise. "Yeah, I saw her. Why? Did *you?*"

I shake my head, quick to dispel it. Fingers playing with the cluster of crystals I wear at my neck, favoring the rough stones over the more polished ones. "Ava did." I shrug, letting go of the amulet, allowing the stones to warm up my flesh. "I'm still unable to see Lina's kind."

"You still trying?" He squints, sitting up briefly, grasping a small pillow by his feet and placing it behind his head before lying back again.

"No." I sigh, my voice wistful, gaze faraway. "Not anymore. I gave all that up a while ago."

He nods, still looking at me, though in a more thoughtful, less intense way. "Well, if it makes you feel any better, I haven't seen her either. Riley, I mean. That is who we're talking about here, right?"

I lean my head back against the cushion and close my eyes. Remembering my adorably feisty, pain-in-the-bum little sister with the penchant for wearing crazy costumes and wigs—and hoping that wherever she is, she's having a truly awesome time.

Pulled away from my thoughts and back toward Jude when he says, "Ever, I was thinking—" He stares up at the wood-beamed ceiling. "Now that things are starting to settle around here, well, it's probably a good time for you to start thinking about heading back to school."

I stiffen, allowing for only the shallowest breath.

"Turns out Lina left it all to me—the house, the store—everything. And since all the paperwork seems to be in order, I figure I can just let the lawyer take over from here, which frees me up to get back to full-time. Not to mention Ava already offered to pick up any stray hours I'm unable to cover."

I swallow hard, but I don't say a word. His expression tells me it's handled, arranged, he's got it all figured out.

"As much as I appreciate your help, and I do—" He peers at me briefly, before returning to the ceiling again. "I think it's probably best for you to—"

But I don't even let him finish before I'm saying, "But, really—it's no—" *Biggie*—I start to say *it's really no biggie.* Start to explain the conclusion I've recently come to regarding school, the normal life path one's expected to follow, and me—and how they no longer mix—no longer make the least bit of sense.

Though I don't get very far before he waves his hand and says, "Ever, if you think for one moment that this is easy for me, well, think again." He sighs and closes his eyes. "Trust me, there's a big, loud, overwhelming part of me telling me to just shut up—to stop talking, and quit while I've got you right here in my house, well within my reach, and more than willing to spend your free time with me." He stops, hands clenching, fingers fidgeting, a sign of the battle that rages within. "But there's also another, far more rational part, that tells me to do just the opposite. And even though I'm probably crazy for saying this, I feel like I have to, so, I just . . ."

He pauses, swallowing hard before he starts again, "I just think its for the best if you—"

I hold my breath, pretty sure that I don't want to hear it, yet resigned to the fact that I will.

"I think you should sort of . . . just . . . stay away for a while, that's all."

He opens his eyes and looks right at me, allowing the sentence to hang there between us like a barrier that cannot be breached.

"Because as much as I love having you around, and I think you know by now that I do, if we have any hope of moving forward, if *you* have any hope of making a decision anytime soon regarding your future—or *our* future—whatever the case may be, well, then, you really need to get back out there. You have to stop—" He takes a deep breath and shifts uncomfortably, obviously having to force the words from his lips. "You have to stop hiding out at the store and deal with your life head-on."

I sit there, speechless, stunned, and a little confused as to how I'm supposed to take that—much less respond to it.

Hiding?

Is that what he thinks I've been doing all week?

And, even worse, is there any chance that it's true? That he's onto something I'm totally unconscious of and worked extra hard to ignore?

I shake my head and drop my feet from the table to the floor. Slipping them back into my wedge-heeled sandals when I say, "I guess I didn't realize . . . I—"

But before I can go any further, Jude abruptly sits up, shaking his head when he says, "Please, I meant nothing by it, I just want you to think about it, okay? Because, Ever—" He pushes his dreadlocks off his face so he can really see me. "I just don't know how much longer I can sit on standby like this."

He drops his hands to his lap, where they remain open, relaxed, like some kind of offering. Holding my gaze for so long my heart begins to race, my gut to dance, and I feel so light-headed it's like all of the air has been sucked right out of the room.

The energy between us building and growing until it's so palpable, so tactile, it's like I can actually *see* it streaming from his body to mine. A thick, pulsating band of desire that expands and contracts, urging us to move closer, to merge as one.

And I'm not sure who's responsible for it—him, or me, or maybe some sort of universal force. All I know is that the pull is so overwhelming, so broad and sweeping, I leap right out of my chair, slap my bag onto my shoulder, and say, "I should go."

Already at the door, fingers twisting the handle when he calls, "Ever—we're okay here, *right*?"

But I just keep going, wondering if he saw what I saw, felt what I felt, or if it was just some stupid thing I made up in my head.

Stepping outside and taking a long, deep breath—filling my lungs with warm salty air as I gaze up at a night sky filled with stars, one in particular that burns especially bright.

One single star that manages to outshine all the rest—as though it's begging me to make a wish upon it.

So I do.

Gazing up at my very own night star, asking for guidance, direction, for some kind of help—and, failing that, to at least provide some kind of nudge that'll push me toward the right one.

eighteen

I drive around Laguna for what seems like forever, unsure what to do with myself, unsure where to go. Part of me—a *big* part of me—longing to go straight to Damen's, barrel right into his arms, tell him that all is forgiven, and try to pick up right where we left off—but I dismiss it just as quickly.

I'm lonely and confused and really just looking for a warm place to land. And as conflicted as I may be about him, I refuse to treat him like a crutch.

We both deserve better than that.

So I continue to cruise, traveling up and down Coast Highway a few times before venturing into the smaller, narrower, twisting and turning village streets. Just meandering around and around, with no real destination in mind, until I find myself at Roman's—or, make that *Haven's*, since according to Miles, she's taken up residence.

Abandoning my car by the curb, far enough away so she won't see it, I creep quietly across the street, hearing the music well before I've even reached the path that leads to the door. The speakers blaring some song by one of those garage bands she's so fond of—the kind Roman hated and I've never even heard of.

I make my way toward the front window, a large bay one lined with hedges on the outside and an unoccupied window seat on the inside. Crouching down beside the bushes, having no intention of going in or being seen, I'm far more interested in observing, learning just what it is that she's up to, and how she spends her free time. The more I know about her habits, the better I'll be able to plan around them, or if not actually *plan*, then at least I'll know how to react when the time comes.

She stands before a blazing fire, her hair long and wavy, her makeup as dramatically applied as the last time I saw her. Though the long, flowy gown she wore on the first day of school has been swapped for a skintight, indigo-blue minidress, while the stilettos she usually favors have been shunned for bare feet. But the tangle of necklaces are still there, minus the amulet of course, and the longer I watch her, the way she speaks, the way she flits around the room, the more I begin to worry.

There's something so manic, so agitated, so tightly wound about her, it's like she can barely contain her own energy, can barely handle herself.

Bouncing from foot to foot in a state of perpetual motion, taking numerous gulps from her goblet, not allowing it to sit empty for even a second before she's dipping into Roman's supply of elixir and refilling again.

The same elixir she claims to be far more powerful than

the one Damen brews, and from the looks of her, and from what I experienced in the school bathroom, I've no doubt it's true.

Even though her words are completely drowned out by the music and the blaring percussion that vibrates the walls, it's not like I need to listen to know what's really going on here.

She's worse than I thought.

She's losing control of herself.

While she may be able to influence her rapt group of listeners, keeping them mesmerized, entranced, and happy to focus only on her—she's far too fidgety, far too frenzied and turbulent to keep it going much longer.

She reaches for the goblet again, tossing her head back and taking a long, deep swill. Running her tongue over her lips, desperate to catch every last drop, her eyes practically glowing as she repeats the sequence again—and again—drinking and pouring, pouring and drinking—leaving no doubt in my mind she's addicted.

Having been to that dark place myself, I know all the signs. Know just what it looks like.

Though it's not like I'm all that surprised. This is pretty much what I expected from the moment she turned against me and went off on her own. Though I am surprised that her new group of friends pretty much consists of every Bay View High School student who's ever been dumped on by Stacia, Craig, or any other member of the A list crew—while the A list itself, the group she was last seen cozying up to on the first day of school, is decidedly absent.

And I'm just starting to get it, just starting to understand what it is that she's up to, when I hear:

"Ever?"

I turn, my gaze meeting Honor's as she pauses on her way to the door.

"What're you doing here?" She squints, carefully eyeballing me.

I glance between her and the house, knowing my hiding place near the bushes and my surprise at being caught pretty much reveals everything that I won't.

The silence lingering between us so long, I'm just about to break it when she says, "Haven't seen you around school lately—I was starting to think you dropped out."

"It's been a week." I shrug, knowing that as far as a defense goes, it's a lame one. Still, I could've been sick, could've come down with mono or a bad case of the flu, so why does everyone just assume I dropped out?

Am I really that big of a weirdo/loser to them?

She juts her hip to the side and drums her fingers against it, taking a moment to really look me over before saying, "Really? A week—is that all?" She bobs her head back and forth as though mentally weighing my words. "Huh. Seems so much longer. Must be the fastest social revolution in all of history."

I narrow my gaze, not liking the sound of that, but determined to not say a word—or at least not yet anyway. I'm hoping my silence will get her so pumped up and carried away, so eager to impress me with whatever it is that she's done, she'll reveal far more than she ever intended.

"Surely you've heard?" She tosses her hair over her shoulder as she starts to move toward me. "I guess I just assumed that's why you're here, spying on Haven and all. But, whatever, all you need to know is that it worked. Stacia is *history* and Haven has taken her place." Her eyes flash as she allows her lip to curl just the tiniest bit, no doubt feeling more than a little pleased with herself. "Things are *very, very* different around Bay View these days. But, heck, don't take my word for it, why don't you drop by and see for yourself?"

I take a deep breath, resisting the urge to react, to pay any real notice to her mocking tone, her sense of superiority. It's exactly what she wants, and I'm not about to comply.

Still, I am hoping to knock her down a notch when I say, "Excuse me, but did you just say *Haven's* taken Stacia's place?"

Honor nods, still smirking, still feeling all puffed up and triumphant.

"*Sooo* . . ." I narrow my eyes, dragging out the word as I take a moment to slowly look her over. Taking in her designer flats, black leggings, and the long-sleeved, clingy T-shirt that hangs well past her hips. My gaze finding its way back to hers when I say, "How does that make you feel?"

She glances toward the window, watching as Haven continues to entertain her minions, before returning to me. Her confidence beginning to waver, to fade, just like her aura, wondering just what it is that I'm getting at.

"I mean, that's not quite the coup you had planned, now is it?"

She exhales loudly, deeply, gazing at the street, the yard, anywhere but me.

"Because, if I remember right, your whole deal was that you were tired of being number two—and now, well, from what you just told me anyway, you actually kind of *missed* the revolution since you're *still* number two. I mean, think about it, Honor, according to what you just said, the only change is that you're now *Haven*'s shadow instead of *Stacia*'s—or at least that's how it sounded to me."

She crosses her arms before her, so quickly, so violently, the bag on her shoulder slips down to her elbow and bangs hard against her thigh. But she pays it no notice, just narrows her gaze on mine when she says, "I was sick of dealing with Stacia's crap. And now, thanks to a little help from Haven, I don't have to. *No one* has to. Stacia is nothing more than a big washed-up has-been who no one pays any attention to. She doesn't matter anymore, and you shouldn't feel sorry for her." She lifts her brow and scowls.

But she can make all the faces and lob all the rebuttals she wants, the fact is, my work is done. I've gotten to her. Reminded her of her one big goal—to take Stacia's place— and pointed out how from everything she's just said, it was a total fail.

Figuring I may as well drive it all the way home when I add, "Because the thing is—" I raise and lower my shoulders casually, as though I have all the time in the world to explain it to her. "The thing about Haven—or at least this *new and improved* version of Haven—is that she's really not so different from your old friend Stacia. No real difference at all. Except for one *major* thing—"

Honor inspects her nails, doing her best to appear bored, uninterested, but it's no use. Her aura is blazing big and bright—her energy streaming toward me as though begging the words to come quicker. Like a mood meter she's not even aware of and couldn't possibly hide if she was.

"Haven is far more dangerous than Stacia could ever be." My gaze locks on hers, watching as she sighs and rolls her eyes.

Addressing me with a major dose of pity when she says, "*Please.* That may be true for you, but it's hardly true for me."

"Yeah? And what makes you so sure?" I cock my head to the side as though I truly need to hear it from her, as though I couldn't just look straight into her mind.

"Because we're *friends.*" She shrugs. "We share a common interest—a common . . . *enemy.*"

"Yeah, well, I'm sure you remember that it wasn't all that long ago when Haven and I were friends too." I glance back toward the window, watching as Haven continues to drink and talk, talk and drink, with no signs of slowing, no signs of ceasing. "And now she's determined to kill me." I turn to face Honor, my voice so quiet it was almost as though I just spoke to myself

But she heard it. The way she sniffs and fidgets and tries so hard to act like I didn't just say what I said, assures me of that.

Her posture stiffening, her resolve hardening, as she heads for the door and says, "Listen, Ever, despite what you may think, the only enemy I share with Haven is Stacia. I really don't want to have a problem with you. Whatever goes on between you and her—stays between you and her. Which means I won't tell her I found you out here spying— *okay*? That can be our secret."

I pluck a stray leaf from the front of my dress, not believing a word she just said. Knowing all too well she'll be unable to resist it, that she'll divulge the whole thing the second she walks through that door.

But maybe that's not such a bad thing. Maybe it's time for Haven to get the long overdue message that her fun is now over—that, as of tomorrow, I'll be back in full swing. She cannot continue to terrorize people—even when those people are Stacia. Or at least not while I'm still around.

"You know what they say about secrets, right?" My eyes fix on hers.

She shrugs, tries to act casual, uninterested, but it's no use. Her face is marred by fear and confusion.

"That two can keep a secret if one of them is dead."

She shakes her head, tries to shake off my words, but she's troubled, that much is clear.

Reaching for the door and looking over her shoulder when I say, "So, if you do decide to tell her I was here, you can also tell her I look forward to catching up with her tomorrow at school."

nineteen

If I were to make an assumption based solely on the look and feel of the parking lot, well, I'd probably assume that all is as fine and well and normal as it ever will be.

I'd also assume that this morning's early training session/workout—the one that left all of my muscles quivering—was a total waste of time and that I should've just slept in instead.

But from everything Miles has told me, I need to venture a little farther than the overcrowded lot that looks more like a luxury car dealership than an area reserved for student parking.

I need to go past the wrought-iron gates and into the heart of the school, where, according to him anyway, the real story lives.

And even then, he says it's probably only truly shocking to those in the know, since all of the teachers and administrators remain pretty much oblivious to the new social order.

"And, Ever," he says, turning to me as I head for my intended space, the best in the bunch, the one Damen used to save for me that now, for some strange reason, has been taken over by Haven. "That's not all. There's a little more to it, something else you should know."

"Sing it." I smile, pulse racing as I focus on Roman's shiny red Aston Martin that Haven now drives.

"Not everything is quite what it may seem at first glance." He studies me, carefully, cautiously, making sure that I'm listening before he goes on to say, "So . . . just try to keep that in mind, okay? Don't rush to judgment. Don't make any snap assumptions should you . . . or, I guess I should say, *when* you . . . come across something like that. Okay?"

I squint, pushing my hair off my face, saying, "Spill it, Miles. Seriously, whatever it is you're dancing around, just say it, simple and clean. Because, honestly, I have no idea what you're getting at." Narrowing my gaze and reading into his energy, his tremulous, wavering aura, a sure sign that something's up, but still maintaining my vow to respect his privacy by stopping right there, not even considering trespassing on his innermost thoughts.

But it's not like he knows that. All he can see is my deep, piercing stare, and it sends him straight into a panic.

"Hey, stop that!" he shouts. "You promised you wouldn't do that without my permission. *Remember?*"

"Relax." I dismiss the thought with a wave of my hand. "I wasn't reading your mind. Not even close. I mean, *sheesh*! What does it take to get a little trust around here?"

Mostly mumbling that last part to myself, but for some reason, it prompts him to say, "Trust goes both ways, Ever, just remember that, okay? That's pretty much what I was getting at earlier."

I shrug, moving past Miles's intentionally coy and cryptic

warning and on to my real mission. Closing my eyes just long enough to do what it takes to prove to a *certain someone* just who's the real boss around here. *Seeing* the red Aston Martin banished to a faraway corner, as I punch the gas and quickly claim the newly vacated space.

Prompting Miles to gasp, turning to me when he says, "Wow. I think I forgot how much I like carpooling with you." He shakes his head and laughs. "In fact, I actually really missed it. I mean, don't get me wrong, I'm eager for the car to get out of the shop so I can get my freedom back and all that, but still, there's nothing like the way you manipulate the traffic light patterns to go green when you need them to and red when you don't, the way you convince all the other drivers to get out of your way and merge into another lane so you can take their place, and how you just *take* whatever parking space you set your sights on, whether it's occupied or not. Like now, for instance." He shakes his head and sighs. "I gotta tell ya, Ever, that sort of thing never really happens when I'm out on my own."

But even though he meant it as a joke, something about it really shakes me. Everything he just mentioned, all of those tricky maneuvers, were taught to me by the stealth-driving master himself—*Damen*. And I can't help but wonder where he stands in all this.

"Miles—" I pause, my voice sounding much smaller than I intended. Dropping my hands from the wheel and clasping them in my lap as I say, "Exactly where *is* Damen these days?" I turn, noting the concern that quickly clouds his gaze. "I mean, why is he allowing Haven to do this—to park here and whatever else she's up to? Why isn't he fighting back in some way?"

Miles looks away, taking a moment to compose himself, his words, before he faces me again. His hand on my arm, squeezing gently when he says, "Trust me, he *is* fighting back. In his own concerned-citizen, good karma kind of way. That's sort of what I meant when I said you shouldn't jump to conclusions. Not everything is as black and white as it first seems . . ."

I stare at him, waiting for more, but he just clamps his lips shut and runs an imaginary zipper across them. And I can't believe he's going to leave it like that, leave *me* hanging like that.

"That's it?" I look at him and shake my head. "That's how you're gonna leave it? All vague and noncommittal, and up to me to figure out on my own, without a heads-up?"

"That *was* your heads-up," he says, clearly committed to leaving it there.

I sigh and close my eyes, but I don't get upset, don't read his mind, don't press any further. He's got my best interests at heart, convinced he's trying to spare me from something. So I decide to let it go. Aware of something he's not—that whatever it is, I can face it.

Nothing can break me anymore.

He flips down the mirrored visor and squints at his reflection, combing his fingers through his longish, glossy, brown hair—the cool new look I'm still getting used to—and checking his teeth, his nostrils, his profile (both sides), before deeming himself ready for the public and slapping the visor back up again.

"Are we ready?" I reach for my bag as I open my door, his nod prompting me to add, "But just so we're clear, whose side *are* you on?"

He tosses his backpack onto his shoulder and shoots me a

look. The glint in his gaze a perfect match for his smile when he says, *"Mine.* I'm on my side."

Well, he certainly wasn't kidding. Nor was he exaggerating. On the one hand, everything is totally and completely different—a radical shift has clearly taken place. While on the other, to the less observant among us (aka the teachers and administrators), everything appears exactly the same.

The "senior tables" are still populated by seniors—only now it's the ones who were never allowed to even walk past, much less sit there before.

And instead of a bitchy, blond fashionista holding court— a bitchy, brunette fascist has taken her place.

A bitchy, brunette fascist whose gaze targets me the second Miles and I step past the gate.

Glancing away from her adoring group of fans just long enough to narrow her eyes and clench her jaw as she quickly takes us in. The look lasting for only a second before she's turned back to them, but it's still enough to give Miles pause.

"Great," he mumbles, shaking his head. "It looks like I've just *unofficially* chosen sides." He winces. "Or at least that's what *she* clearly thinks."

"No worries," I whisper, gaze scanning the area, searching for Damen even though I try to pretend I'm merely refamiliarizing myself with the school grounds. "I promise I won't—"

I see him.

Damen.

"—I promise I won't let her—"

I swallow hard and drink him right in.

Lounging on a bench, long legs splayed out before him, resting back on his hands as he tilts his gorgeous face toward the sun . . .

"—I promise I won't let her hurt—"

I struggle to finish, but it's no use. I know the instant I see it that *this* is what Miles was so covertly trying to warn me about.

Not wanting to state it bluntly, correctly assuming I'd freak—pretty much just like I am—but not wanting me to just stumble upon it either and feel sucker-punched in the very worst way.

Miles did what he could—I'll give him that. He did his best to spare me this brand of pain. But still, no matter how much he tried to prepare me, there's just no denying a sight like this.

When I said that nothing could break me, I was wrong.

Dead wrong.

But then again, I never really imagined I'd find him like this.

He talks to her softly, his face gentle and kind, distracting her from the cruel comments and looks that come from just about everyone who passes by. But as long as Damen's there, that's as bad as it'll get. No one will dare venture anywhere near. His presence alone is what keeps them away. Keeps her safe.

As long as he's with her, she's spared from their wrath.

But it's not like understanding why he does it makes it any easier to watch. And every second I stand there—a part of me withers.

A part of me dies.

Miles grabs hold of my elbow, determined to steer me away, but it's no use. I'm stronger than him and I refuse to be swayed.

Knowing it's just a matter of moments until he'll sense my presence, my energy. And even though my insides are churning, my heart breaking, my hands shaking, even though I'm terrified of what I might find in his gaze once he does locate me—I still need it to happen.

Need to know what it means.

Need to know if she now occupies the space I once filled in his life.

When he sees me, when his eyes go wide and his lips part in a way that completely transforms him—my breath stalls in my throat.

The moment feeling like forever, like it's somehow suspended in time. Though it's not long before she sees it too, following his gaze all the way to me before quickly looking away. Her former surplus of confidence now diminished for good.

"Ever—*please*," Miles urges, his voice at my ear. "Remember what I told you. *Nothing* is what it seems. Everything's been turned upside down. The former D list is now the A list—and the old A list, well, they've pretty much disbanded, most of them are in hiding, some have even left. Nothing is the same anymore."

But even though I hear it, the words flow right through me.

I don't care about any of that. I only care about Damen and the way his gaze circles mine.

And though I wait for it—a tulip, either real or imagined, or some other kind of sign—nothing comes.

Nothing but the infinite silence that stretches between us.

So I lean into Miles and allow him to lead me away.

Lead me right past the sight of them.

Right through my pain.

twenty

He calls out my name, his voice coming from behind me. Right behind me. Causing me to turn, instinctively, automatically, moving toward him without thinking.

"You're back." He looks at me, the words a statement, his gaze a question.

I nod. And then I shrug. And then I struggle to cease all outright modes of fidgeting as I try to decide where to take it from here.

But clearly he's far more up to the task than I am, because barely a moment passes before he says, "It's good to see you."

"Is it?" I narrow my gaze, instantly regretting the tone, the words. Seeing the way he flinches, the way his eyes pull down at the sides, but now that I've said it, there's no taking it back.

"I've missed you." He gestures toward me, his hand lifting, reaching, but only briefly before it falls back to his side. "I've missed the *sight* of you, the *scent* of you. I've missed *every single thing* about you." He allows his gaze to move over me slowly, circling, like the warmest of hugs. "And even if you decide to never talk to me again, it won't change a thing. Nothing can ever change how I feel about you."

My insides turn to jelly—a quivering mass of indecision. Torn between bolting—getting myself as far from him as I possibly can—and running straight into the shelter of his warm and wonderful arms. Wondering how I can possibly feel so totally empowered to deal with Haven and all of her crap, to do whatever it takes to get a handle on her—but *this*, this thing with Damen, seeing him with *her*, and now standing before me like he is—well, it instantly unearths every last trace of my old insecurities and self-doubt.

Leaving me to wonder why it's always so much easier to train the body than the heart.

I mean, out of all the girls in this school, why *her*? Why Stacia? Surely there's someone else he could play the white knight for . . .

But just after thinking it, the reason becomes clear. And I watch as she ducks out of class, makes her way down the hall, head lowered, shoulders slumped, gaze fixed on a distant point just in front of her, not daring to risk any accidental eye contact with her tormentors, as she cowers against their onslaught of hate—the slew of harsh words, cruel looks, and the occasional water bottle aimed at her head.

And even though my mind hates the fact that he's the only one who can protect her, my heart knows I have nothing to worry about, nothing to fear.

"As it just so happens, she needs protecting more than anyone else," Damen says, nodding toward the scene I just witnessed. "A lot's changed since you were last here. The whole school's turned against her. And even though you may think she deserves it, trust me, no one deserves that, no one deserves what Haven's put her through."

I nod, knowing it's true, wanting him to know that I know it's true, but unable to actually voice the words. It hurts too much to speak.

"But, Ever." He pauses, gaze holding mine. "I'm merely looking after her here at school, nothing more. It's not at all what you think, or what you might fear. It's always been you. I thought you knew that."

"I do know that," I say, finally finding my voice again. "But does she?" I cringe at the statement, hating the sound of it, the weak, disgusting, totally embarrassing sound of it. Still, it's not like I can't see the way she gazes at him. Same way she always gazes at him. Same way *most* girls gaze at him. The only difference is, with Stacia, there's history.

"She does." His face is grave, his eyes never once straying from mine as his hands hang open, loose by his sides. "Trust me, I've told her. She knows."

I swallow hard and study those hands, remembering all of the wonderful things that they're capable of and longing to feel them again. Knowing from the way they tremble ever so slightly that it's taking every last ounce of his strength to stay right where he is, rooted in place. That all I have to do to bridge the terrible chasm gaping between us is take one step toward him—one step away from the past, Stacia, and everything else.

If only it were that easy.

While I know our past lives don't define us, I still can't make peace with some of the more undeniable facts. Like his penchant for pulling me away from my loved ones so that he can have me all to himself—having done so twice that I know of. And I can't help but wonder how many other times he's resorted to that, and how many people have suffered because of it.

The bell rings, the sound trilling loudly, but neither one of us moves.

We just stand there together, allowing a scurry of students to move all around in a blur of color and sound. Our gazes locked, bodies still, his mind streaming tulips toward me until I'm surrounded by a glorious halo of them only we can see.

The spell broken when someone bumps into me—*hard*—one of Haven's minions who's severely misjudged me. Tossing me a belligerent gaze and a few choice words to go with it, until she reads the look on Damen's face and swiftly cowers away.

"I understand." I nod, watching as a wadded-up piece of paper bounces off the side of Stacia's head as she ducks into class. My gaze shifting from her to him when I add, "Really, I get it. It's good of you. Kind of you. It's the right thing to do. So don't worry about me, you just continue to protect her, and I'll . . ." I search the hall, watching it empty as everyone races to beat the tardy bell. "And I'll do what I can to keep it from getting any worse—to keep Haven under control."

"And *us*? Is there any hope for us?" he asks.

But I leave the words behind.

His thoughts drifting from behind me, around me, curling up inside me, as I turn and make my way down the hall.

Reminding me that he's here.

Will always be here.

All I have to do is let him in.

twenty-one

I figured she'd try to avoid me 'til lunch.

Figured she'd want to hold off on any sort of confrontation until she had her groupies all gathered around her and she could show me the full brunt of the big, bad thing she's achieved.

Figured she mistook my weeklong absence, my wanting to get my head straight about Damen, for fear.

Fear of her and all she's accomplished.

Which is exactly why I made sure to run into her well before that.

Appearing by her side without warning, I slide up alongside her, tap her on the shoulder, and stare straight into her heavily made-up, slightly startled eyes, saying, "Hey, Haven." I keep my expression benign, if not outright friendly. Wanting her to know that I'm back, that it's time for her to rein it in, but not wanting to challenge her directly, since nothing good will come of that. "Just thought you should know that your car has been moved. I needed the space."

She looks at me, mouth curling up at one side, obviously far more amused than mad, ridiculously delighted to know the game is still on.

"But then again, that shouldn't really surprise you, since you know that's not your space. It belongs to Damen and me. Has for almost a year now."

She laughs, a short burst of sound that ends almost as soon as it begins. Slipping out of her shorts and T-shirt, she tosses them into her locker in exchange for the navy-blue dress she starts to yank over her head. "Yeah, well, you weren't here and Damen didn't seem to mind all that much. But then again, from what I've seen, he's been a little *preoccupied* lately."

She pulls the dress down, her eyes meeting mine as her face emerges from the swath of fabric, then she shimmies from side to side, getting herself all situated. Taking a moment to eyeball me, her derisive gaze raking from my head to my toes before venturing back up again, searching for a reaction that just doesn't come.

Her comment glides past me, doesn't affect me in the least. Damen and I have come to an understanding, and *this* confrontation with her, well, it's everything I've trained myself for.

"I thought you hated P.E." I drop onto the scarred wood bench, cross my legs, and clasp my hands on my knee. Gazing around the girls' locker room, a place she's made a point to avoid after a particularly brutal hazing incident she was forced to suffer at the beginning of freshman year.

"Well, it's true that I used to." She shrugs, readjusting the jumble of necklaces she now favors in place of the amulet I gave her. Her eyes blazing, face radiant when she looks at me and says, "But then, as you well know, things change, Ever.

Or, more specifically, *I've* changed. And because of it, I've finally come to realize something I could've only guessed at
before." She pauses for a moment to slip on her shoes, wrapping the ties around her ankles, once, twice, before tying
them in a knot that reaches halfway up her tiny, well-muscled
calves. "Once you've made it to the top of the pyramid, once
you're beautiful, powerful, *and* graced with both strength
and speed, well, there's really no reason to dislike *anything*.
Except for maybe those pathetically jealous losers who are
determined to bring you down. But, seriously, other than
that, it's *all good*. You can't even imagine what it feels like to
be me right now." She fluffs her hair, smoothing her hands
over the front and sides of her dress, gazing at herself admir-
ingly in the mirror across the way, as she makes sure everything is perfectly in place.

Stealing a moment away from her reflection to reflect
upon me, sighing deeply, loudly, her gaze full of pity when
she says, "I meant that *literally* by the way. You seriously cannot imagine what it's like to be me. What it's like to be on top
of the world—at the top of your game." She smirks, reaching
into her locker, toward the top shelf, where she's stashed all
her rings. "I mean, let's face it, not to be cruel or anything,
but you've pretty much been a big loser your whole, entire
life, and even now, when, technically speaking anyway, you
can have anything or anyone you choose—you still choose
to be a big dork." She shakes her head and stacks her rings on
her fingers, a task that takes longer than you'd think due to
the sheer number of them. "I mean, if it wasn't so funny, it
would be sad. But still, I have to admit, there's still a small
part of me that pities you."

"And the other part?" I look at her, watching as she arranges her hair, getting it settled and smoothed around her shoulders and face.

She laughs. Satisfied with her hair, she pilfers through her bag for some lip gloss before casting a quick glance my way. "Why, the other part is going to kill you. But then, you already knew that."

I nod, so casually you'd think she'd just made some harmless, throwaway comment rather than an actual threat on my life.

"I mean, don't get me wrong, originally I'd planned to kill Jude first, you know, hurt him real bad while making you watch—that sort of thing. But then, once I really thought about it, I realized it would be so much more fun to switch it around and do away with you first. You know, leave him totally defenseless and alone, with no one *able*, much less *willing* to save him. I mean, surely Damen won't be volunteering for that. And not just because he's so busy protecting Stacia, but because, well, let's face it, as good and noble as he likes to think he is, I doubt even he'll be all that sad to see him go, considering everything that's gone down recently." She shrugs, running the wand over her lips, once, twice, before rubbing them together, making a kissing face at the mirror, then grinning as she drops the gloss back into her bag. "I don't know, just an idea. What do you think?"

"What do I think?" I lift my brow and tilt my head, allowing my hair to spill down the front of my dress.

She looks at me, waiting.

"I think—*bring it on.*"

She breaks into laughter, deep, belly-clutching laughter. Struggling to catch her breath as she smooths her hair again, tosses her bag over her shoulder, and continues to check herself out in the mirror, tilting her head from side to side and clearly admiring the view when she says, "You couldn't possibly be serious. You actually want to start this, here? *Now?*" She looks at me, face full of doubt.

"Seems as good a time and place as any." I shrug. "I mean, why delay the inevitable, right?"

She holds my gaze as I rise from the bench, standing before her without a trace of fear, completely assured of my surplus of strength. Taking a moment to remind myself of the promise I made—that it's up to her to make the first move. I don't bait her, don't do anything more than stand there and wait. The consequences are far too serious, far too permanent, for a reckless move like that. My only goal is to teach her a lesson, knock her down a notch or two. Show her that I'm stronger than she thinks, that it's time for her to pull back, to retreat. Hoping it'll prompt her to rethink all of this, to realize her big, bad plan is not such a wise move.

She shakes her head, rolls her eyes, mumbles something indecipherable under her breath, and tries to push past me, dismissing the whole thing with a wave of her hand. "Trust me. It'll happen, when it happens." She glances over her shoulder and narrows her gaze. "All you need to know is that you will *not* control it, you will *not* determine it, and you will *not* see it coming. Makes it *way* more fun that way, don't ya think?"

But just as she reaches the door, sure she's in the clear, I appear right before her, barring her exit. "Listen, Haven, you so much as lay a finger on Miles, Jude, or anyone else, and so help me you will not like what happens to you . . ."

Her lip curls, while her eyes go dark, darker than I've ever seen them before. "And what if I go after Stacia?" She smiles, though it's more like a leer. "What're you gonna do about that? You gonna risk your life—your very *soul*—to protect her too?" Pausing long enough to allow the words to penetrate, before slapping her hand over her mouth in a feigned bout of shame. "Oh, never mind. I totally forgot she has Damen for that now. My bad." She smirks and shoves past me, pushes right through the door.

Leaving me there on my own, knowing the victory may have been small, but having no doubt I succeeded in getting my message across.

The next move is hers.

twenty-two

It's hard to get used to this new lunchtime routine—with Haven holding court at table A, while Miles and I sit at our usual table C. Both of us pretending not to look anywhere near table D, where Damen sits beside Stacia, even though we're both pretty much blatantly gaping at it.

Though as hard as it is to watch, Damen and I have come to a new understanding—one where we accept our respective responsibilities in the present, while I take some time to try and accept the sins of his past. Still, I know inside that it's worth it. Worth the pain of seeing him like that—the way he gazes at me, the way he keeps watch over her—worth it because as long as I'm here, as long as Damen is there, Haven is contained.

Out of control but contained.

And no one gets hurt.

I twist the cap off of my elixir and take a deep swig. My eyes darting around the area, seeing Honor work overtime to maintain her place beside Haven—working harder than she ever had to work with Stacia, while Craig and some of his friends seem clearly relieved to have gotten off easy—reduced to sitting at a lesser table, but still, it could be worse. If it wasn't for his connection to Honor, and the fact that she still has feelings for him, I've no doubt he'd be as bad off as Stacia.

"It's like we've landed in upside-down bizarro world," Miles says, between slurps of vanilla yogurt, eyes tracking the area as anxiously as mine. "I mean, everything's backward, everything I thought I knew about this school, the good, the bad, and the completely hideous, is now totally different, and it's all because of *her*." He nods toward our former friend, watching her for a moment before turning to me. "Is this what it was like for you when Roman took over?"

I turn, wide-eyed, caught completely off guard. We never really talk about that time, back when Roman hypnotized everyone and turned them all against me. Those were some of the darkest days of my life—or at least this life anyway.

Still, I just nod and say, "Yeah, it was pretty similar." My gaze drifting toward Damen, remembering how he sat with Stacia then too. "*Very* similar, in fact."

I play with the cap on my elixir, twisting it on and off, off and on, as my mind revisits the past. Choosing the more hurtful scenes to play over and over again, before reminding myself that I got through that time just as I'll get through this time. As Ava always says: *And this too shall pass.*

Though she's also quick to remind me that the phrase works both ways. That it's true for the good times as well as the bad.

Everything passes. Everything experiences the birth and death cycle. Unless, of course, you're like Damen and me, in which case you get stuck in the same eternal dance.

I shake the thought away, and finish my elixir. Tossing the empty bottle back into the bag I hike onto my shoulder as Miles gazes up from stirring his yogurt and says, "Going somewhere?"

I nod, and one look at his face tells me he does not approve.

"Ever—" he starts, but I stop him right there. I know what he's thinking—that I'm leaving because it hurts too much to see Damen with Stacia, having no idea of the deal Damen and I made.

"I just thought of something, something I need to take care of while I still have the chance," I mumble, knowing I haven't convinced him as I watch Haven parade around table A, laughing and flirting, clearly enjoying her new role as queen bee.

"Cryptic much?" Miles narrows his gaze.

But I just shrug, eager to get moving, not wanting Haven to see me leave and, gawd forbid, decide to follow me.

"Well, can I at least come?" He looks at me, spoon dangling in midair.

I shake my head, gaze still on Haven when I say, "No." Not even pausing long enough to consider it, which doesn't go over so well.

"And why not?" His voice rises as his face drops into a frown.

"Because you have class." The sound of my own voice making me wince, I sounded way more like a teacher than a friend.

"And you don't?"

I sigh, shaking my head as I look at him. That's different. *I'm* different. And now that he's aware of it, I shouldn't have to explain it.

Still, he's not about to give up, he just continues to gaze at me with those big brown eyes, holding the look for so long I finally give in and say, "Listen, I know you think you want to come, but trust me, you *so* don't. You really, really don't. And it's not that I don't want you with me, or that I'm trying to ditch you or anything like that, it's just that, well, what I'm planning to do, it's not exactly considered legal. So really, I'm only trying to protect you."

He looks at me, spooning a glob of yogurt into his mouth, not the least bit swayed by the case I just pled. Covering his face with his hand as he looks at me and says, "Protect me from who—*you?*"

I sigh, fighting to keep a straight face, though it's kind of hard when he looks at me like that. His brow rising in suspicion, the flat-edged tip of his spoon bobbing up and down in his mouth. "Protect you from *the law*," I finally say, cringing at how dramatic that sounds, even though it's true.

"O—*kay* . . ." He drags out the word, eyes squinted as though seriously considering it. "And just what brand of illegal are we talking here?" He looks me over, clearly having no intention of letting it go 'til he's uncovered every last detail. "Larceny, bribery, usury, or some other illegal act that ends with a *y?*"

I sigh again, longer and louder this time, but still, in the end I just shrug and say, "Fine, if you must know, I've got a little harmless B and E I need to take care of, okay?"

"Breaking and entering?" He tries not to gape but doesn't really succeed. "But of the *harmless* variety?"

I nod. And shrug. And make a big point of rolling my eyes. Clock's ticking, lunch is shrinking, bell's gonna ring, and if it wasn't for this, I'd be long gone by now.

Seeing him lick his spoon clean, toss it into the trash, and rise from his seat as he says, "Well then, count me in." I start to protest, but he'll have none of it. He just flashes his palm and adds, "And don't even try to stop me. I'm coming, whether you like it or not."

I hesitate, hating the idea of involving him in this but also thinking it might be nice to have a little company for a change. I'm tired of playing the solo act.

I squint, looking him over as though I'm still weighing my options, even though I've already decided in favor of it. Shooting a quick glance at Haven, making sure she's still occupied, still engrossed in her own little world on Planet Haven, before I say, "Fine. But just act normal, okay? Act like you're just casually getting your stuff together because you know the bell's gonna ring in exactly two and a half seconds and you want to get to class on time and then—"

The bell rings, interrupting my speech as Miles gapes at me and says, "How did you—?"

But I just shake my head and motion for him to follow, warning him not to look anywhere near Haven's table, as I steal a quick glance at Damen's.

"And just remember, whatever happens, you asked for it," I add, as we make our way through the gate.

Aware of Damen's heavy wondering, questioning gaze—having no idea that what I'm about to do, well, if I'm successful anyway, could change our lives forever.

For better.

And if not, if I don't get what I'm looking for, well, maybe that alone will provide the answer I seek.

"Now, *this* is what I'm talkin' 'bout." Miles grins, face practically glowing with excitement. "*This* is what senior year is supposed to be like. You know, ditching classes, playing hooky, having fun, indulging in a little illegal activity—"

I peer at him, making sure he's all settled in before I punch the gas hard. There's no need for pretense, he knows exactly what I am, what I'm capable of. And after a few moments of white-knuckle-gripping silence from him, we're there.

Or at least, *almost* there, since I make a point to park half-way down the street, just like I did the last time I was here, figuring it's safer, if not smarter, to walk the rest of the way. No need to park on the drive and announce my arrival.

"Last chance to back out." I glance at my friend, white faced and panting beside me, struggling to get his equilibrium back.

"How can I back out?" he gasps, still catching his breath. "When I don't even know what I'm potentially backing out *of*?"

"Roman's house, which is now Haven's house, is just up the street. And you and I are going in."

"We're breaking into *Haven's*?" He gasps, finally starting to get the potential seriousness of all this. "*Seriously?*"

"Seriously." I push my sunglasses up on my forehead. "And I'm also serious about you backing out, since there's really no good reason for you to take part. I'm perfectly fine with you waiting right here. You can be my lookout. Not that I think I'll need one, but still."

But before I can finish, he's already climbing out of the car, already made up his mind. "Oh, no, you are not talking me out of this." He shakes his head in a way that allows his hair to flop right into his eyes. "If I'm ever up for a role as a cat burglar, or an art thief, or something like that, I can to-tally use this experience." He laughs.

"Yeah, except it's not exactly *art* that we're after." I motion for him to follow as I make for the walkway that leads to the door. Glancing over my shoulder to add, "And trust me, it doesn't really feel all that much like breaking and entering when you just walk up to the front door and open it with your mind. Though technically, since we weren't exactly invited, the term still applies."

He stops in his tracks, face expressing major disappointment. "Wait—seriously? That's it? We don't get to do a stealthy tiptoe as we slip around back? No sneaking through a cracked window or arguing over who gets to crawl through the doggie door to let the other one in?"

I pause, remembering the time I snuck into Damen's house in much the same way, back in the beginning when I was so confused by all of his strange ways I was desperate to determine what he was—only to find out later that I'm exactly like him.

"Sorry, Miles, but it's not gonna be nearly as exciting as that. It's pretty straightforward stuff." I stand before the door, *seeing* the lock retreat in my mind as I hold my breath and wait for the sound of that telltale *click*—but it doesn't come.

"That's weird." I frown, trying the handle for myself and surprised when the door springs wide open. Thinking either Haven's feeling ridiculously overconfident these days, leaving her house unlocked, or we're not the only ones here . . .

I glance over my shoulder, motioning for Miles to stay quiet, to stay behind me, as I pause in the threshold, taking a moment for my eyes to adjust, to scope out the space, making sure it's all clear before I signal for Miles to join me.

But the moment he steps into the hall, the floor creaks so loudly the sound seems to blare. Prompting us to freeze, instinctively holding our poses as we listen to the unmistakable sounds of glass breaking, voices whispering, feet scrambling, and a back door slamming so hard it sends the walls shaking.

I bolt. Racing toward the kitchen, and reaching the window just in time to see Misa and Marco making their getaway. Marco running somewhat clumsily as he cradles an unzipped duffle bag filled with elixir, as Misa follows with her own empty bag slung high over her shoulder. Turning just long enough to meet my gaze—holding the look until she breaks away, hops the fence behind Marco, and they both disappear down the alleyway.

"What the *hell*?" Miles says, finally catching up and coming into the room. "Did you seriously just move as fast as I think you did?"

I turn, taking in the jagged shards of glass scattered all across the floor, and the deep, dark red liquid that races across the tiles and seeps into the grout.

"So, what's the deal? What did I miss?" he asks, glancing between the mess and me.

But I just shrug. I have no idea what's going on here. No idea why Misa and Marco would resort to stealing the elixir. Why they were so panicked they actually broke a bottle. Not to mention why Misa looked so frightened to see me.

Only one thing is clear—they weren't exactly invited to help themselves to the supply.

Still, none of that has anything to do with us or our reason for being here. So as soon as I've cleaned up the mess simply by *wishing* it to disappear, I look at Miles and say, "So, what we're looking for is a shirt. A white linen shirt. With a big green stain on its front . . ."

twenty-three

The weeks go by, but nothing much changes. Jude continues to avoid me until I come to a decision, Damen continues to guard Stacia at school, Miles continues to guard my feelings regarding Damen guarding Stacia at school, and Haven continues to rule the school, while I continue to remain on high alert, waiting for the moment when she decides to go after me.

But that's just on the surface.

Because a closer look reveals more than a few cracks that are starting to show.

For one thing, there's just no hiding the fact that Honor's just as miserable being Haven's number two as she was being Stacia's number two—maybe even more so.

For another, while I can't be too sure, since it's not like we actually talk or anything, but by the way Stacia keeps glancing at table A with such determination and longing, well, it's pretty clear she's getting sick of being protected by a guy who's immune to her charms and truly only wants to protect her.

And as for Haven, after having hooked up with and discarded just about every guy who's ever snubbed her in the past, she's clearly getting bored with the game. She's also growing increasingly annoyed with the way everyone copies the various looks she works so hard to create, forcing her to invent new, more outrageous ones that ultimately get copied too.

I guess being the alpha chick isn't quite what she thought it would be. The reality is starting to wear thin, like a job she doesn't particularly enjoy and wasn't really all that qualified for in the first place.

I can tell by the way she snaps at her supposed new friends, by the way she rolls her eyes dramatically, heaves these big loud sighs, and sometimes even resorts to foot-stomping tantrums when she's really, really frustrated and wants them all to know it.

Life at the top is dragging her down, and from what I can tell, Honor is really starting to resent her being there, just like I predicted she would.

Yet it's also clear that neither one of them has any plan to forfeit their positions. Haven has too much to prove, and Honor, well, while I have no idea what level she might've reached in her magick skills now that Jude's taken a break from tutoring her, regardless of what she's managed to learn, she's still no match for Haven and there's no doubt she knows it.

And even though Miles and I don't really discuss it, even though I pretty much just stick to the same ol', day in, day out, boring routine—of training in the morning, remaining vigilant at school, and then training again before bed, only to get up and do it all over again—I know I'm not the only one who notices.

Damen sees it too.

I can tell by the way his gaze is always on me—following me wherever I go. He feels anxious, worried about me.

Worried that she's starting to lose it—that she'll blow without warning and decide to come after me.

Worried that I'll fail to alert him when it happens, even though I promised I would.

And he probably has good reason to worry. She's strung out. Unruly. She's a complete and total wreck.

Like a bomb only seconds from detonating.

A thread that's *this* close to snapping.

And when it happens, I'll be the first one she seeks.

Or at least I hope it's me.

Better me than Jude.

On my way home from school I stop by the store. Despite the fact that Jude asked me to stay away, claiming he can't bear to have me around until I make a firm decision either way.

Still, I convince myself it's my duty—that I have a serious obligation to look after him and make sure that he's safe and okay and all that.

But when I catch myself manifesting a cute new dress and shoes to go with it, just before checking my hair and makeup in the rearview mirror, I know that's only part of it. The other part is I need to see him. Need to see if being around him will spark something in me.

Something I can build on.

Something strong and tangible and defined enough to steer me in the right direction.

I stop just outside the door, fussing with my clothes and

my hair once again, before taking a deep breath and going in. Half expecting to find Ava behind the counter, since it's such a warm and beautiful day, I figure the siren song of all that good surf will be pretty hard for Jude to ignore, but thrilled to find him right there behind the register instead. Laughing and joking as though he hasn't a care in the world, his face relaxed, his aura green and easy, as he goes about the business of ringing up a customer.

A *cute* customer.

One whose blazing pink aura tells me she's only partly there for the books that she's buying and mostly there to see Jude.

I pause, wondering if I should just leave and come back later, when the door closes behind me, the bell clanks hard against it, and Jude looks past his customer to find me standing only a few feet away. Prompting his eyes to darken, his smile to falter, as his aura grows wavy and dim—pretty much the opposite of how he looked when he was talking to *her*.

As though the mere sight of me is enough to suck the joy right out of the room.

He shoves her stuff in a bag and sends her on her way so hastily, so abruptly, she can't help but notice the change. Giving me a quick up and down, chased by an accusatory frown, she mumbles something under her breath and makes her way past, while Jude busies himself behind the counter as though I'm not there.

"She likes you," I say, watching as he takes an extra long time to handle his copy of the receipt.

"She likes you *and* she's cute," I add, getting no more than a grunt in reply.

"She likes you *and* she's cute *and* she's got good energy," I insist, urging him to look at me as I make my way toward him. "Which makes me wonder, what's wrong with *you*?"

He stops. Stops with the fumbling, and the busy making, and the pretending I'm not standing right there in front of him when we both know I am.

Stops with all of that and finally looks at me and says, "*You*." Stating it so openly, so simply, I'm not sure what to do. "*You* are what's wrong with me." I gaze down at my feet, unable to look at him, feeling foolish for coming here like this, and barely daring a breath when he adds, "Isn't that what you wanted to hear?"

I nod, slightly, barely, because he's right. It is what I wanted to hear. It's exactly why I came here.

He sinks down onto the stool, shoulders slumping as he buries his face in his hands. Rubbing his eyes, the pads of his fingers digging in deep, before lifting his head and squinting at me when he says, "Ever, what's this about? Seriously? What're you doing here—what do you want from me?"

I swallow hard, knowing I owe him an answer, owe him the truth—in both of its forms. Venturing to do just that when I say, "Well, first of all, I wanted to make sure you're okay. I haven't seen you in a while and—"

"*And—?*" he snaps, clearly in no mood for games.

"*And . . .* I just really wanted to see you. *Needed* to see you, I guess you could say."

"You *guess?*"

His eyes rake over me, leaving me feeling raw, exposed, and weirdly traitorous toward Damen. Still, I need something from him. I'm all out of options. I mean, I can't find the shirt, the Great Hall refuses to help me, the wish I made on my night star has yet to come true, and so far there've been no omens or signs of any kind—all of which has led me right here, left with only one way I can think of to get to the bottom of it.

A way that's only been attempted but never actually completed.

A way that just might steer me toward the right one.

"Jude," I start, my voice sounding raw, unused. "Jude, I—"

I move closer, thinking: *This is ridiculous—this whole thing is ridiculous.*

I mean, he loves me, and I know I once loved him, or, even if it wasn't exactly *love*, I know for a fact I felt *something* for him. And maybe a kiss is all it'll take to reveal it to me. Just like when I first kissed Damen, how we felt so connected, so bonded, before all the other cruel realities moved in.

I move around the counter and reach for his hand, moving so quickly barely a moment passes before my fingers are pressed against his and a soothing rush of his cool, calm energy streams through my limbs. Quieting my mind—causing my body to soften and yield—watching as his face veers closer, gaze probing, burning, as my fingers curl around the lean tautness of his arm.

My entire being flushed with anticipation as I pull him right to me, waiting for the swell of his lips against mine, needing to experience this once and for all, needing to know just what it is we've been missing throughout all of these centuries.

At first shocked by the feel of it, the unexpected coolness, the pillowy firmness of his kiss—so opposite Damen's perfect blend of tingle and heat. Aware of the low groan escaping his throat as he cups the back of my head and presses me to him.

His mouth parting softly, his tongue seeking mine, as the door swings wide open, crashes hard against the wall, and sends the bell ringing and scattering across the floor.

We turn.

Jolted apart in surprise.

Only to find Haven, looking dark, sinister, cruelly shadowed by the light at her back, blocking the doorway and glaring at us.

Her lip curled, eyes narrowed, a hand perched on each hip as she says, "Wow. Would you look at that? This must be my lucky day. Two birds, one stone, and neither one of you standing a chance."

twenty-four

I turn to Jude, urging him to run, hide, to do whatever it takes to get away from her. Knowing we have only a second, two at the most, before she's on us—before it's too late for him to go anywhere else.

But even though I'm not at all joking, even though I shoot him a look that tells him I'm one hundred percent serious—he stays right where he is. Planted behind the counter, planted right behind me. Mistakenly thinking our brief, barely-there kiss somehow obliges him to stick around and protect me.

And I'm just about to repeat my request, when she's already crossed the room, already standing before us wild-eyed, crazed, wearing an out-of-control look on her face.

I move to cover Jude, seeing the way she smiles, slowly running the tip of her tongue around the rim of her lips as she peers over my shoulder and says, "Do yourself a favor and don't listen to Ever. You're much better off staying right where you are. You can never outrun me, no matter how hard you try. Besides, you're definitely gonna need that energy for later."

She takes a quick step to the right, as though she's planning to reach right around me and snatch him away, but I'm quick to block her, my eyes narrowed on hers, reminded of our unfortunate encounter in the school bathroom—when she controlled me—pinned me up against the wall—against my will—and knowing that if I'm barely a match for her, then Jude will never survive it.

"Sorry to interrupt your little make-out session." She laughs, her red-rimmed eyes darting between us. "I had no idea you two had decided to take it in *that* direction." She reaches toward me, pricking my shoulder with the sharp edge of her long, blue-painted nail before pulling away. The cold, bitter chill of her energy stinging, lingering, though there's no mistaking the effort it took to keep the hand trembling to a minimum.

She cocks her head to the side, grabs a chunk of hair that spills over her shoulder, and twirls it around and around her raised index finger. Her gaze focused solely on Jude when she says, "Before you get too overly excited about having made it to first base, you should probably know that the only reason Ever's allowed you to even get that far is because Damen's abandoned her for Stacia. *Again.*" She shakes her head and purses her lips, eyes darting between him and me. "And, well, I guess she's just looking for someone to fall back on. You know, so to speak."

I steal a quick glance at Jude, hoping he's not really listening to this, not taking her seriously, but his gaze is so clouded, so conflicted, it's nearly impossible to read.

"Don't you ever get tired of it?" She abandons the hair

twirling in order to admire the stacks of rings she wears on each finger. "You know, of Ever's constantly using you as a shoulder to cry on, using you to do her dirty work for her? I mean, seriously, when you think about it, a kiss is like, well, pretty much the *least* she can do when she's the number one reason why your life is destined to come to such a tragic, untimely end."

But even though she's prepared to go on and on, dragging this out for as long as she pleases, I've heard enough. Jude's heard enough. And I don't want him to get distracted by her or, worse, start to believe her.

"What do you want?" I steady my breath, center myself, and prepare for whatever it is she plans to dish out.

"Oh, I think you know." Her eyes flash with irises that were once a beautiful, tortoiseshell swirl of bronzes and golds but are now dark, ominous, gloomy, and mottled with red. "I think I've been quite clear about that." She smirks. "But what I can't decide is who to kill first? So maybe you can help me out here, which would you prefer—you or Jude?"

I hold her gaze, doing what I can to temper and soothe Jude's increasingly agitated energy, while keeping her attention and the brunt of her anger directed at me. "So, this is it?" My brow lifts as I glance all around. "Your big plan, the big scary move you've been threatening to make for—what's it been—weeks, months?" I lift my shoulders as though it's hardly worth remembering. "Is actually going to go down in a quaint little neighborhood bookstore?" I shake my head as though I couldn't be more disappointed by her mundane choice of venues. "I gotta tell ya, Haven, I'm a little surprised. I mean, I really would've thought you'd go for something with way more drama and flair. You know, some big, bold move in an overcrowded mall or something. But, then again, you are looking a little—what was that word Roman used to use?" I narrow my lids as though I'm actually trying to re- member, making a show of slapping my forehead when I say, "Oh, that's right—*peckish*. You're looking a little *peckish* these days." My gaze meets hers. "You know, strung-out, tired, a little—*edgy*—even. Like you're desperately in need of a good meal—and, well, yeah, maybe even a *hug*."

She scowls, scowls and rolls her eyes. Taking an unsteady step toward me when she says, "Oh, I've had lots of hugs lately—don't you worry about that. And if I find myself in need of another, I can always get one from Jude here." She leers at him, her face so creepy, her gaze so predatory, I can feel his energy contract from behind me. "Oh, and as for the lack of drama and flair, don't you worry, Ever, there will be plenty of that. Besides, it's not the stage that matters but the scene that plays upon it. And even though I'm not about to reveal any plot spoilers, because, let's face it, it's gonna be way more fun to surprise you, let's just say that in the end, I'm definitely going to make you pay for all of the horrible things that you've done to me, including your latest—"

I squint, having no idea what she's getting at.

But she just frowns and says, "Um, *duh*. You think I don't know it was *you* who broke into my house and stole my elixir?"

I gaze at her, shocked that she'd even think it was me.

"You think I don't keep track of my supply?" Her voice rises in outrage. "You think I wouldn't notice a *nearly empty fridge*? You think I'm an *idiot*?" She shakes her head. "It's pretty obvi- ous why you did it. It's the only way you think you can be equal to me. But news flash, Ever, you will *never* be equal me. *Never*. And drinking my elixir won't change that."

"Why would I want your elixir when I already have my own?" I squint, aware of Jude still behind me, aware of the way his muscles tense and his energy wavers, two very bad signs that he's planning something foolish that I can't let him go through with.

I push back against him, trying to keep Haven from noticing while still using enough force that he'll hopefully get the message to just lie low and let me handle this.

"Face it, Ever." Her eyes move over mine as her limbs begin to shake. "Mine is better, stronger, and far, far superior to yours. But it still won't help you, no matter how much you drink, you'll never match me."

"Why would I want to, when it's turned you into this?" My voice is scornful, scathing. "Seriously, Haven, just *look* at yourself." I motion toward her bloodshot eyes, twitchy fingers, and scary pale face. Drawing a line with my finger all the way down her skinny, shrunken form and back up again. And suddenly, after I really do look at her, I realize I can't do this anymore. Can't keep this up no matter what she's threatened to do.

This is *Haven.*

My old friend Haven.

The one I used to hang out with, laugh with. The only one besides Miles who was willing to let me sit with her on my very first day.

She's clearly in trouble, clearly needs help, and it's up to me to try to reach her, to help her, to try to dissuade her from what she's about to do before it's too late and I lose her forever.

"Haven, *please.*" I lift my palms before me, softening my tone along with my gaze. Wanting to make it clear that I'm switching gears, that I'm sincere, that I mean no harm here. "It doesn't need to be this way. You don't have to do this. We can stop right here, right now. What you're planning to do will only take a terrible tragedy and make it even worse. So please, please, at least think about that."

I take a deep breath, filling myself with all the light I can hold before exhaling slowly and sending it to her. Cocooning her in soft, soothing waves of green healing energy, watching as it hovers, attempting to penetrate, only to bounce right back—repelled by her hate-filled, rage-fueled exterior.

"It's not too late to call a truce," I say, keeping my voice low, steady, as though talking her down from the ledge, and hoping it'll work to calm Jude as well—keep him from going forward with whatever crazy suicidal act he has planned. "You're not looking so good. You've lost all control. Take it from someone who's been there, it doesn't have to be like this, there's a way out, and I'd really like to help you find it, if you'll let me."

But despite my calm, soothing words, she laughs in my face. The sound harsh, abrasive, her gaze dancing crazily, unable to hold still, hold it together, when she says, "You? Help *me*? *Please*." She rolls her eyes and bobs her head from side to side. "Since when have you ever helped me? All you ever do is *take* from me. Over and over again. But *help* me? Yeah, right. You've got to be joking."

"Fine." I shrug, determined to get past her words, to get through to her, to stop her from self-destructing. "If you feel you can't trust me, then let someone else help you. You still have a family, you know. You still have friends. *Real* friends. People who care about you, unlike the ones you've *manipulated* into being your friends."

She looks at me, blinking rapidly, swaying from side to side ever so slightly. Thrusting her hand deep into her bag, fumbling for her elixir but finding only a growing supply of empty, drained bottles she tosses all around her.

And I know I have to hurry, hurry up and get to it. We don't have much time, she'll erupt at any second. My words are rushed when I say, "How about Miles—he'd be more than willing to help you. And your little brother, Austin, he totally looks up to you, he *depends* on you. Heck, I bet even Josh is still crazy about you. Didn't you tell me he even wrote you a song in an attempt to win you back? Which means I seriously doubt he's over you yet. I'm sure he'd be there in a heartbeat if you called him. And—" I start to mention her parents, but I stop just as quickly. They've never really been there for her, and that's a pretty good part of the reason why we find ourselves here.

But I hesitate for too long, long enough for her to glare at me and say, "And *who*, Ever? Who are you gonna add to that list? The *housekeeper*?" She rolls her eyes and shakes her head. "Sorry, but it's way past all that. You robbed me of the one and only person I ever truly cared about, the one and only person who truly cared back. And now you're going to pay for that. *Both* of you are going to pay for that. Because make no mistake, neither one of you will be leaving here in anything other than a body bag! Or, in your case, Ever, a dustbin."

"It won't bring him back." But the words come too late. I've lost her. She's gone. No longer listening. Having already drifted deep into the darkest recesses of her own troubled mind.

I can tell by the way her gaze goes hazy, by the way her

whole body stills as she tunes in to the red-hot rage flaming within.

I can tell by the way the walls start to shake.

By the way the books begin to fall from the shelves.

By the way a flock of angel figurines soar through the room and crash into the walls before splintering toward the ground.

There's no getting through to her.

No turning back.

She stands before me, eyes blazing, hair lifting, as her entire body trembles with fury. Fists clenched tightly as she rises up onto her toes and reaches for Jude.

So I start to say: *Run!*

Start to say: *Make the portal and get the heck out of here!*

But before I can get to the words he's already leaped out from behind me.

Already charged her.

Already foolishly gone ahead with his plan to protect me at the expense of himself.

And as I reach for him, desperate to stop him from going any further, Haven reaches for me.

Snapping the amulet right off my neck, her face contorted, eyes burning bright, as she smiles and says, "So, Ever, how you gonna defend yourself now?"

twenty-five

She dangles the amulet before me, the crystals glinting, taunting, leaving me vulnerable, exposed, defenseless, and bare. Tossing the amulet over her shoulder as the sickening shrill of her laughter echoes through the room.

Jude clamors, hands and feet grasping, at the ready, but he's no match for her. With barely a flick of her wrist, she's shoved him aside, paying no notice as he flies across the store and crashes straight into the wall.

Paying no notice to the horrible sound of bones snapping and popping as he crumbles to the floor in a sad broken heap.

But as much as I long to run to his side to see if he's okay, I don't do it. Can't do it. That'll only lead her to follow, and I can't afford to let her get anywhere near him. For his safety, I need to keep her focused on me.

Still, I shoot him a look, mentally urging him to make the portal, to hurry up and do it while he still can, hoping he can somehow hear me. Unable to tell if his refusal to comply is due to the severity of his injuries, the gruesome mask of agony he wears on his face, the trickle of blood that flows from his mouth, or the fact that he refuses to leave me with her, determined to be there for me, no matter the cost to him.

She moves toward me, striving for slow and intimidating but nailing unsteady and shaky instead. Which, truth be told, is far more nerve-wracking than if she moved with purpose. Making it impossible to read her energy, to guess what she'll do next, when she doesn't even know yet herself.

She takes a swing, her fist rising, arcing, 'til it centers on me. But I duck just as quickly, moving right out from under it as I make for the other side of the room. Prompting her to turn and go after me again, tongue lodged against the inside of her cheek, her rage-fueled energy growing and expanding in a way that causes the lights to flicker, the floor to buckle, and all the glass fixtures, including the counter, to shatter and splinter.

Following me clear to the other side of the room as she says, "Nice try, Ever. But trust me, you're only delaying the inevitable. Every time you evade me, you just make it more fun. Still, I'm in no hurry, I can play this all day if you want. But you should know that the longer you drag this out, the longer he"—she hitches her thumb over her shoulder in the general direction of where Jude lies in a barely-breathing heap—"well, the longer he'll suffer."

My teeth grind together, as I press my lips tightly. I'm done trying to reason with her. I did all I could. And now it's time to put my training to use.

She charges me again, but she's so off balance, I just step to the side at the very last moment, causing her to crash into a CD display in a way that sends her skittering across the floor right along with them. Landing hard on a pile of jagged shards of glass she broke earlier, causing a spray of blood to spatter the walls as they slice deeply into her.

But she just laughs and rolls onto her back, taking a moment to pluck the pieces from her torn flesh, her eyes glinting as she watches the cuts mend, picks herself up, brushes herself off, and faces me again.

"How does it feel to know you're gonna die soon?" she asks, her voice raspy, ragged, revealing the effects of her efforts.

But I just look at her, shoulders lifting as I say, "I don't know. You tell me."

I move back just a little, realizing too late I'm pressed up against the wall—not really the best place to be when I need to keep myself open, unencumbered, with plenty of room for escape. Still, I only plan on being here for a moment, only until I can get to the other side where my amulet waits. As soon as I can get hold of it, I'll secure it back on my neck, and do what it takes to put this whole thing to rest.

She stands before me, arms loose, fingers twitching, feet planted wide, and knees slightly bent—preparing to move, preparing to pounce.

I use the moment to study her closely, get a feel for her energy, and try to determine which way she'll swing. But she's so out of whack, so disconnected from herself and from everything else, it's like trying to see through a cloud of static—she's impossible to read.

So when she does charge, her fist held high, angling down toward my stomach, I instantly move to block it.

Never once imagining she'd switch at the very last moment.

Never once imagining that anyone so strung out and unsteady could actually maneuver like that.

Catching the crazed look of triumph in her eyes as her fist plunges straight into my throat.

Slamming right into the sweet spot—my fifth chakra— the center for a lack of discernment, misuse of information, and trusting all the wrong people.

Nailing it so hard and fast, it's a moment before I realize what happened.

A moment before I'm overcome with staggering pain.

A moment before I'm out of my body, floating, swirling, gazing down at Haven's leering gaze, Jude's collapsed form, and the beautiful but fleeting cloud of blue sky that expands all around me—before everything shrinks, and collapses, and the whole world goes black.

twenty-six

You know how they say that when you die your whole life flashes before you?

Well, it's true.

That's exactly what happens to me.

Not the first time though. The first time I died I went straight to Summerland.

But this time, this time is different.

This time I see *everything*.

Every major, defining moment from my most current life, as well as all the others that came and went before it.

The images swirling around me as I free-fall through a solid dark space devoid of all light, overcome by a feeling both terrifying and familiar, as I struggle to remember when I could've possibly experienced it before.

And then it hits me:

The Shadowland.

The home for lost souls.

The eternal abyss for immortals like me.

That's exactly where I'm headed, and it's just like it was when I experienced it through Damen.

Except for the show.

That part he failed to let me see.

Though it's not long before I know why.

Know why he was so haunted after his own trip to the Shadowland.

Why he came back so different, so humbled and changed.

Plummeting so quickly, I'm buffeted by a sort of reverse gravity, feeling as though my gut's about to burst through my shoulders and head, as the images unfold all around me.

At first coming in glimpses, mere flashes of myself in all of my former life guises, but as I grow used to the sensation, accustomed to the movement and speed, I learn to temper it, to slow it down, to focus. Taking them in one at a time as they continue to stream past me.

Clean.

Unedited.

Including all of the parts Damen didn't want me to see.

Starting at the beginning, my first life in Paris, back when I was a poor, orphaned servant named Evaline, and wincing as I watch some of the more unsavory tasks I was made to perform—the kind of stomach-curling stuff Damen definitely spared me from. Everything unfolding just as he'd told me all along, until I notice Jude who lived as a cute, young stable boy with a lean, muscular build, sandy blond hair, and piercing brown gaze. And I watch as we begin to dance around each other, starting slowly, a look here, a brief word there, until we grow more comfortable and begin to seriously consider each other—make serious promises to each other. Promises I fully intend to keep until Damen appears and sweeps me right off my feet.

Sure he used a bit of trickery, summoning all of his immortal charms and putting them to good use. Always managing to show up at just the right time, in just the right place. Always managing to impress me in some big and showy spectacular way. But still, it's not like any of that was really necessary, because the truth, the truth that I couldn't see clearly until now, is that it wasn't the magick that enabled him to capture my heart—magick had absolutely nothing to do with it.

Damen won me over from the very first moment. From our very first glance.

Damen won me over long before I even knew who he was or just exactly what he was capable of.

His powers of attraction, the reason I fell for him so quickly wasn't because of the magick—it was because Damen was just simply being, well, *Damen*.

After watching our entire courtship together—scenes we've relived in Summerland, and those we have not—including my horrible death at Drina's hands—I move on to my next life. Back when I was a Puritan with a strict father, a long-dead mother, a wardrobe consisting of three drab dresses, and an even drabber existence. The only bright spot on the entire horizon of my boring life being a fellow parishioner with dark shaggy hair, a generous smile, and kind eyes I instantly recognize as belonging to Jude—a parishioner my father approves of, pushes me toward, until the day I spot Damen sitting in a pew and my whole world, my entire future, is turned upside down. And it's not long after meeting him, not long after getting to know him, when I promise to abandon my life of humble obedience for his far more glamorous one. Until, of course, Drina brings it to an untimely end.

Drina always brought it to an untimely end.

Leaving my father devastated, Jude shell-shocked, and Damen to scour the earth plane in a prolonged state of grief, waiting for my soul to recycle so we can reunite once again.

I watch my other lives as well, watch as my soul merges into the body of a well-coddled and extremely pampered baby who will grow up to be a frivolous, spoiled daughter of a wealthy land baron. Carelessly casting aside Jude, a British earl everyone assumes I'll marry, in favor of a tall, dark stranger who arrived seemingly out of nowhere. Though once again, thanks to Drina, my life ends tragically before I have a chance to make the choice public, but my heart knows the score.

Then on to Amsterdam where I lived as the beautiful, sultry, alluring artist's muse with the amazing mane of long titian hair. Flirting with Jude, just like I've done with so many who came and went before him, until Damen arrives and steals my attention.

Not by resorting to any sort of trickery, no overt magick acts were used. He won me simply by being who he is. No more, no less. From the moment I first laid eyes upon him, no one else stood a chance.

But the life I'm most interested in is the life that's revealed last.

My Southern life.

Back when I lived and worked as a slave.

Back when Damen freed me at the expense of my happiness.

Watching that whole miserable lifetime unfold, from a

childhood that never really was, to the only bright spot in that entire existence—a brief kiss from Jude.

The two of us slinking off to meet behind the barn just as the sun begins to fall. Unsure what's causing my heart to flutter more—the excitement of what I hope will be my first kiss or the fear of being caught sneaking off the job. Knowing the penalty for such an act will be a severe beating—or worse.

But still, determined to keep my promise to meet him, I'm overcome with a rare feeling of joy, an unexpected surge of happiness, when I see that he's already there.

He smiles awkwardly, and I nod in return, suddenly overcome by an extreme bout of shyness, a fear of appearing overeager. Though it's not long before I notice the way his hands shake, the way his eyes dart, and I know I'm not the only one feeling this way.

We exchange a few pleasantries, the kind of automatic words neither of us pays any real attention to. Then just when I'm thinking I've been gone for too long, that I'll have no choice but to head back before my absence is noticed, he does it.

He leans toward me, his large brown eyes peering at me with such love and kindness it robs me of breath. Then he closes them softly, leaving me with a view of curly dark lashes resting against glossy dark skin, and a pair of enticing lips moving toward mine. The cool sweet press of his mouth so soft and familiar, it causes a wonderful wave of calm to flow through my body.

Even after it's over, even after I push him away, turn on my heel, lift my skirts, and run back toward the house—the kiss lingers.

The taste and feel of it continuing to play, as I silently repeat the whispered promise we made to meet up the very next day, same time and place.

But just a few hours before that's scheduled to happen, Damen appears.

Seemingly arriving out of nowhere, just like he has in all of my previous lives, only this time he spares no time for a prolonged courtship, or even a few pleasantries of any kind, his intentions are far too urgent for that.

He's determined to buy me. To *free* me from a painfully harsh life of brutality and servitude, in exchange for one so opulent, and so privileged, and so opposite of everything that I'm used to, I'm convinced that he's lying, that it's a trick, that there's no way it could possibly be true.

So sure that my life has just taken such a major turn for the worse that I cry out for my mother, my father, strain my fingers toward Jude's—wanting him to hold me, protect me, not let me go to wherever it is I'm about to. Convinced I'm being ripped away from the only form of happiness I ever could know for something far worse, I'm terrified, caught in a state of overwhelming turmoil and fear. Deeply suspicious of this new, soft-spoken master who whispers to me gently, who treats me respectfully, and who gazes upon me with the kind of reverence I've never known before, that I'm sure isn't real.

Carefully setting me up in my very own room, in my very own wing of a house far bigger and fancier than the one I was made to clean. Faced with no task more demanding than sleeping, eating, dressing, and dreaming, with no threat of demeaning chores or painful beatings.

He gets me settled in, pointing out the features of my

quarters—my own private bath, a canopied bed, a wardrobe full of beautiful dresses, a vanity lined with the finest imported creams and perfumes and silver-handled brushes— telling me to take all the time that I need, that supper will hold until whenever I'm ready.

Our first meal together spent in absolute silence as I take the seat just opposite him, dressed in the finest gown I ever have seen. Focusing on the soft feel of the fabric, the way it eases against my subtly scented skin, as I pick at my food and he sips his red drink. Staring off into the distance, occasionally peering at me when he thinks I don't notice, but mostly distracted by the thoughts in his head. His brow furrowed, his mouth grim, his gaze telling, heavy, and just conflicted enough to tell me he's struggling with something, some kind of choice he must make.

And though I wait for the other shoe to drop, it never comes close. I simply finish my meal, bid him good night, and return to a room that's warmed by a well-tended fire and the finest cotton sheets.

Waking early the next morning and rushing to the window just in time to see him riding off on his horse, my eyes following anxiously, sure that this is it, that he's brought me all this way only to abandon me to someone who will find me and beat me 'til my death in some kind of sick, twisted game.

But it turns out I'm wrong, he returns that very same evening. And though he smiles when he greets me, his eyes betray a tragic story of devastating defeat.

Torn between telling me the truth and not wanting to upset me or scare me any more than I already am, he decides to keep the news to himself, to bury the awful truth he just learned, figuring there's no reason for me to ever know, it won't do me any good.

But even though I never learned the truth in that life, Shadowland generously reveals everything that he failed to.

Showing me exactly what happened when he rode off that day, where he went, who he saw, who he spoke to, the whole sordid scene.

He returned to the plantation, fully intent on buying my mother, my father, Jude, and all the rest of them and bringing them back to the house to enjoy their freedom, offering an exorbitant amount of money, a sum completely unheard of even among the very rich in those parts, only to have it refused. Taking no time to consider it, before he was quickly sent away. So eager to be rid of him, a foreman was sent to escort him off the property.

A foreman who, I can tell at first glance, isn't at all what he seems.

It's in the way he moves, the way he lives in his skin—overconfident, overly perfect, in every single way.

He's an immortal.

Though not the good kind—not Damen's kind—he's a rogue. Long before Damen even realized Roman still existed, that he'd made his own elixir and was freely turning people. Still, I can see by the worried look in his eyes that he senses it too.

Not wanting to cause any problems, not wanting to make a scene or make it any worse for my family or Jude, Damen leaves. Tuning in to my fear at being alone in the mansion, he's eager to comfort me, while vowing to revisit the plantation later, under the cover of night, when he plans to sneak them all out.

Having no way of knowing it'll be too late by then.

Having no way to see what I see—Roman lurking in the background while the master's away, running the entire show, sight unseen.

Having no way of knowing that the fire was purposely set long after he left, when it was already far too late to stop it, far too late to rescue anyone.

The rest of the story unfolding just as he said—he takes me to Europe, proceeding slowly, cautiously, allowing me all the time and space that I need until I eventually learn to trust him—to *love* him—to find true, but fleeting, happiness with him.

Until Drina finds out and quickly does away with me.

And suddenly, I'm aware of what I should've known all along:

Damen's *The One*.

Always has been.

Always will be.

A fact made even clearer as I relive the scenes from my most current life.

Watching as he finds my body by the side of the road, just after the accident. Not just witnessing but also *feeling, experiencing* the full impact of his grief at having lost me yet again. His pain becoming my pain, the full brunt of his sorrow leaving me gasping, as he begs for guidance, as he grapples with the choice of whether or not he should turn me like him.

Completely consumed by his gut-wrenching loss, the day I shout at him, reject him, tell him to go away, to leave me alone, to never speak to me again, just moments after he's finally found the courage to reveal what he made me—what I am.

Experiencing the full force of his confusion when he found himself under Roman's spell. His numbness, his inability to control his own actions, his own words, everything carefully orchestrated by Roman who manipulated him into being cruel, into hurting me, but even though I already guessed it, here in the Shadowland I can *feel* it, and I know, now more than ever, that no matter what he said or did, his heart wasn't in it.

He was just going through the preprogrammed motions, his body and mind dancing to Roman's tune, while his heart, refusing to be controlled, never once strayed from mine.

Even when he leaves me to choose between him and Jude, he loves me as much as ever before. So much that he's unsure if he can actually withstand the pain of losing me again, and yet he's so convinced of his actions, so convinced he's doing the right and noble thing, he's fully prepared to lose me if that's what I choose.

I watch how he spends those days without me, feeling lost and lonely and bleak. Haunted by the scenes from his past, sure that he deserves nothing less, and though he's clearly overcome with joy when I return, deep down inside, he's not entirely sure he deserves it.

I feel the fear he held in check when I was taken over by the dark magick I brought upon myself—just as I feel his eagerness to forgive me for all of the things that I did while under its influence.

Experiencing his love in such a deeply profound way, I'm left completely hollowed and humbled by the sheer abundance of it—by the way it never once shrank in its intensity, never once wavered throughout all of these passing centuries, throughout this past tumultuous year.

Humbled by the way he never once questioned his feelings for me in the way that I've questioned mine for him.

And yet, despite my occasionally turning him away—I now know something I failed to realize before:

My love for him also stayed true.

I may have questioned, second-guessed, veered a good ways from the path now and then, but all of that confusion existed only in my head.

Deep down inside, my heart knew the score.

And I know now that Haven was wrong.

It's not always a case of one loving more than the other.

When two people are truly meant to be, they love equally.

Differently—but still equally.

The irony being—now that I realize all of this, finally realize the truth of him and me, I'm forced to spend the rest of eternity suspended in the abyss, reflecting on all that I missed.

Swathed in a never-ending cloak of darkness, completely disconnected from anything and everything around me. Haunted by the mistakes of my past that forever swirl by. Like an infinite show set on permanent repeat, taunting me with all that I could've been, if I'd only chosen differently.

If only I'd followed my heart instead of my head.

One thing made abundantly, blindingly clear—while it's true that Jude's always been there, always been kind and giving and loving toward me—Damen's my one and only true soul mate.

I open my mouth, desperate to shout out his name, desperate for the feel of it on my lips, my tongue, hoping to reach him in some way.

But nothing comes.

And even if it did, there's no one to hear me.

This is it.

My eternity.

Disconnected.

Dark.

Repeatedly tormented by a past I can't change.

Aware that Drina is out there somewhere. Roman too. Each of us trapped in our own version of hell with no way to reach each other, with no end in sight.

So I do the only thing that I can—I close my eyes and surrender. Thinking that if nothing else, at least now I know.

At least I found the answer I sought for so long.

Soundlessly whispering into the void, my lips moving quickly, silently, without ceasing. Calling his name, calling him to me.

Even though there's no use.

Even though it's futile.

Even though it's way past too late.

twenty-seven

The sound of his voice floats over me, through me, all around me. Like a vague and distant hum that crosses oceans, continents, and galaxies to reach me.

But I can't reply, can't respond in any way. It's useless. Unreal.

A trick of the mind.

A Shadowland jeer.

No one can reach me now that I'm here.

My name a plea on his lips when he says, "Ever, baby, open your eyes and look at me—*please*." Words so familiar, I'm sure I've heard them before.

And just like before, I struggle to meet them. Slowly lifting my lids to find him gazing at me. Brow slanted with relief as those deep dark eyes bore anxiously into mine.

But it's not real. It's a game of some kind. Shadowland is a cruel and lonely place and I can't afford to buy into this.

His arms slide around me, surrounding me, cradling me,

and I allow myself to accept it, to sink into their depths, because while it may not be real, it's just too good to resist.

I try once again, struggling to call out his name, but he presses his finger to my lips, pushing softly. He whispers, "Don't speak. It's okay. *You're* okay. It's all over now."

I start to pull away, still gazing at him, not entirely convinced. My fingers seeking my throat, searching for evidence, exploring the exact same space where Haven's fist plowed into me.

Ended me.

Remembering exactly how it felt to die for the second time in this life.

Remembering how it was nothing at all like the first time.

My eyes grazing his face, seeing the concern that plays at his brow, the relief that creeps into his gaze, eager for him to comprehend what really, truly happened here. "She killed me," I tell him. "Despite all of my practice and training, in the end, I was no match for her."

"She didn't kill you," he whispers. "Honestly, you're *still* here."

I struggle to sit, but he just holds me that much closer. So I gaze around the shop, taking in the piles of broken glass, the knocked-over bookshelves—like a scene from the most over-the-top disaster flick, featuring earthquakes, tornadoes, a full-on assault.

"But I went to the Shadowland—I saw—"

I close my eyes and swallow past the lump in my throat, pausing long enough for him to say, "I know. I could *feel* your despair. But even though it probably felt like a long time to you, or at least I know it did for me, it wasn't nearly long enough for the silver cord to break and detach your body from your soul. Which is why I was able to coax you right back."

But even though he speaks with such confidence, even though he nods and meets my gaze with complete and total assurance, I know better. Despite my cord staying attached, I know for sure that I died. And there's only one reason I'm back.

I rose above my weak chakra.

The moment I realized the truth—about me—about *us*— the moment I made the right choice—I was somehow restored.

"She hit me right in my weak spot—my fifth chakra—and then—I saw everything." I gaze up at him, wanting him to know, wanting him to really hear me. "I saw *every single thing,* every single moment from all of our lives. Including the stuff you tried so hard to keep hidden from me."

He takes a deep breath, his gaze full of questions, one in particular that looms large between us.

And I waste no time in answering, circling my arms around his neck and bringing him to me, vaguely aware of the energy veil that dances between his lips and mine, as my mind streams into his. Informing him of all that I saw and what I now understand.

That I've accepted the one real truth.

That I will never doubt him again.

We stay like that, our bodies pressed together, intensely aware of the miracle that just occurred.

I'm more than just reborn—I'm truly, newly awakened.

Pulling away a moment later, my gaze posing a question he immediately answers when he says, "I sensed your distress. I got here as soon as I could, only to find the shop destroyed, and you . . . essentially . . . dead. But it wasn't long before you came back—though I'm sure it felt like an eternity to you. That's how the Shadowland works."

"And Jude?" My heart sinks to my stomach as my eyes scan the room, unable to find him, no matter how hard I look.

Then plummeting even further when Damen's voice drops as he says, "Jude's no longer here."

twenty-eight

The first thing I see when we arrive is pretty much the last thing I expected:

The twins.

Romy and Rayne standing side by side, with Romy in head-to-toe pink and Rayne in head-to-toe black, their jaws dropping in unison the moment they see me.

"Ever!" Romy cries, running up to hug me, her skinny body barreling right into mine, practically knocking me over from the force, as she wraps her scrawny arms around me and holds tight.

"We thought for sure you were stuck in the Shadowland," Rayne says, shaking her head as she blinks back her grief. Coming forward to stand quietly beside her sister, who's still attached to me. And just when I'm sure she's going to chase it with some kind of sarcastic crack, some derisive dig about how disappointed she is that I made it out in one piece, she looks right at me and says, "I'm so glad we were wrong." And her voice warbles so badly, she can barely eke out the words.

Recognizing a peace offering when I see one, I slide my arm around her, amazed by the way she lets me, the way she leans into me. Not just returning the hug but holding it for much longer that I ever would've expected. Pulling away a few moments later, she clears her throat, combs her fingers through her razor-slashed bangs, and wipes her nose with her long cotton sleeve.

And even though I'm dying to know how they got here, for now, it'll have to wait. There are far more pressing concerns.

But I don't even have a chance to voice them, before they nod their heads solemnly and say, "He's here." They turn and point toward the Great Halls of Learning just behind them. "He's with Ava. It's all good."

"So . . . he's *healed* then?" My voice catches, cracks, hoping that's what they meant, and instantly flooded with relief when they confirm it. "And you? Do you guys live here again?"

They look at each other, eyes meeting, faces still wearing the same somber expression, though it's quickly replaced with shaking shoulders and great peals of laughter. The two of them falling all over each other, enjoying some kind of private joke, before Rayne can calm down enough to say, "Do you *want* us to live here again?" She quirks her brow and looks me over, right back to being her normal self, well, for the most part, anyway.

"I just want you to be happy," I tell them, not wasting a single second in answering. "Wherever that takes place for you."

Romy grins, lifting her shoulders when she says, "We're sticking with Ava. Now that we know how to come here and visit whenever we want, well, we don't really feel like we need to live here again. Besides, we really like school."

"Yeah, and school likes us back." Rayne flashes a rare and brief smile that makes her eyes dance. "I've been voted class president."

I nod, not the least bit surprised by that.

"And Romy made cheerleader," she adds, rolling her eyes.

"I think all that practicing with Riley, you know, back when she lived here and used to hang out with us, well, I think it must've really helped." Romy shrugs modestly.

"Riley helped you with cheerleading?" I squint, more than a little surprised to hear that, though I'm not sure why.

Seeing Romy nod when she says, "She wanted to be just like you, you know that, right? She memorized every single cheer you ever did, and then she taught them to us."

I press my lips together and lean against Damen, enjoying the shelter of his strong solid warmth, of his hand squeezing mine. Knowing for sure, now more than ever before, that I can have this anytime I want, anytime I need it. He will always be there for me.

Focusing on the twins again when I say, "And speaking of missing people—"

They peer first at each other, then me.

"I know someone who'd really like to see you again."

Picturing the old British man I ran across the time I stumbled upon the cottage where they both used to live. Back when I first discovered the truth about their connection to both my sister and Ava, and telepathically sending the image to them.

"Though he seems to be more than a little confused. Somehow he's gotten it into his head that Romy's the stubborn one, while Rayne's the easygoing one, but I think we all know that's not true . . ."

They look from me to Damen, then burst into a whole new fit of giggles. Leaving Damen and me to just stand there, having no idea what they're carrying on about, but quickly pushing it aside to focus on each other.

And that's how Ava and Jude find us when they exit the Halls and make their way down the steep marble steps.

The twins giggling.

Damen and me communing—my head on his shoulder, our hands clasped tightly together.

And that's all Jude needs to see to know that the choice has been made.

To know that it's Damen and I who are meant to be together.

That whatever happened between us was long over before it could ever get started.

He stops, pauses right there on the very last step, allowing Ava to move past him as his gaze locks on mine. Holding it for what feels like a very long time, though no words are exchanged, no telepathic thoughts of any kind.

Though words aren't really necessary when the message is clear.

Then he takes a deep breath, takes a moment to collect himself, before nodding his acknowledgment. Both of us knowing this is it, my decision is made, and that it won't be up for consideration ever again.

Switching his focus to Ava and the twins, he decides to join them on their journey to revisit all their old haunts, if for no other reason than to distract himself from what he thinks he just lost.

And they're just about to head off when I turn toward the twins and say, "Hey—how'd you guys do it? How'd you get back here?"

Seeing the way Ava beams proudly, as the twins glance first at each other, then me, with Romy choosing to take the lead. "We took the focus off ourselves and put it on someone else for a change."

I squint, not quite understanding what they're getting at.

"We were with Damen when he found you," Rayne explains. "And when we saw Jude and the condition he was in, well, we knew there was only one way to save him, and that was to get him here, to Summerland."

"Which meant that our whole focus on getting here was no longer about *us*, it was about *him*. Our only goal was to help *him*." Romy smiles. "And it worked."

"Just like Ava always told us it would," Rayne says, gazing up at her with admiration. "It's like she always says—" She stops and motions toward Ava. "Well, you should probably say it, since it's your phrase and all."

Ava laughs, taking a moment to ruffle Rayne's hair, before she pulls her close to one side and Romy to the other, her gaze locked on mine when she says, "It all comes down to your *intention*. When you put all of your focus on a problem, you just get more of the problem. But if you put your focus on being of help, then your energy is directed toward the *help* instead of the problem. So before, when the twins were unable to return to Summerland, it was because they were too focused on themselves and their problem of getting here. But this time, their only concern was for Jude, and they got there in an instant. So basically, whenever you're looking for a solution, you are feeling *positive* emotion—and whenever you're looking at a problem, you're feeling *negative* emotion, which, as you know, never gets us anywhere. But once you take the focus off yourself and your wants, and instead turn it toward how getting what you want might also benefit someone else, well then, you can't help but succeed," she says, voice soft and sweet. "That's the key behind any success."

Rayne shrugs, smiling and shaking her head. "Who would've thought?" she says.

Yeah, who would've thought? I smile, briefly catching Ava's eye, watching as she glances between Damen and me and instinctively knowing she approves of my choice, then switching my focus to Jude, who, thanks to the wonderful healing magick of Summerland, is back to being as strong and cute and sexy as ever.

Looking as though Haven hadn't just broken his body.

As though I hadn't just broken his heart.

The kind of guy any girl would be lucky to get.

The kind of guy I've been lucky to know for as long as I have.

Then I close my eyes and manifest my very own night star, hanging it high in the Summerland sky, just over his head. Knowing that wishes don't always come about in the way that we think, but if you believe and keep your mind open, there's a really good chance they will manifest in some way. Because even though I didn't realize it at the time, that's exactly what my night star did for me.

By sending me to the Shadowland, I was able to find the answer I needed.

And before they move on, before my star can fade, I take a deep breath and make a wish for Jude.

Wishing for him to remain open and hopeful and willing to believe that there's someone out there who's far better suited for him than I ever could be.

Wishing for him to find the one and only person who'll love him as equally as he will love them.

Wishing for him to find what I've found with Damen.

And I leave him with that wish. Leave my star shining high in the sky for as long as it lasts. Watching as they go off in one direction, while Damen and I take another, the two of us strolling hand in hand, quiet and content, as I lead him toward the pavilion.

"Are you sure?" he says, standing just outside of it, clearly conflicted about trying this again.

But I just nod and pull him inside. I'm more than sure. In fact, I can't wait to get started.

There's so much about that Southern life we've yet to explore, and from what I saw in the Shadowland, there were definitely some really nice parts I'd love to revisit.

I hand him the remote as I stand before the screen, smiling at him as I say, "Just fast-forward to the good part, after you've secured my freedom and trust and you whisked me away to Europe . . ."

twenty-nine

By the time we get out of there I have no idea how much time has passed.

Since Summerland exists in a perpetual mode of hazy daylight where everything happens in an eternal state of now, it's impossible to tell.

All I know for sure is that my lips are tender and swollen, and my cheeks pink and slightly abraded from the swath of stubble that lines Damen's jaw—a condition that should disappear in just a matter of seconds.

Far quicker than Sabine's outrage over my extended absence back home on the earth plane.

Far quicker than Haven's triumphant glee over thinking she succeeded in killing me.

Still, even though I know I need to get home and face both of those things, I'm reluctant to leave, reluctant to give up the magick so quickly. And since Damen's clearly reluctant too, he manifests a single white stallion for us to ride. Allowing the horse to meander of its own free will as we enjoy the passing scenery.

I rest my chin on Damen's shoulder and wrap my arms loosely around his waist as we ride beside swiftly moving streams, down empty cobblestone lanes, through large sprawling meadows filled with chirping birds and deliciously fragrant blooms, alongside the shore of a beautiful beach made of white sand and turquoise waters, up a steep and winding trail that leads to a mountainous peak with a wondrous view, then back down its other side before wading through a barren desert's sands.

We even ride through the streets of all our former lives, as Damen manifests replicas of Paris, New England, London, Amsterdam, and, yes, even the antebellum South. Going so far as to give me a glimpse of his early life in Florence, Italy. Pointing out the tiny home where he lived, his father's workshop off the alleyway, the favored stalls where his mother frequently shopped.

He makes fleeting images of his parents, soulless forms that waver in and out of focus before us. Knowing I've seen them before, back when I spied on his life in the Great Halls of Learning but still wanting me to see them as he sees them. Eager to share every last trace of his life, of our shared lives, until there are no secrets between us—until all of it comes neatly together—until the entire story of our lives is complete.

And because I feel closer to him than ever before, because I'm completely secure in the knowledge that we're in this together for better or worse, I decide to show him something I'd previously kept from him.

Closing my eyes and urging our mount to take us to that

place—the dark side of Summerland—the side I kept hidden, kept to myself. Convinced for some reason I can't quite explain, that now's the right time to share it with him.

The horse immediately following my lead, instantly switching course as I press my lips to the curve of Damen's ear and say, "There's something I haven't told you—something I need you to see."

He turns, glancing over his shoulder, smile fading to concern when he takes in my serious gaze.

But I just nod and urge the horse forward, knowing we're getting closer when his pace begins to slow and I have to urge him to keep going. Knowing by the way the air suddenly changes, the sky darkens, the mist thickens, and what was once a blooming, thriving forest of vibrant plants and flowers becomes a drooping, rain-drenched, mud-filled swamp.

Our horse stops. Swishing his tail from side to side and throwing his head back in protest, refusing to go any farther. And knowing it's useless to force him, I slide off his back and motion for Damen to join me.

Answering the question in his gaze when I say, "I found this place a while back, the time I was in Summerland with Jude and ran into you. Strange, isn't it?"

He squints, glancing from the mud-soaked ground to the malnourished trees. Their branches brittle, graying, devoid of all foliage, of any sign of growth or life, despite the never-ending supply of rain.

"What is it?" he asks, still taking it in.

"I don't know." I shrug, shaking my head. "Last time I was here, I just sort of stumbled upon it by accident. I mean, I guess it wasn't really an accident, since there are no accidents here, but still, it wasn't like I was looking for it or anything. I was just killing time, waiting for Jude to come out of the Great Halls of Learning. And so, just to keep busy, just to have something to do, I asked Summerland to show me the one thing I'd never seen before, the one thing I really needed to know about—and my horse brought me right here. But when I tried to venture farther and explore a little more, she totally refused, just like our horse did now. So I tried to go off on my own, but the mud was so deep I kept sinking down to my knees, and it wasn't long before I gave up. But then, just now I thought—"

He looks at me, curiosity piqued.

"Well, it seems bigger than before. Like it's—" I pause and gaze all around. "Like it's growing or expanding or something." I shake my head. "I don't know, it's hard to explain. What do you make of it?"

He takes a deep breath, his gaze clouding at first, as though he's trying to protect me from something, but then it's gone just as quickly. That's our old way of communicating. We no longer keep secrets.

His fingers playing at his chin when he says, "Honestly? I have no idea what to make of it. I've never seen anything like it or at least not here anyway. But I gotta tell ya, Ever, it certainly doesn't leave me with a very good feeling."

I nod. Gazing at a flock of birds just off to the side, watching the way they carefully keep to the perimeter, refusing to soar anywhere near the darker bits.

"You know, Romy and Rayne once told me, not long after we met, that Summerland contained the possibility of *all things,* and you even said it once too."

Damen looks at me.

"So, if that's true, then maybe this is like—the *dark side*? Maybe Summerland is like the yin and the yang—you know, equal parts dark and light?"

"Hopefully not *equal*," he says, a look of alarm overtaking his gaze. Sighing as he adds, "I've been coming here for a long time, a *very* long time. And I certainly thought I'd seen it all, but this—" He shakes his head. "This is entirely new. It's nothing like the Summerland I studied or read about. It's nothing like the Summerland I ever experienced. And if it didn't start out this way, if this part of it is, in fact, new . . . well, something tells me that cannot be good."

"Should we explore? Have a quick look around and see if we can learn anything more?"

"Ever—" He squints, clearly not nearly as curious to get started as I am. "I'm not sure that's such a good—"

But I won't let him finish, my mind is made up and now it's just a matter of convincing him too. "Just a quick peek around, then we'll go," I say, seeing the waver in his gaze and knowing I'm close to succeeding. "But I gotta warn you, that mud runs deep, so be prepared to sink down past your knees."

He takes a deep breath, hesitating for a moment even though we both know it's as good as done. Finally grabbing hold of my hand as the two of us venture slowly into the muck, stealing a quick glance over our shoulders to see our horse, ears pinned back, pawing at the ground, snorting and grunting while shooting us a *you're crazy if you think I'm following you* kind of look.

Pushing through the relentless driving rain, until our clothes are soaked through and our hair clings to our faces and necks. Occasionally stopping to glance at each other, eyebrows rising in question, but still we keep going, keep forging ahead.

The mud pooling up to our knees when I remember something from the last time I was here, and I look at him and say, "Close your eyes and try to manifest something. Anything. Quick! Though try to make it something useful like an umbrella or a rain hat."

He looks at me, and I can see it in his gaze, and even though it's not at all useful, it's definitely lovely. A tulip. A single red tulip. But it just stays right there in his mind, refusing to materialize for us.

"I thought it was maybe just me." Remembering that bleak and dreary time when I first found myself here. "I was so confused back then, I actually thought maybe this whole place existed *because* of me. You know, like it was a physical manifestation of my inner state—or—*something*." I shrug, feeling more than a little stupid for having voiced that out loud.

Just about to take another step forward when Damen stretches his arm out before me and stops me dead in my tracks.

I follow his gaze, follow the length of his pointing finger, all the way across the muddy gray swamp. Gasping in surprise when I spot an older woman just a few feet away.

Her hair hanging in wet, white wisps that fall way past her waist and cling to a thin, gray cotton tunic that's a perfect match for the gray cotton pants she wears tucked into tall, brown rain boots. Her lips moving incessantly, mumbling softly to herself, as she stoops forward, her fingers digging deep into the mud—as Damen and I look silently on, wondering how we could've possibly missed seeing her until now.

We continue to stand there, unsure what to do or even what to say should she happen to notice us too. But so far she remains oblivious, focused intently on whatever it is that she's doing. Finally taking a break from all the digging when she reaches for a small, silver can and begins to water the already thoroughly drenched area.

But it's not until she turns, turns to face us, that I see how old she really is. Her skin so fine, so thin and translucent, it's practically see-through, while her hands are gnarled and bumpy, with large bulging knuckles that look painful to the touch. But it's her eyes that tell the real story—their color resembling a faded-out, sun-bleached light denim. Appearing rheumy, filmy, clustered with cataracts, but even from this distance, there's no mistaking the fact that they're trained right on me.

Her fingers loosen, dropping the watering can to her feet, not seeming to care when it's quickly swallowed whole by the mud. Her arm slowly lifting, finger shaky but still pointing right in my direction, when she says, *"You."*

Damen instinctively moves to cover me, to block me from view.

But it's no use. Her gaze remains firm, unwavering, as she continues to point, continues to repeat to herself, again and again:

"You. It's really you. We've been waiting for you for so long now . . ."

Damen nudges me, whispering between clenched teeth. "Ever, don't listen to her, just close your eyes and picture the portal—now!"

But even though we try, it doesn't work. There's no quick escape. No magick or manifesting to be had in these parts.

He pushes into my shoulder, grabbing hold of my hand as he urges me to run, turning on his heel and sloshing through the mud, doing his best to pull me along. The two of us stumbling, falling, taking turns picking each other up, as we continue to move forward. Doing whatever it takes to get back to our horse, to get out of here.

To gain some distance from the voice that continues to chase us.

Taunt us.

Repeating the same phrase over and over again:

From the mud it shall rise
Lifting upward toward vast dreamy skies
Just as you-you-you shall rise too . . .

thirty

The moment we walk through the gate, we start searching for Haven. But she sees us first.

I can tell by the way she stops—stops talking, stops moving, practically stops blinking and breathing—and settles for gaping instead.

She thought I was dead.

She left Jude for dead.

But apparently that didn't turn out quite as she'd planned.

I nod in acknowledgment, taking a moment to push my hair over my shoulder to provide a clear view of my neck—still free of the amulet, just like she left it. Wanting her to know that I'm no longer vulnerable. No longer ruled by a weak spot. No longer endangered by a lack of discernment, trusting all the wrong people or misusing knowledge.

I've totally and completely risen above it.

Leaving her no choice but to deal with me now that she can't do away with me.

And when I'm sure she's had enough time to process all

that, I lift the hand that's clasped with Damen's, raising it high enough for her to see. Wanting her to know we're still together, that we weathered the storm, that she cannot defeat us, nothing can, so it's best not to try.

And even though she quickly turns away, turns back to her friends and tries to carry on as though everything's normal, we both know it's not. I've put a major dent in her plans, and if she doesn't get the full extent of it yet, she soon will.

We move past her, through the quad, and all the way over to the bench where Stacia sits by herself with a hoodie pulled over her head, earbuds shoved in her ears, and a pair of over-sized designer sunglasses shielding her face in an attempt to deflect and ignore the stream of insults coming from just about every single student that passes, while she waits for Damen to show up and defend her from them.

I stop, struck by the way she looks just like me, or at least the old me, wondering if she sees it too, if she's managed to tune in to the irony of it.

Damen squeezes my hand, his gaze questioning, having misread my hesitation as an unwillingness to go through with it, even though we've been over it a million times already.

"I can handle it." I nod, glancing at him as I add, "Seriously. No worries. I know exactly what to say."

He smiles and leans in to kiss me, his lips soft, sweet, as they brush across my cheek. A quick and easy reminder that he loves me—that he's with me, always will be. But while it's definitely nice, and while I definitely appreciate it, I no longer question those things.

Stacia gazes up from her iPod, wincing the second she sees me. And I can't help but notice the way her mouth goes grim, the way she involuntarily hunches her shoulders and pulls them way in when I claim the space just beside her.

Having no idea what I could possibly want, but clearly convinced that whatever it is, it cannot be good, she pushes her glasses onto her forehead and shoots Damen a quick, *help me* kind of look, but he just claims the space right beside me, as I shake my head and say, "Don't look at him, look at *me*." My gaze holds on hers. "Believe it or not, *I'm* the one who's going to get you out of this mess. *I'm* the one who's going to put everything back the way it was. Or at least, *almost* the way it was."

Her eyes dart between us as her fingers pick at the rolled hem of her dress. Unsure if I'm actually being sincere or if she's being played in some sort of payback plan that I've made.

Just about to get up and leave, take her chances with the hostile masses, when I stop her by saying, "But, as I'm sure you've already guessed, there is one condition."

She looks at me, gaze wary, assuming the absolute worst.

"The condition being that when I return you to table A, you use your popularity for good and not evil."

She shakes her head, then bursts into a nervous laugh that ends almost as quickly as it begins. Unable to determine whether I'm joking or serious, and again looking to Damen for the answer, but the only answer he gives is a casual shrug as he motions toward me.

"I'm not joking. I'm one hundred percent serious. In case you haven't noticed, in case you've already forgotten, you've been nothing but a complete and total bitch to me from the very first day I arrived at this school. You took *way* too much pleasure in making my life a living hell. And I'm willing to bet you spent more time plotting against me than you did studying for your SATs."

She gazes down at her knees, cringing at my list of accusations and flushing under my scrutiny, though wisely choosing not to speak. I'm far from through with her yet, and there's plenty more where that came from.

"Not to mention how you tried to steal my boyfriend right out from under me—on more than one occasion." My eyes narrow on her, devoid of all mercy. "But let's not pretend I was the only one you tortured, because I think we both know that's hardly the case. Pretty much anyone you perceived as either weaker than you or somehow beneath you or, heck, even some kind of threat to you, was a target as far as you were concerned. You even went after your supposed best friend." She looks at me, nose scrunched, eyes squinty, prompting me to say, "Um, hel-*lo*, *Honor*?" I shake my head, wondering if I'm not just wasting my time, if it's actually possible to get through to someone as vain and selfish and emotionally clueless as her. "Why do you think she turned against you? You think it's all Haven's fault? Think again. She's been planning this for some time now, mostly because you treated her like crap—the same way you treat everyone. But also because you even tried to steal her boyfriend, and from what I heard, that was the last and final straw."

She swallows hard, combing her fingers through her hair, rearranging it in a way that partially covers her face. Completely unwilling to look at me and reluctant for me to see her, but at least she's not trying to deny what we both know is true.

"But I also hear you were as successful with that as you were when you tried to steal Damen." I narrow my gaze and shake my head, though I leave it at that, figuring I've gloated enough as it is.

"And despite the fact that your behavior is so completely cruel and calculating and totally uncalled for, I'm still gonna help you get your old position back."

She searches my face, trying to determine if it really is true, then quickly returning to the intense study of her spray-tanned knees as soon as I confirm it.

"And it's not because I like you—because I really, truly *don't*—and it's not because I think you deserve it—because I definitely *know* you don't—it's because what Haven is doing, believe it or not, is even worse than what you used to do. And since I have no interest in being the queen bee of the school, I've decided to return the position to you. But, like I said, it comes with conditions. The main one being that starting right now, from this moment on, you're gonna have to find another way to build yourself up. You're gonna have to stop tearing everyone down in order to make yourself feel bigger and better because that's pretty much the lowest, cheapest thing a person can ever do. And if this experience of yours, this reversal of your social fortune, hasn't taught you that, then I don't know what will. I mean, now that you've experienced what it's like to be on the other side, now that you know firsthand how it feels to be ostracized and treated as badly as you used to treat everyone else, I can't imagine you'd really want to make anyone go through that again. But then, maybe you do. There's really no saying with you."

She continues to sit there, shoulders hunched, hair hanging in a curtain between us. Her head bobbing as she taps the toes of her expensive designer sandals together, the only clue that she's listening, taking me seriously, and that's all I need to continue.

"Because the thing is, you're smart and pretty, and you

have all the advantages anyone could ever want in this world, and honestly, that alone should be enough to empower you. So maybe, just maybe, instead of acting like such a greedy little brat and trying to steal everything you know you can't have, you can concentrate on finding a way to use your gifts to be a good influence on others. You may think it's corny, you may think I'm ridiculous, but I'm totally serious. If you want to go back to being the rock star of this school, then that's exactly what you're going to do. Otherwise, I have no interest in helping you. For all I care, you can spend the rest of the year like this, and neither Damen nor I will lift a finger to help you."

She takes a deep breath, then glances between us, sighing and shaking her head, directing her words mostly at Damen when she says, "Is she serious? Is this for real?"

But Damen just nods, slides his arm around me, and pulls me even closer. "It is. So you should probably listen to her and take notes if you need to."

She sighs, taking a moment to gaze around a school she used to rule and now fears. And even though it's clear she's far from converted, that she's only gone along this far because she's hit rock bottom and has nothing left to lose, nowhere else to go but down even further, it's still a start.

Still good enough for me.

So I give her another moment to let it really sink in, waiting for her to turn to me and nod her agreement, when I say, "Okay, so here's where you start . . ."

If I'd had my way, she would've started right then and there. And Damen and I would've watched as she walked right up to Honor and put the plan in motion.

But Stacia needed more time.

Time to think it over, time to get used to the idea. Even though she clearly wanted to be on top again, she was so un-used to the concept of apologizing, she ended up requiring not only a good deal of convincing but also quite a bit of coaching to find the right words.

Still, as much as I pushed her, as much as I tried to con-vince her it was the right thing to do, deep down inside, I really didn't expect it to work—or at least not right away. I was more interested in getting her used to the idea of being a better person, and if I'm going to be perfectly honest, then I also have to say that I wanted her to have no doubt in her mind that I meant what I said.

My help came with conditions. And if she wanted it, well, she'd have to earn it.

I wasn't to be messed with again.

So by lunch, when Haven and her minions stroll out of class only to find their table occupied by me, Damen, Miles, and Stacia—well, they're not quite sure what to make of it.

And it's pretty clear that Haven's not quite sure what to make of *me*.

But then, neither is Honor, for that matter.

They just sort of stand there, loitering awkwardly, gawk-ing in disbelief as Craig and his friends slowly move toward us, gratefully taking the seat Damen just offered. Acknowl-edging the gesture with a *"Hey"* and a nod, which may seem simple on the surface but is definitely something they never would've bothered with before.

And while Haven continues to stand there, hands shaking in fury, eyes narrowed and red, I pretend not to notice. Look-ing right past the storm cloud of hate that emanates from her when I say, "You're welcome to join us if you want, as long as you behave yourself, that is."

She rolls her eyes, mumbles a slew of obscenities under her breath, and starts to turn away. Fully expecting her flock of minions to follow, but her power over them is no longer what it once was. It's waning. And to be honest, it's pretty clear that they're all getting a little sick of her. So when they accept Damen's offer to join us instead, she turns to Honor, eyes blazing, virtually daring her to choose.

And just when Honor starts to turn away from us and move toward Haven, Stacia jumps up from her seat and says, "Honor, wait—I'm—I'm really sorry!"

The words sounding so shrill, so uncomfortable, so foreign coming from her that Miles instantly bursts out laughing, and I have to squeeze his knee—*hard*—to get him to stop.

Stacia looks at me, eyes narrowed, brows merged, as if to say: *See, I tried, but it doesn't work!*

But I just nod toward Honor, seeing the way she's stopped, the way she's turned, her head tilted, gaze full of questions, wavering between two supposed best friends, neither of whom she particularly likes.

Hesitating for so long that Haven storms off in a huff. And even though I'm tempted to go after her, tempted to try to calm her, find a way to help her or at least talk some sense into her, I don't. Maybe later I will, but not now. For now I've got to see this thing through.

I nudge Stacia, nudge her with my eyes, with my mind, shoving my energy up against hers, urging her to keep going, to not stop now, even though the territory may seem scary and unfamiliar.

And a moment later, they're gone.

Walking side by side, Honor shouting, hurling the long list of accusations, all the very good reasons why Stacia *should* apologize, while Stacia patiently listens, just like I coached her to do.

"Are you eavesdropping?" Miles says, elbowing me and pointing toward them.

"Should I?" I look at him.

"Well, *yeah.*" He squints. "I mean, what if it's not what you think? What if they're both plotting against you?"

But I just smile, watching Stacia's aura shift and change, becoming just a bit more vibrant with each passing step. Knowing she still has a long way to go, that she may never really arrive, but still secure in the knowledge that auras never lie. And hers is off to a semi-decent start.

Taking a sip of my elixir and looking at Miles when I say, "Trust works both ways. Aren't you the one who told me that?"

thirty-one

Even though it shows all the signs of turning into an insanely uncomfortable situation, Damen still insists on going to Mystics and Moonbeams. And this time, just before we climb out of my car and head in, I'm the one who questions him on whether or not he truly wants to go through with it.

But he just looks at me and says, "Ever, for four hundred years we've been circling each other. Don't you think it's finally time to call for a cease-fire?"

I nod, not doubting for a minute that it is indeed time, though I'm not at all sure that Jude will agree. It's a lot easier to be logical and reasonable about these things when you're the one on the winning team.

He holds the door open as I make my way in. Spotting a few familiar customers milling about—the woman who collects angel figurines, the guy who's always bugging us to get an aura video station, even though from what I've seen of his, he's bound to be disappointed by the results, and the older woman with the beautiful purple glow all around her who Ava's currently assisting with the meditation CDs—while Jude sits behind the counter, taking small sips of coffee. His aura flaring the moment he sees us—especially Damen—though it's not long before it settles and calms, and I sigh in relief. Knowing it was just the result of an age-old, knee-jerk reaction, the kind that may require some time to phase out, but someday, if Damen has his way, it will.

He moves ahead of me, eager to get this thing started. Making straight for the counter with a ready smile and a softly spoken *"Hey,"* as Jude takes another sip of his coffee and merely nods in reply. His gaze dancing between us, apprehensive and unsure, and I really hope he doesn't think we came here to gloat.

"I was wondering if we could maybe talk." Damen motions toward the back. "Somewhere private, perhaps?"

Jude hesitates for a moment, taking a series of slow contemplative sips, before tossing his cup and leading us into his office. Settling himself behind the old wood desk, while Damen and I claim the two seats on the opposite side.

I watch as Damen leans forward, his gaze intent, face earnest, determined to get right to the point when he says, "I'm guessing you really must hate me by now."

But if Jude's surprised by the words, he doesn't show it. He just shrugs, leans back in his seat, and rests his hands flat against his stomach. His fingers splayed across the colorful mandala symbol that blazes across his white tee.

"And it's not that I'd blame you if you did," Damen says, eyes steady, focused on Jude. "Because I've no doubt committed my share of hateful acts over the last—" He glances briefly at me, still unused to voicing it out loud, even though he finds himself doing so more and more these days. "Over the last six hundred and some odd years." He sighs.

Both of us watching as Jude tilts his seat back as far as it will go, taking a moment to gaze up at the ceiling, pushing his fingers into a steeple, before the whole thing collapses and he drops forward again, his gaze boring into Damen's when he says, "Dude, seriously, what's that about?"

Damen squints, as I shift uncomfortably in my seat. This was a bad idea. We never should've come here like this.

But Jude just leans forward, sliding his elbows across his desk, pushing his dreadlocks off his face as he adds, "Really, what's that *like*?"

Damen nods, making some kind of sound between a grunt and a laugh, instantly relaxing as the tension drains from his face and he settles farther back in his seat. Propping his foot on his knee, snapping the bottom of his flip-flop back and forth against his heel, he shrugs and says, "Well, I guess you could say it's been—" He pauses, searching for just the right word. "*Long.*" He laughs, eyes creasing at the sides. "It's been . . . really, *really* long, in fact."

Jude looks at him, nodding in a way that shows he wants to hear more, and Damen obliges, picking at the frayed and broken hem on his faded old jeans, when he adds, "And, to be honest, well, sometimes it's a little exhausting. And sometimes it feels more than a little defeating—especially when you're forced to watch the same old tired mistakes being made over and over again with the same lousy excuses to support them." He shakes his head, lost in a stream of memories most people only learn about through history books. His expression instantly transforming, brightening, when he smiles and says, "And those are just the mistakes *I've* made." He meets Jude's gaze. "But then, there are also moments of such extreme beauty and joy that, well, it really does make it all seem worthwhile, you know?"

Jude nods, more in contemplation than agreement, as though he's still taking it in, considering the statement.

Though it's enough to prompt Damen to say, "Why, you interested? You want to give it a go?"

Jude and I both look at him, eyes wide, unable to tell if he's serious.

"Because I can set you up. I know a guy . . ."

And it's not until his lips curl into a grin, that I realize he's joking, and I settle back with relief.

"But the thing is," Damen says, back to being serious again. "In the end, it's pretty much all the same. I may live for centuries, you may live for three quarters of a century, but both of us will always find ourselves preoccupied with whatever's immediately before us—or, more often than not, whatever seems just out of reach . . ."

We sit there in silence, the words hanging heavy between us, as I gaze down at my knees, too uncomfortable to look anywhere else. Knowing that this is the moment we came for, that Damen's fully prepared to offer whatever explanation or apology Jude might demand.

But Jude just sits there, picking at a stray paper clip he found on his desk, twisting, and bending, and totally reshaping it until it's completely unrecognizable from its original form.

Finally looking up when he says, "I get it." He glances between us, focusing on me until I lift my head and meet his gaze. "Really, I do." His face so sincere I've no doubt he means it. "But if you came here to apologize or try to make up for it or—*whatever*—you should probably forget it."

I suck in my breath, as Damen sits perfectly still, waiting for him to continue.

"I mean, I'm not gonna lie, the whole thing sucks for me." He tries to laugh but doesn't quite make it. His heart isn't in it. "But still, I really do get it. I know it wasn't just a matter of playing fair or not playing fair. I know it wasn't just about your immense wealth and magick tricks. And I also know it was probably extremely unfair of me to pretend that it was. Because the thing is, Ever isn't that shallow. Neither was Evaline or any of the rest of them." His eyes meet mine, and they're filled with such warmth and kindness and love, it's impossible to look away. "The only reason I never stood a chance with her is because it was never meant to be me. It was always supposed to be the two of you."

I exhale slowly, my shoulders sinking, stomach settling, releasing a tension I wasn't even aware I was holding 'til now.

"And the fire—" Damen starts, desperate to explain that as well.

But Jude dismisses it just as quickly, waving his hand before us. "I know about that too—thanks to Summerland and the Great Halls of Learning." He shrugs. "I've been spending a lot of time there lately, maybe too much time, or at least that's been Ava's concern. But, sometimes, well, sometimes, or at least lately anyway, I'd rather be there than here. I guess that's why I'm so fascinated by your extra long life. I mean, I don't know how you do it when there are definitely times when the regular life span feels like more than enough, you know?"

Damen nods. Telling Jude he most certainly does know, knows all too well. Then he launches into the story about his first trip to Summerland, back when he was lost, and lonely and looking for some sort of deeper meaning, and found himself studying in India alongside the Beatles. And having already heard it myself, like a thousand times before, I quietly get up, let myself out, and head back into the store, curious to see what Ava's been up to.

Finding her off in the corner, restocking a shelf full of crystals when she turns to me and says, "All's well that ends well, right?"

I shrug, having no idea what she's referring to.

"Your choice." She smiles, turning back toward the shelf. "It must feel good to have that all figured out, no?"

I sigh. Because while there's no doubt that it definitely does feel good to put it behind me, the thing with problems is, there's never any shortage in the supply. As soon as one gets solved, another crops up in its place.

She digs her hand into a bag of rose quartz crystals, the crystal of love, balancing a generous pile of chunks in her palm when she glances at me and says, *"But . . ."* Purposely dragging the word out for as long as she can.

"But . . ." I shrug, hand darting forward, catching a falling stone and handing it back to her. "There's still Haven, who's getting more and more out of control, and then, of course, there's still the antidote, and the fact that Damen and I can't really, truly touch . . ." *Not outside of the pavilion anyway, but I'm not about to let her in on that.* "And then there's—"

She looks at me, brow raised, patiently waiting, as I quickly weigh whether or not I should confide in her about the dark side of Summerland I've discovered, and the strange, seemingly demented old lady Damen and I ran across.

But something keeps me from doing so. Something tells

me not to go there with her. Or at least not yet anyway. Not until we've had a chance to investigate a little further.

So I take a deep breath, lift an amethyst cluster off the shelf and carefully inspect it from all sides, as I say, "Well, you know, that whole drama with Sabine is still alive and well." Shaking my head as I return the stone to its place, knowing that while it wasn't exactly a lie, it wasn't quite the truth either. It's not bothering me nearly as much as it used to. Sadly, I'm getting used to living like that.

"Would you like me to speak to her?" she offers, but I quickly dismiss it.

"Trust me, it won't work. Her mind is made up, and I have a feeling time may be the only cure."

She nods, wiping her hands on the front of her jeans as she stands back to inspect the shelf. Head tilted, mouth twisted to the side, as she switches the apache's tear with the phantom quartz, then smiles approvingly.

And when I look at her, I mean *really* look at her, I can't help but wonder why she's always alone. I mean, she has the twins to look after, so I guess she's not really alone-alone, but still, ever since I met her, she's been decidedly single, and from what I can tell, she hasn't gone out on even one date.

And before I can stop it, I say, "Do you think everyone has a soul mate?"

She turns, regarding me seriously.

"I mean, do you think everyone has that *one person* they're destined to be with—like Damen and me?"

She's silent for a moment, as though she's really taking the time to consider. And just when I'm sure she's not going to answer, she does something I definitely wasn't expecting— she bursts out in laughter.

Her whole face lifting, her eyes glinting, when she looks at me and says, "Why? Who are you worried about more here, Ever, me or Jude?"

I flush. I hadn't realized I was that obvious, but knowing that she's a pretty gifted psychic and all, I should've figured she'd see through me.

"Well, both." I smile feebly.

Watching as she turns back to her work, folding up the now empty bags, and piling them on top of each other before folding the stack in half and stashing them inside a bigger bag. Her voice soft, just barely audible, when she says, "Well, for the record, yes, I do believe that. But whether or not you're able to recognize them and do something about it is a whole other story."

thirty-two

"So, how'd it go?" I glance at Damen, watching as he settles into the passenger seat and closes his door as I pull away from the curb.

"Good." He nods, shutting his eyes for a moment as he lowers the top with his mind, taking a long deep breath of cool evening air before he looks at me and says, "We're going surfing this weekend."

I gape, more than a little surprised to hear that. I mean, I originally thought he'd be lucky to get the cease-fire he was after, I never even considered they might become friends.

"So, is this, like, a *date*?" I tease, wondering how long it's been since Damen's been able to have a friend—a real and true guy-type friend—one who actually knows the truth about him.

"Never." He glances at me. "I've never had a friend who knew the truth about me. And, to be honest, it's been a very, very long time since I even tried to connect in that way." He averts his gaze, taking in the shops, the trees, the pedestrians crowding the crosswalks and streets, before he turns back and says, "Friendships for me were always short-lived since I had no choice but to move on after a certain number of years. People get suspicious when you stay exactly the same while they age, and after a while, well, it just seems easier to avoid those types of things."

I swallow hard and concentrate on the drive. Even though it's not the first time he's said it, it doesn't make it any easier to hear. Especially when I relate it to me and my life and the long list of good-byes I have to look forward to.

"Do you mind taking me home?" he asks, the request jolting me right out of my thoughts as I gape at him in surprise. I was sure he'd try to drag me off to the pavilion again, and to be honest I had no plans to deny him.

"Miles is meeting me back at the house. I told him I'd help him run some lines for a play he's auditioning for."

I shake my head and laugh, making a right on Coast Highway before stealing a quick peek at him. "Got any time in there for me, you know, amongst all of these playdates of yours?" Only partially teasing as I press the accelerator and cruise along the winding curves.

"Always." He smiles, leaning in to kiss me but ending up distracting me so badly I nearly run the car off the road.

I push him away and right the wheel again. Gazing out at the ocean, watching the waves turn to foaming white froth as they crash against the shore, and clearing my throat as I turn to him and say, "Damen, what are we gonna do about the antidote?" Seeing the way his shoulders stiffen, feeling the way his energy shifts and changes but still forging ahead, knowing it has to be said. "I mean, I'm fully committed to you, to *us*, I think you know that by now. And as much as I enjoy our time in the pavilion, well—" I swallow hard, I've never been much good at discussing this kind of thing, I always end up a red-faced, embarrassed, sputtering mess, but still, I'm determined to get to it. "I *miss* you. I miss being able to touch you in *this* life. Not to mention I was hoping that someday we could break this four-hundred-year-old-dry spell and—"

I pause before his gate, waving at Sheila, who motions us in. Taking the hill and the series of turns that lead to his street, before braking in his driveway and swiveling in my seat until I'm fully facing him.

Just about to finish the thought when he says, "Ever, I *know.* Believe me, I do." He reaches for me, cups his hand to the side of my face, as his eyes fix on mine. "And I haven't given up. I've even gone so far as to turn the wine cellar into a sort of chemistry lab—and I've spent every spare moment in there hoping to surprise you."

My eyes go wide, trying to calculate just how long it's been since I last poked around Damen's house, realizing it's been a while. When I haven't been avoiding him for one reason or another, we've been either training or making out in the pavilion.

"But if the wine cellar is a chem lab, then where do you store the elixir?" I ask, frowning as I try to picture it for myself.

"In the new wine cellar, where the laundry room used to be."

"And the laundry room?"

"Gone." He laughs. "But then, I never really saw the point of it anyway, when I can just manifest new, clean stuff whenever I need it." But his smile soon fades when he says, "But, Ever, I don't want to get your hopes up, because while I haven't given up trying, well, so far at least, it's been pretty slow going. I have no idea what Roman put in that drink, but everything I've tried up to this point has failed."

I sigh, pushing my cheek hard against his palm, aware of the *almost* feel of his skin upon mine. Telling myself it's enough, that it will always be enough, but even though I'm fully committed to that, I still can't help wishing for *more*.

"We have to get that shirt." My gaze meets his. "We *have* to find it. I *know* she still has it. There's no way she'd get rid of it. She's either keeping it for sentimental reasons or because she knows what it's worth to me, or both. But, either way, it's pretty much our only hope at this point."

He looks at me in the exact same way he did the last time we discussed it—in full agreement that it is indeed important but completely unwilling to pin all of his hopes upon it.

"Surely it's not our *only* hope?" he says.

But I shake my head. I'm not patient like him. I don't want to spend the next several years enjoying brief respites in the various guises of my former self, just so we can enjoy a chaste smooch now and then, while he fiddles around in his former wine-cellar-turned-chem-lab on the side. I want to enjoy *this* life. The one I'm in now.

I want to enjoy it as fully and normally as any other girl would.

And I want to enjoy it with *him*.

"I can't talk you out of this, can I?" he says, his voice as resigned as his sigh.

I shake my head again.

"Then I'm going with you."

"Going where? I haven't admitted to going anywhere."

"Aw, maybe not, but a plan is surely forming, I can see it in your eyes. So you better make room for one more, because I'm coming with."

"No, you hang with Miles, I'll be fine. Really."

But despite my protest, he's already grabbing his phone, already texting Miles and telling him he's got an errand to run so he'll be a little late.

"So, where should we start?" he asks, pocketing his cell.

"The store." I nod, having just confirmed it for myself. "But really, you don't have to come, I'll be fine on my own," I add, giving him one last chance to back out.

"Forget it." He buckles his seat belt again. "I'm coming along whether you like it or not. And just so you know, all this refusal, well, it's really starting to give me a complex."

I look at him, having no idea what that meant.

"Last time? When you broke into Haven's house and chose to drag Miles along instead of me?"

I look at him, thinking I hardly *dragged* Miles, not to mention that I really didn't have a chance to invite him since he was guarding Stacia. But then again, that's not really the point. What I really want to know is how he happened to know about that when I hadn't quite gotten around to filling him in on all of those details just yet.

"Miles mentioned it," he says, answering the thought in my head.

I glance out the window, my eyes narrowed as I say, "Is this what it's going to be like now that you're Mr. Popular with all your new friends?" I turn toward him. "You're gonna spend all your free time coaxing them to spill my secrets?"

"Only the good stuff." Damen smiles, pressing his lips briefly to mine as I back out of his drive and make my way toward the gate. "Only the stuff I really need to know."

thirty-three

We drive past Roman's old store, Renaissance!, even though I have no plans to go inside since it's too early for that. The last thing I need is another confrontation with Haven or any of the other immortals that work in the place. Yet I still slow as I near it, quickly calculating just how long it's been since the last time I was there, and more than a little curious to see what's become of it now that Roman's no longer around.

But even though I expected to find some kind of change, I never expected to find it boarded up the way it is. The windows empty, the once elaborate displays dismantled and gone, with a door that's not just locked but also bearing a sign that reads: CLOSED! With the additional, hand-scrawled scribble of: FOR GOOD! Just underneath.

"I know I shouldn't be surprised, but still, I didn't see that coming," Damen says, his voice soft and low, his eyes fixed on the sign. "I thought for sure Haven would've taken it over, or even Marco, or Misa, or Rafe."

I nod in agreement, ditch the car by the curb, as the two of us scramble out, crossing the street until we're standing before it. Peering through the window at some of the bigger pieces of furniture—the couches, tables, and display cases—that, for whatever reason, were left behind. Seeing that, for the most part anyway, with a few exceptions here and there, all of the smaller items like clothes and jewelry and such are all gone.

And I can't help but wonder just whose decision this was, just who decided to shutter it for good. Not to mention just who Roman might've possibly left control of it to.

Being immortal and all, I somehow doubt he ever thought to make a will.

I take a quick look around, making sure no one's paying any attention to us, before I close my eyes and open the door with my mind. Forgoing my original plan to wait until dark, figuring with the way things are going, this place could be empty by then, so it's best to just strike while we can.

"You've become increasingly comfortable with the breaking and entering," Damen says, his lips at my ear as he follows me inside. "Should I be concerned?"

I laugh, a startling burst of sound that echoes in this vast, high-ceilinged space. Motioning for Damen to close the door behind us as I place my hands on my hips and take a good look around—taking a moment to close my eyes and employ all my senses, trying to get a read on the place, tune in to where a stained white shirt might be hidden, as Damen stands beside me and does the same.

But not getting much of anything, we decide to start right where we stand. Peeking inside antique armoires, wobbly old chests of drawers, sorting through everything quickly, methodically, but not finding the one thing we need. Damen heads for the back, the space Roman once used as an office and, once inside, calls for me to join him.

It's a mess. An absolute mess. Like a tornado blew through it. Like the fault lines recently slipped. Reminding me of the way Jude's store looked the day Haven left us for dead—and I take it as a sure sign that she's responsible for this.

We pick our way through massive piles of papers all strewn across the floor. Damen stepping lightly, gingerly, while I'm not quite so graceful and accidentally go skidding and surfing a few times only to have him catch me and keep me from falling.

I dodge an overturned chair, scoot around a set of truly hideous, green paisley cushions pulled from the small love seat that's shoved in the corner, pausing long enough for Damen to remove an emptied file cabinet from my path, before we make for a desk that's almost as littered as the floor, covered in a mess of papers, and cups, and books, and debris so thick you can barely make out the fine inlaid wood underneath. The two of us pilfering through every last drawer, every last nook, until we're sure it's not here—convinced it's not hidden anywhere.

Damen stands beside me, wearing an expression that's closer to resolve than disappointment, since he never allowed himself to believe we might find it so easily. And even though he makes to leave, I'm not quite ready to join him. I can't seem to keep from staring at the small wine fridge in the corner—its plug pulled, its door not just left open but hanging haphazardly off its hinges.

A small, innocuous fridge with nothing special about it, except for the fact that I'm sure it was once filled with elixir, though I've no idea who might've emptied it.

Was it Misa and Marco, who were last seen hopping a fence with two duffle bags filled with stolen juice?

Was it Rafe, who, well, I haven't seen in so long I have no idea if he's even still around?

Or was it Haven, who, from what I've seen anyway, seems to have developed a serious elixir addiction problem?

And, even more importantly, does it really matter anyway, considering my only real concern here is obtaining the shirt?

Damen nudges me, ready to move on. And since there's no reason to stay, nothing to be gained here, I take one last look around, making sure I haven't missed anything, then follow him out the door, the two of us slipping out just as quickly and covertly as we came.

No closer to obtaining what we need, though more assured than ever that we're definitely getting closer, definitely making progress of some sort.

Haven's world isn't just showing signs of wear—it's also starting to crumble all around her. And now it's just a matter of time until she either reaches out for help or completely self-destructs.

Either way, I intend to be there.

thirty-four

Since the store ended up being such a complete and total bust, I drop Damen at his house so that he can help Miles rehearse, then decide to head home so I can regroup and hopefully come up with a new plan of attack. Feeling more determined than ever to locate that shirt, especially now that Damen and I are so solidly back on track.

I pull into the garage, heaving an immediate sigh of relief when I see that it's empty. Sabine's vacant space signaling that she's either still at work or out with Munoz, and knowing that either way it allows me the promise of an empty house, some much needed time on my own, and a few hours of calm and peaceful, non-arguing silence, which is exactly what I need before I head out again.

And I've just walked through the side door and am about to make my way up the stairs to my room when it hits me:

A cold blast of energy.

The effect so stinging and frigid it could mean only one thing:

I'm not nearly as alone as I'd thought.

I spin on my heel, not the least bit surprised to find Haven standing behind me. Her body fidgety, twitchy, her formerly beautiful face reduced to a shockingly pale arrangement of sunken cheekbones, a sharply angled nose, grim shrunken lips, and eyes so narrowed and hollowed and red, it's like gazing upon a crime scene photo.

Her lips twisting in a way so gruesome, it instantly transforms her into a vision even more lurid than she was just a moment ago. Scowling at me when she says, "Where is it, Ever?"

And suddenly I know exactly who dismantled the fridge in the store.

Know exactly what she's here for.

Misa and Marco broke into her house to steal her elixir—it all makes sense now.

Roman never passed on the recipe, and without him, the rogues' supply is cut off. And now it's only a matter of time before their powers dwindle, and ultimately their youth and beauty are lost.

I'm Haven's only hope of retaining her new powers.

Her new life.

Still, it's not like I'm about to make it easy on her. Not when this could turn out to be just the solution I need.

She wants something I have—and I want something she has. So, under the circumstances, that leaves me pretty well positioned to broker some kind of deal.

I'll just have to tread carefully, cautiously. I can't afford to alert her to the true significance of the shirt, just in case she hasn't realized it yet.

Lifting my shoulders casually, I say, "I don't know what

you're talking about." Then I smile, stalling for time, trying to get a better read on her as I formulate a plan in my mind.

But she's not about to play along, she's in much too big a hurry for that. She's fading fast, barely holding on, and she doesn't have time for this particular game.

"Quit fugging around and just *give it to me!*" She rolls her eyes and huffs under her breath, shaking her head in a way that throws her completely off-balance, forcing her to grab hold of the stair rail in order to steady herself.

I narrow my gaze, taking a moment to really study her, noting the way she appears so edgy, so jumpy, so out of whack and unsteady, she can barely stand still, can barely hold herself up without some kind of support. Focusing on her solar plexus, seeing it like a bull's-eye smack dab in the center of her torso, fully prepared to take her out if I have to, though still hoping it won't really come to that. Then I try to tune in to her energy, tune in to her head, try to get some kind of read on just where she's at, and just how far she's willing to go to get what she wants—but getting nothing for my efforts.

She's not just shut off from me—she's shut off from everything around her as well.

Belonging to no one and nothing.

Barely belonging to herself.

She's like a walking talking Shadowland.

Dark.

Alone.

Totally caught up in a past she's hell bent on avenging, even though the truth of it is nothing at all like the version she's chosen to convince herself of.

"The *elixir*, Ever! Give me the fugging elixir already!" Her voice is shaky, high-pitched, raspier than ever, revealing just how much her desperation has come to define her. "I've already checked all the fridges—the one in the kitchen, the one outside by the barbecue, the spare one in the laundry room, and I was just about to head up to the den off your room, when, well, you came home and beat me to it. So, I figure as long as you're here, I may as well ask nicely—seeing as what good friends we used to be and all. So, come on, Ever, for old time's sake, for old *friend*'s sake, hand over the fugging elixir you stole!"

"That's you asking nicely?" I lift my brow, noticing the way she eyeballs the space between the banister and me, as though plotting to sneak through it, prompting me to quickly grab hold of it, blocking all access.

She mumbles under her breath, gripping the stair rail so tightly her knuckles blanch to an impossible shade of white, looking at me with eyes so red they're practically bleeding from the effort, leaving no doubt that she's *this* close to snapping when she repeats, *"Just give it to me already!"*

I take a deep breath, and concentrate on surrounding her with a stream of calming energy. Hoping it will help to pacify her, cool her, ease some of the anger, temper and tone down the rage. The last thing I need is for her to go off, to explode in some sort of meltdown. Even though she poses no real threat to me anymore, she's still a very real threat to everyone around her, and I can't afford to let it get to that point.

But when I see the way my bubble of peace once again fails to penetrate, bouncing right off her in much the same way it did the last time I tried, I decide to give her what she needs instead. Figuring a couple sips of elixir can't hurt—if anything, from what I can see, it should go a very long way toward taming the beast.

I turn, slowly, cautiously, careful not to alarm her or set her off in any way, heading up the stairs and motioning for her to follow, when I glance over my shoulder and say, "I'm happy to share, Haven. I've got more than enough, so no worries there. Though I am curious—" I stop on the landing and face her. "Why do you need *my* juice? What happened to *yours*?"

"I ran out." She shrugs, glaring at me as she adds, "I ran out because you stole a bunch of it, and now I'm gonna take it back."

She grins, the promise of a drink seeming to appease her just the tiniest bit, though her words leave me chilled. I have no idea how much juice Roman might've kept on hand, but if he was anything like Damen it must've been a pretty healthy supply, a year's worth at the very least. Since it's forced to ferment under the proper moon phases, it's not like you can just whip up a batch spontaneously. And the fact that Misa and Marco only made off with a bagful means she's managed to plow through the rest of it in such a short amount of time it's not only alarming but goes a long way toward explaining the state that she's in.

I head for my den and over to the mini-fridge that's placed just behind the wet bar. Reaching for a fresh new bottle as I say, "I didn't steal your elixir. I have no interest or need for that kind of thing."

Seeing her stand before me, hands shaking in outrage. "You're such a liar! You think I'm stupid? How else did you survive? I know all about the chakras—Roman told me and Damen told him! It was back when Roman was controlling him, back when he convinced him to spill all kinds of secrets. I hit you in your weak spot and you *know* it. I hit you before you went down and after you went down, and I even hit you one last time for good measure just before I left you for dead. It should've *killed* you! I thought it *did* kill you. I was sure the only reason you didn't disintegrate into a big pile of dust is because you weren't as old as the rest of them. But now I know the real reason for why you're still here—"

I look at her, knowing full well what that reason is—the fact that I watched my lives unfold right before me. The fact that I witnessed the *truth*. And because of it, I made the right choice, the only choice, which allowed me to rise above my weak chakra. No more, no less. Still, I'm interested in hearing her take on it.

"You drank Roman's elixir." She shakes her head, allowing the blue gemstones on her earrings to chime softly together. "It's *way* more powerful than yours, as you well know, which is exactly why you drank it. It's the *only* thing that saved you!"

I shrug, catching our reflections in the mirror on the far wall behind her—noting the difference between us—her darkness versus my light. The contrast so stark, it takes my breath away. Then averting my gaze just as quickly, determined not to overfocus on her sad, sorry state. I can't afford the sympathy, not when I may be forced to kill her at some point. Switching my gaze back to hers when I say, "If that's so true, then how come it can't seem to save *you*? And how come it couldn't save Roman either?"

But Haven's done chatting. She's determined to get what she came for.

"Give me the elixir." She takes a slow, unsteady step toward me. "Give me the elixir and no one gets hurt."

"I thought we just covered that." I keep the bottle behind me, holding it well out of her reach. "You can't hurt me anymore, remember? No matter what you do or how hard you try, you can't get to me, Haven. So just maybe, instead of threatening me, you should try a whole new approach and try to get on my good side."

But she just smiles. Causing her face to widen and lift in a way so ghastly it only serves to emphasize her hollow, red eyes. "Maybe I can't hurt you, but trust me, Ever, I can still do some serious damage to the people who are near and dear to you. And, as good and fast as you may be, well, it's not like you can be in *all* places at *all* times. It's not like you can save *everybody*."

And that's when she does it—that's when she takes advantage of my momentary shock at hearing her words and lunges straight for the elixir grasped in my hand.

And that's also when I react just a little bit quicker than she planned.

Tossing the bottle aside, watching as it lands clear on the other side of the room, well out of reach, I pounce on her. Descending so sure and so fast she doesn't see it coming until it's way too late to react.

Throwing her down to the carpet as my fingers eagerly circle her neck. Wriggling through the tangle of necklaces, immediately noticing how her amulet is still gone.

But despite the fact that her face is turning blue, despite the fact that I'm slowly cutting off her air supply, she just laughs. The motion of it pushing her throat hard against the palm of my hand, as she emits a sound so gruesome, so awful, I'm tempted to kill her just to put an end to it.

But I can't act rashly. Can't afford to do anything of the sort. Not until I get what I want, and if the price is a few bottles of elixir, then so be it.

"Give me the fugging elixir!" she screams, the second I loosen my hold. Her body thrashing under mine, moving frantically, violently, thrusting from side to side, as she scratches and claws with sharp, pointy, blue nails.

Lashing out like a rabid animal.

Like a junkie gone too long without a fix.

Scrambling across the floor the moment I lift myself off, grasping the bottle, popping the top, and shoving it against her lips so hard and fast her front teeth break off from the force.

But she doesn't miss a beat. Doesn't pay it any notice at all. She just continues to gulp and glug, draining it so quickly it's just a matter of seconds before it's completely emptied, and she's tossed it aside. A hint of color returning to her cheeks, though her teeth still haven't re-formed—not that she seems to notice or care. She just looks straight at me, licking her lips, as she says, *"More.* And make it the good stuff this time. The stuff you stole. Your juice tastes like crap."

"Didn't seem to stop you." I shrug, having no intention of handing over anything more until I get what I want. "You can have my entire supply for all I care. I'm not addicted, like you." I slowly look her over, leaving no doubt just how troubled I am by the view. "But just so you know, I didn't steal your elixir. Misa and Marco did." I study her face, noting the way it changes, transforms, as she stops and considers my words, calculates the possibility of them actually holding even a smidgen of truth.

"And you know this *because* . . . ?" She quirks her brow and places a hand on each hip, as she cocks her head to the side.

I meet her gaze, knowing I have to say something quickly, though not quite sure what that is. If I tell her I was there, that I saw it, then she'll know I was looking for something else, something she might not yet recognize the significance of. So, instead, I just shrug, forcing my voice, my entire demeanor to stay cool, calm, and collected when I say, "Because *I* didn't steal it. And because *Damen* didn't steal it either. And because that is hardly the reason why I survived your attack. And because it only makes sense, if you'll stop long enough to think about it."

She looks at me and frowns. And that's all I need to see to know she's not buying it. That she's still convinced it was me.

"Or—or maybe it was Rafe?" I say, having temporarily forgotten about him. "I mean, when was the last time you even saw him anyway?"

But when I look at her again, it's clear it's not working. Even though everything I just said makes sense, it's not quite getting me where I want to go, *need* to go, and thanks to the elixir she drank, she's now just alert enough to realize it.

She smooths her heavily jeweled fingers over the front of her dress, plucks some stray carpet lint from her sleeve. "Not a problem," she says. "I'll deal with them. But in the meantime, since I'm here and all, what do you say you just give me the rest of your supply?"

thirty-five

Just as she's leaving, clutching a single bottle of elixir tightly to her chest, Sabine marches through the side door.

Juggling her briefcase in one hand and a bag of groceries in the other, she stops, does a quick double take, and says, "Haven? I haven't seen you in . . . *ages*. You're looking . . ." Sabine pauses, brow slanted as she slowly looks her over. And even though Haven's in much better shape than she was when she arrived, she's still a long way from being anywhere even close to presentable. And for those not used to seeing her new look—well, she's downright scary.

But Haven just laughs, shooting Sabine a friendly, broken-toothed smile when she says, "No worries. Trust me, my mom's not crazy about it either. Which, by the way, is just one of the many reasons I'm divorcing her."

Sabine glances between us, clearly confused by the statement.

But Haven's quick to fill in the blanks. "I'm divorcing all of them actually, both my parents and my little brother. I'd divorce the housekeeper too if I could." She laughs, the sound so unnatural, so disturbing, it instantly sets Sabine on edge. "Anyway, long story short, I moved out. I'm in the middle of getting emancipated so I don't have to deal with their crap anymore."

Sabine frowns, eyes narrowed in a look I've come to know all too well, a look that clearly signals her outraged disapproval.

But Haven's immune to all that. If anything, it only seems to egg her on even further. Causing her to smile that much brighter when she says, "They just refused to accept me as I am, so, I just packed up my stuff and said—*adios!*"

Sabine glances between us, probably wondering if I'm somehow playing a role in this, if I fed Haven the lines, told her just what to say and when. But even though the words clearly apply to the way Sabine's been treating me, I had nothing to do with it. Haven's a one-woman show.

"Well, I'm sure they miss you very much." Sabine nods, reverting to her courtroom litigator's tone.

But Haven's not playing that game, the one where everyone acts all polite and politically correct and pretends that what was just said really wasn't, and that everything will work out in the end despite a load of evidence piling up against it.

She's also way past playing the parent and/or guardian game where you work overtime trying to put your best manners on display, so your friends' parents will like you, trust you, and invite you to come back again.

Because Haven and I aren't friends.

And she couldn't care less what Sabine thinks of her or if she's ever invited back.

So she shrugs and rolls her eyes and sings, *"Doubtful!"*

Causing Sabine's gaze to immediately harden and switch over to me as though I'm somehow responsible, that my silence, my not saying a word, my not doing anything to stop it, signals consent of some kind. When really, I'm just waiting for this whole thing to end. Waiting for Haven to finally shut up, for Sabine to finally give up, head into the kitchen, and put the groceries away, so I can finally make some progress toward closing the deal Haven and I made.

Though, unfortunately, Haven's far from done. Clearly relishing every last bit of tension she's introduced and eager to add to it, she says, "But then, I don't miss them either, so I guess that makes us even."

Sabine looks at me, ready to speak, but Haven just waves her hand in the air, temporarily losing control of the juice and watching as it hurtles toward the floor—sparking and flaring as it splashes up the sides, until she casually reaches out, flattens her palm, and catches it in midair. Her eyes glinting when she sees the way Sabine blinks, shakes her head, and instantly talks herself out of what she just saw, convincing herself that no one can actually move that fast, that it didn't happen at all like she thought.

"Whoops!" Haven laughs. "Well, anywho, don't mean to keep you. Just came over to grab some of Ever's elixir here." She holds the bottle before her, tilting it from side to side, causing it to spark and flare, before pointing at the box I grasp in my arms, the one that houses the rest of the supply.

"You came to get her . . . *what*?" Sabine squints, struggling to make sense of it, glaring suspiciously between the bottle and me, before rising up onto her toes and peering inside the box, wondering why she failed to pay it any real notice until now. She places her bag on the entry table and reaches for the bottle Haven happily offers. If it means trouble for me, Haven will gladly hand it right over.

But this has gone far enough, and there's no way I can let it continue.

I can't allow Sabine to get her hands on the juice.

Can't allow Haven to play me like this.

"It's *nothing*," I say, shoving the box into Haven's side, pushing hard against her. "It's just that energy sports drink I like."

But Sabine's not buying it. One look at her face is all it takes to know that she's launched into a full-scale alert. Suddenly making the connection between my strange behavior, my refusal to eat, and all of my other strange, unexplainable, and just plain weird habits, assuming, somewhat correctly, that it all stems from this one single thing.

Haven laughs, thrusting the elixir toward her, taunting her, tempting her, urging Sabine to try a little sip so she can see for herself just how *good*—just how *refreshing*—just how *energizing* and life *changing* one sip can be.

And Sabine's just about to do it, lured by the pull of Haven's gaze, the spark of the elixir, and just about to take the bait, when Haven laughs even harder and snatches it away.

Causing Sabine to shake her head, straighten her shoulders, and quickly pull herself together when she says, "I think you should leave." The words ground between tightly clenched teeth. "I think you should go *right now*. And while I'm sorry to have to say it, Haven, you're obviously very troubled and in need of some serious help, and until you find a way to get your behavior under control, I really don't want to see you hanging around here anymore." She reaches for the shopping bag, lifting it off the table and balancing it back on her hip as she continues to eyeball her carefully.

"Oh, no worries." Haven smiles, turning to leave. "You

will *not* be seeing me again anytime soon. I have absolutely no need to ever return, now that I got what I need."

She reaches for the door and I'm right there behind her, determined to get this over with as quickly and seamlessly as I can, before the calming effects of the juice wear off and Haven starts raging again.

But just as I'm about to step onto the stoop, Sabine stops me by grabbing hold of my arm. She has no intention of letting me leave, not now, and certainly not with a friend she just banned from her house.

She narrows her gaze, fingers slipping down to my wrist, circling tightly, as she says, "And just where do you think you're going?"

My gaze meets hers, and I know I have no choice but to say it as calmly and succinctly as I can. Leave no doubt whatsoever that whether she likes it or not, she will not keep me from going through with my plan.

"Sabine—I have to go somewhere with Haven. It won't take long, and when I get back, we can talk all you want, but for now, I *have* to go."

"You'll do nothing of the sort!" she cries, her voice high-pitched, shrill, as she grips me that much tighter, my wrist turning an angry shade of red that won't even have time to bruise before it's healed again. "Didn't you hear me? You are *not* to hang around with that girl anymore. I thought I made myself clear?"

I'm just about to yank free, just about to agree that yes, she has made herself clear, but that it's not really her choice to make, when Haven smiles, lifts the box right out of my arms and says, "No worries, Ever. You stay with your auntie. She's obviously very upset. I can get it from here."

And I watch as she heads for her car—Roman's car—dumping the box on the passenger seat before settling in, revving the engine, and laughing hysterically as she waves good-bye and backs down the drive.

Sabine's fingers still on me, still clutching me, still keeping me from doing the one thing I need to do most—the one thing that could end this horrible curse and put my life on a whole new course of complete and total happiness—shouting, "Go to your room!" Her cheeks red, eyes blazing, face so full of outrage it makes me feel terrible for causing it.

But that's nothing compared to how I feel when I yank myself free. Pulling so hard and fast that the bag of groceries slips from her grip and sends a barrage of cans and fruits and vegetables and egg cartons and cottage cheese containers scrambling all across the floor, leaving a trail of curds, pulpy bits, and runny yellow yolk all over the polished travertine stone.

Nothing compared to how I feel when I catch her expression—a horrible mix of hurt, outrage, surprise, and even worse—*fear*.

Nothing compared to the regret I feel when I glance between the mess and her, wishing I could just make it disappear with my mind, erase it entirely, make it seem as though it never did happen—but knowing that'll only serve to make things worse, I turn my back on it all, and head out the door.

Desperate to catch up with Haven who's just used the opportunity to renege on our deal. Having no idea where to start but knowing I need to start somewhere, and I need to start now.

Calling over my shoulder to say, "Sabine, I'm sorry. Really I am. But there are things you just don't understand—don't *want* to understand—and, as it just so happens, this is one of them."

thirty-six

As soon as my foot hits the stoop, I start running. Not wanting to waste the time it'll take to go into the garage and get my car and start it up and back out of the drive and all the other steps in the whole "normal" routine I work so hard to keep up if for no other reason than to appease Sabine (even though pretty much all of my actions so far have done just about anything *but* appease her), but also not wanting to manifest anything while she's still watching from the window. Knowing that'll only result in a whole new slew of questions—questions I have no intention of answering.

Her gaze follows me. I can feel the weight of it wrapping all around me in a horrible mix of anger, worry, and fear.

Thoughts are things. Made of a very tangible form of energy. And hers are shooting straight to the heart of me.

But despite feeling terrible about everything that just happened, it's not like I can take the time to stop and worry about it now, there'll be plenty of time for that later. I'll no doubt have my work cut out for me trying to find a way to make it up to her, but for now, my only concern is finding Haven.

I turn off my driveway and onto my street, thinking I'm finally home free, only to be confronted with the sight of Munoz slowing his Prius as he heads right toward me.

Great, I mumble, watching as he lowers his window and calls out my name, his face clouded with a look of genuine concern when he asks, "Everything okay?"

I stop, stealing a second to look at him and say, "Actually, no. Pretty much nothing's okay. In fact, not even close."

He scrunches his brow and glances between the house and me. "Can I help?"

I shake my head, starting to take off again, but then I think better, so I turn to him and say, "Yeah, please tell Sabine that I'm sorry. That I'm really and truly sorry for everything . . . for all the trouble I've caused, for hurting her in the way that I have. She probably won't believe it, probably won't accept it, and I can't say I blame her, but, well, anyway . . ." I shrug, feeling more than a little foolish for having shared all of that, but it's not like that stops me. "Oh, and failing that, you can always greet her with these . . ." I close my eyes and manifest a large bouquet of bright yellow daffodils, knowing I shouldn't have done it, knowing it'll only spawn a whole new slew of questions I have no time to answer, but still thrusting them upon him when I add, "They're her favorite— just don't tell her how you got 'em, okay?"

And before he can reply, before I can take in the full impact of the shock on his face, I'm off.

Having wasted more time than I can afford, I take one more second to manifest a black BMW for myself, just like the one Damen drives. Aware of Munoz's bewilderment, his outright astonishment, as he continues to watch me from his rearview mirror. *Seeing* his jaw dropped down to his knees in a bug-eyed, *did I really just see what I think I did* kind of stare when I speed out of sight.

Making my way toward Coast Highway, figuring I'll find a way to deal with him later, as I accelerate along the series of curves and try to determine where Haven might've gone.

My gut sinking the second the answer appears in my mind.

The shirt.

Now that she got what she wanted—thanks to Sabine's interfering—she has no plans to make good on her end of the deal. She hates me so much, she'd much rather destroy the one thing I want, the one thing I didn't just ask for but insisted upon in return for the juice, even though it clearly holds great sentimental value for her.

Even though I'm pretty dang sure she has no idea of the promise it holds for me.

But that's hardly the point. As far as Haven's concerned, the fact that I want it, the fact that I was willing to bargain for it, is reason enough to destroy it.

I could tell by the way she looked at me. She may have been shaky, more than a little unsteady, but she'd had just enough elixir to allow her to think and act somewhat logically.

So when I offered to provide her with a nice supply of juice if she gave me something in return, she just shrugged and said, "Fine. Whatever. Just go ahead and spill it already. What's this big thing you so desperately need?"

"I want the shirt," I'd said, moving until I was standing right before her, seeing her squint in reply as I added, "the one Roman wore on his very last night. The one you snatched right out of my hand before you threatened me and told me to leave."

Her gaze narrowed, and the way she looked at me, well, it was clear she still had it. But it was also clear she had no idea why I'd want it, what the significance could possibly be. And I can only hope it stays that way, at least until I can get the shirt safely within my possession.

"You mean, the shirt he was wearing on the night when *you killed him*?" she'd said, brow quirking crazily.

"No." I shook my head, keeping my voice steady and sure, my gaze focused on hers. "I mean the shirt he wore on the night he so tragically died *an accidental death* at Jude's hands." My gaze holding, making sure I had her full attention, when I added, "You hand over that white linen shirt he was wearing, and I mean that *very same one*, because trust me, Haven, I will know if you try to swap it for a fake, but anyway, you give me that and in exchange I'll give you all the elixir you need."

She glanced between the box of elixir I'd just filled—the box I referred to as a good-faith down payment, since it was all that I had on hand—and me. Wanting so badly to deny me, but so completely overcome by her own dependency, her own raging need, in the end, she was unable to do anything but reluctantly agree.

Finally nodding her consent when she said, "Fine. Deal. Whatever. Let's just get this over with, okay?"

And that's when we headed downstairs. Haven carrying a fresh new bottle she was well on her way to draining, and me lugging the box for safekeeping, determined to keep it from her until the exchange was complete.

But then Sabine came home and wrecked everything.

I sigh, switching my focus back to the present, just about to stop by her old house, the one where her parents and little brother still live, wondering if she might've stashed it there for some reason, primarily because it seems like the last place anyone would look, when I have this overwhelming urge to head somewhere else instead.

Not knowing if it's a message of some sort, a sign of some kind, or maybe even just some crazy powerful intuition, I follow it anyway. Every time I ignore one of my stronger instincts I live to regret it, so this time I pull a quick U-turn and follow its lead.

Disappointed when I find myself at a place I've already checked. That Miles and I already checked, but still going ahead with it anyway. I approach the door, thinking how even though she claims it's hers, having lived here for months now, I can't help but think of it as Roman's, as a flood of memories come rushing back.

Remembering all the times I came here before—the times I knocked down the door, the times I fought with him, nearly succumbed to him, the time I watched Jude kill him—then pushing the thoughts aside as I make my way around a confusing maze of furniture. Stuff that up until recently lived in the store, and now that it's been moved here, allows for only the slimmest path down the hall and into a den that's also so jam-packed it requires a moment to take it all in.

My gaze roaming among the antique armoires, the silk and velvet settees, the shiny Lucite coffee table that looks like a reject from the eighties, and over to the huge stack of oil paintings in ornate gold frames, all piled up against each other, leaning against the far wall, while various items of clothing, from all different time periods stretching back hundreds of years, are strewn over practically every available surface, including the bar where Roman kept the crystal goblets he filled with elixir, as well as the couch where I, ruled by the dark flame within me, tried to shamelessly seduce him while wearing a façade that made me appear to be Drina. The same couch where everything changed the night I made Haven drink Roman's special brew.

My gaze traveling past all of that and all the way over to the blazing, stone hearth, where Jude cowers. Looking scared, shocked, defeated, and confused, while Haven stands before him, clutching the stained white linen shirt in one hand and Jude's arm in the other. Having made the transformation back to a slightly healed version of herself, or at least where her teeth are concerned, though she's still a long way from the old Haven, still completely ruled by her own overwhelming addictions and anger.

"Well, well," she says, turning to me, her eyes red and squinty. "Did you actually think you could trick me?"

I shake my head. I'm as confused as she is as to what's really going on here.

My gaze darting between them, seeing the way Jude cowers, caught in her grip, clearly horrified at having been caught doing—well, doing what I'm not sure. I can't quite make sense of what I'm looking at or what his goal could've possibly been.

Has he figured out the truth behind the shirt—the promise it holds—and he's trying to obtain it as a sort of peace offering for Damen and me?

Or, even worse, and far more likely, is he here to steal it, destroy it, having only pretended to be friendly with Damen, to forgive him for the past, when really he's been planning for this moment all along, refusing to give up on his final revenge?

And before I can do anything to stop it, she's on him. Fueled by the juice that rages within her, the juice that I gave her, she lets go of his arm only to catch him by the throat. Lifting him high into the air as his feet kick and dangle beneath him, shaking the shirt before her, shaking it at me when she says, "What the fug is going on here?"

"I don't know," I say, careful to keep my voice low, steady, slowly approaching her with my hands held where she can see them. "Really. I have no idea what he's doing. Perhaps you should ask him?"

She glances at Jude, sees the way his eyes bulge, the way his face grows swollen and red, and she drops him just as quickly, her grip switching to his arm to keep him from bolting, as he sputters and coughs and fights to catch his breath.

"You two plan this?" She glares at me.

"No." I glance between her and Jude, wondering why he always has to show up at all the wrong times.

Why he *always* wrecks everything.

Knowing one thing for sure—it's not a coincidence. There's no such thing. The universe is far too harmonious for such randomness as that.

So what then? Why is it that every time I'm so close to getting exactly what I want, Jude shows up at just the right moment to thwart all my plans?

There's got to be something more to it—some sort of reason or meaningful explanation behind it—but what that reason or explanation could be, is completely beyond me.

Haven holds up the shirt, scrutinizing it, inspecting it,

trying to determine why I'd want it, why Jude would risk so much to get it, what possible significance it might hold for anyone other than her.

Then she switches her gaze between us, noting how he gazes at the stain, noting how I watch him gazing at the stain—and that's when she knows.

That's when the lightbulb goes on and it all comes together.

That's when she loses herself in peals of shoulder-shaking laughter.

Laughing so hard she can barely contain herself. Bending forward, one hand on her knee, she heaves and coughs in a series of thigh-slapping spasms, until she finally gets hold of herself, rights herself, and says, "I totally get it now." She dangles the shirt from the tips of her fingers as a hideous grin spreads across her cheeks. "I do, I do indeed. But, unfortunately for *you*"—she points at me—"or, maybe, even possibly *you*—" She jerks her head toward Jude. "It seems like Ever here has a very big decision to make."

thirty-seven

She turns, eyes darting between us as she says, "You know, at first I kept the shirt with me all the time. Carried it everywhere I went. To school, to the store, I even slept with it just so I'd never have to be far from his scent." She shrugs. "I pretty much looked upon it as my last connection to Roman—the one remaining thing I'd ever truly have of his. But now I know differently. Everything you see here is *mine*. Roman never planned on dying, so he didn't bother making a will. Which means no one else has any claim to his things, and I dare them to try. *This* is my connection to Roman." She waves the shirt through the air, the fabric gently swaying as she points at the collection of antiques. Using her other hand to tighten her grip on Jude's sleeve as she adds, "This *house*, these *things*, everything, all of it, belongs to me. I have reminders of him everywhere I look, so it's not like I need some dumb white shirt anymore. No, you're the one who needs it, Ever. This is all about the stain, right? It's left over from that infamous antidote you came *so* close to getting if it wasn't for this guy." She grips Jude harder, causing him to flinch, but he refuses to cry out, refuses to give her the satisfaction of knowing she's actually causing him pain. "And now it seems he's done it again." She turns to Jude, *tsking* as she shakes her head. "If this guy hadn't gotten in the way, you'd be living happily ever after now, wouldn't you? Or, at least that's been your version of the story anyway. So I ask you, you still will-ing to stand behind that? You still willing to blame him for *everything*?"

I look at her, keeping my gaze steady, my body tensed, ready for anything, though refusing to answer, refusing to fall into whatever trap she has set.

But she just rolls her eyes, not at all dissuaded by my silence, saying, "Well, it's not like it matters anyway, because what's done is done, and it's not like I need you to know what's really going on here. You honestly managed to convince yourself that all the answers live *here*." She wags the shirt before me. "In a big, green blob of a stain on a white linen shirt. You hon-estly plan to drop it off at some crime lab or, better yet, take it to the science lab at school so you can get extra credit for breaking down all the components, as well as finally getting your hands on the recipe that'll allow you and Damen to, as Roman would say: *shag your bleedin' hearts out!*" She laughs and shakes her head, her Ouroboros tattoo flashing in and out of view as she shoots me a pitying look, as though she can hardly believe the foolishness of it all. "So tell me, Ever, how am I do-ing so far? Am I right? Am I pretty much on track?"

But even though she continues to eyeball me, even though she pretty much nailed the truth on its head, I don't answer, and I'm careful not to let on. I just continue to stand there, warning Jude with my eyes not to do anything as rash and stupid as the last time, while keeping watch over Haven, who's still a long way from being at the top of her game, but is still able to do a good bit of damage and wreak a good bit of havoc, from what I've seen.

Taking great care to not let her catch me as I covertly call for backup. Sending a telepathic message to Damen that consists of nothing more than the image unfolding before me.

Knowing it's just a matter of time before he appears.

All I have to do is stall until then.

"Listen, Haven—" I start, but I don't get very far.

She's seen it.

Seen the shift in me.

And because of it, she's not about to indulge me any further.

And before I can do anything to stop it, she's got Jude by the neck again, while she kicks the screen away from the fire and dangles Roman's white shirt just over the blaze.

Her fingers shaking as the shirt dangles precariously. Allowing the flames to spark and lick and blacken the hem, as she looks at me and says, "No use wasting any more time here, is there? So whaddya say we just cut to the chase, shall we? Time to decide, Ever. The choice is yours and yours alone to make. What'll it be—a lifetime of nonstop, happy shagging or—*Jude* getting to enjoy a long life?"

Jude gasps and struggles against her, but when he looks at me, instead of a plea for help, his gaze begs only forgiveness. His oxygen supply becoming more and more scarce the tighter she grips, yet he still allows me to see inside his head.

He came here for me.

Only for me.

He wanted to make good on his word, to prove that he really does just want to see me happy. He wanted to make up for what he did all those months before, right here in this house. And now, he's ready to die for it if it should come to that. He's fully prepared to sacrifice himself to see that I finally get what I want, to see that it's done.

Do it! he urges, his gaze holding mine, the feel of it so warm, so loving it robs me of breath. *Please, I just want you to be happy. And because of everything you've shown me, everything I've learned in Summerland, I'm free of all fear. Think of it as my final gift to you. I was wracking my brain, trying to think of a way to make up for everything, when I remembered Roman's shirt, remembered the way you reacted the day I spilled my coffee and soaked it up with my sleeve. And after putting the two together, I realized this would be the perfect way to erase my mistakes.*

He closes his eyes, but the thoughts don't stop there, he continues to think: *But now I've only made it worse, and I'm so sorry. I really, truly am. I just want you to know that my love has always been true and my intentions good. I've never once meant to harm you.*

I choke back a sob, work past the knot in my gut, blink back my stinging wet tears, and glance between him and the shirt Haven holds just shy of the flames.

And I know that all I have to do to get the one thing I've sought for so long is to make the choice they're both begging me to make.

Jude's already given his consent. He's practically pleading with me to do it already.

And Haven, well, Haven can hardly contain her excitement. This is exactly the sort of thing she's come to live for.

Exactly the kind of thing she's come to enjoy most in this world.

So I take a deep breath, allowing the words *forgive me*, to stream from my mind to Jude's as I turn to Haven and say, "You know, this is the exact same kind of crap Roman used to play. And like I told him, I'll tell you, I don't play this game anymore."

thirty-eight

She looks at me, clearly unable to believe what she just heard.

So I repeat it, leaving no room for doubt when I say, "Seriously. I'm not choosing. I'm not playing this game. So it looks like you're gonna have to come up with something else—and hopefully it'll be something a little more original, a little more unique. Take your time, though." I lift my shoulders in a way that's deliberately calm and cool. "I'm in no hurry. Though you might want to lighten up on poor Jude, unless, of course, you've decided to kill him after all, in which case, feel free to grip even tighter and finish the job. Either way, I'll be right here. I'm not going anywhere 'til I get what I came for."

She looks at me, hands beginning to shake from the effort, rage taking over again. Her scathing, hate-filled gaze moving over me as she says, "So help me, Ever, I will burn this shirt *and* kill Jude, and there's *nothing* you can do to stop it."

"No you won't." My voice remains firm as my gaze holds steady on hers. Noticing how she's loosened her grasp just the tiniest bit, though doing my best not to let on that I saw, for fear that she'll only tighten up and cause him great pain yet again. "I know of at least two very good reasons why you won't even try."

She looks at me, her entire body growing increasingly shaky as she quickly loses whatever grip she'd managed to hang onto until now.

"One, because it's been a little too long since your last drink, and you're already starting to suffer withdrawal." I shake my head and cluck my tongue against the inside of my cheek, wearing an expression of disapproving pity. "Just look at yourself, Haven, you're a hollow-eyed, sunken-faced, shivering wreck. It took years—centuries probably—for Roman to build up the kind of tolerance to drink as much as you have in just a few months. You can't handle it, you're in way over your head. Just look at yourself, will you?"

"And *two*?" she says, voice raspy, acid-tinged, broadcasting her extreme displeasure with me.

"And two." I smile, eyes never once leaving hers. "You're about to be outnumbered. Damen is here."

I can *feel* his presence, *feel* him pulling into the drive, rushing through the front door, down the maze in the hall. Warning Miles to stay back, to not get involved or venture any further, as he storms into the den and Haven gazes upon them. Seeing Damen, standing right beside me, while Miles peers in through the doorway, having refused to listen to Damen's warning to stay out of the way.

Narrowing her eyes when she says, "Oh, would you look at that—Damen brought his own backup. That's so cute!"

I turn, glimpsing Miles, his aura dimming, his shoulders cringing, regretting the moment he decided to enter this room when he takes in the gruesome sight of his former best friend.

Haven glares, her eyes blazing with fury when she says, "You chose the wrong side, Miles." She narrows her gaze even further, until all I can see are two slits of red. "I can't believe what a traitor you turned out to be."

Miles meets her gaze, and if he's scared, he doesn't show it. He just straightens his spine, squares his shoulders, and combs his fingers through his hair, his aura beaming, strengthening, when he says, "I haven't chosen at all. I may not agree with your more recent choices, I may have chosen to distance myself a bit, but as far as I'm concerned we never stopped being friends. I mean, seriously, Haven, so far I've made it through your ballerina phase, your preppy phase, your goth phase, your emo phase, and now your super-scary immortal witch phase." He shrugs casually as he takes a moment to glance around the room. "And the fact is, I'm not going anywhere. For one thing, I haven't yet given up on you, and for another, well, I'm way too curious to see which role you'll decide to play next."

She rolls her eyes, voice raspier than ever when she says, "Well, I hate to break it to ya, but there is no *next*, Miles. Whether you like it or not, this is it. This is the new and improved, infinite version of me. I'm completely self-actualized. I'm everything I was ever meant to be."

Miles shakes his head. "I really wish you'd rethink this or look in a mirror at least."

But if she hears it, she chooses to ignore it and instead turns her attention back to Damen. "So, Damen Auguste *Esposito*." She smiles, her face garish, eyes red and flashing, using a name that was thrust on him a very long time ago, back when his parents were murdered and he was turned over to the orphanage where he lived until the black plague ravaged the area and he spared himself by making the elixir. A name he hasn't used for several centuries at least, and it takes me a moment to recognize it. "I know *all* about you. I'm not sure if Ever mentioned it or not, but Roman kept *very* good records, very *detailed* records. And you, well, let's just say you've been a very, very naughty boy, now haven't you?"

Damen shrugs, careful to keep his face still, his emotions well hidden. "I brought you more elixir. I left a big box by the door, and believe me, there's plenty more where that came from. So why don't you come with me and have a look, okay? You can even have a taste if you'd like."

"Why don't you save me the steps and bring it to me instead?" She bats her eyes, attempting to smile in the way that she used to—cute, charming, flirtatious, with a hint of adorable quirkiness. But she's veered so far from that old version of herself, it just ends up looking creepy instead. "As you can see, I'm a little busy here. Ever and I were just working through the details of a little deal that we made, and if I'm not mistaken, the fact that she summoned *you* means she no longer trusts me. Which is pretty ironic if you consider that not only did she *make* me this way, but, from everything I saw in Roman's journals, well, she really has no good reason to trust you either, now does she?"

"Enough with the journals," I say, eager to move away from all this. "I know *everything*, Haven. There's nothing left for you to lord over us, so why don't you just—"

"You sure about that?" Her eyes dart between us, as though she knows something I don't and can't wait to reveal it. "You know about his past with Drina? How he faked his own death in a fire? About *the little slave girl he stole from her family*? You know about all of that?" She glances between us, including Jude, but he just meets her gaze and gives nothing away.

"She does." Damen looks at her. "And, by the way, I didn't *steal* the slave girl, I *bought* her in order to *free* her. Unfortunately, that's how it was done back then. It was a very dark time in our history. But I don't think you're really all that interested in reliving that. So please, don't waste any more of our time with this nonsense. Just let go of Jude and hand over the shirt. *Now.*"

"*Now?*" She balks, lifting her brow. "Oh no, I don't think I'll be doing that *now* or any other time, for that matter. That's not the way this game is played. In fact, that pretty much goes against all the rules. And since you're so late to the party, allow me to explain it to you. Basically, a choice must be made. You can either, *A*, choose to save Jude, or *B*, choose to save the shirt. So Damen, what'll it be—a person's life or your own self-interest? Kind of like what Roman made Ever do when she made me drink, right here in this room, well, at least according to Ever anyway. I can't say for sure since I was so out of it. Though I do remember how the whole thing went down right there on that couch." She jerks her head toward it. "Which, I guess, is probably why she's refusing to play this time around. Must be a painful reminder since it's pretty obvious how much she regrets her decision. It's pretty obvious how she wishes she'd just let me die instead. But just because she won't play doesn't mean you can't. So tell me, Damen, which one will it be? Just tell me and it's yours and yours to keep!"

Damen looks at her, preparing to charge, to take her down

and put an end to all this. I can *feel* it in the way his energy shifts. I can *see* the plan forming in his head. But I quickly warn him against it—pleading with him to stay calm and still and to not do a thing. She's baiting him, expecting no less than an ambush, and there's far too much at stake to play it that way.

"Haven, no one's *choosing* anything," I say. "Because no one's playing your stupid little game. So why don't you just let go of Jude, hand over the shirt, and try to get a grip on your-self—on your *life*. Believe it or not, I'm still willing to help you. I'm still willing to put all the bad stuff behind us, so you can recover. Seriously. Just—just give me the shirt and let go of Jude and—"

"*Choose!*" she screams, her whole body shaking so badly my gut jumps into my throat when I see how closely the shirt veers toward the flames. "*Fugging choose already, sheesh!*"

And even though she means it, even though her eyes blaze with rage, I just look at her and shake my head.

"Fine." She glares. "If you two won't choose, then I'll choose for you. But just remember, you had your chance."

She turns toward Jude, her lips parting as though she's about to say something, something that might be *good-bye* or *good luck* or *good riddance* or—or anything of the sort.

But it's not real.

She's trying to throw us all off.

Make us think Jude's not long for this world when she couldn't care less about him.

It's *me* she wants to hurt.

It's *me* she wants to destroy.

And she's determined to take all of my hopes and dreams along with it.

So I lunge.

Just as Damen lunges to save Jude, and Jude lunges to kill Haven.

Coiling his fingers into a fist, aiming right for the very center of her torso—her third chakra—her one major weak spot—just like I taught him.

Only it doesn't connect.

Damen inadvertently catches him in midflight and knocks him off course at the very last second.

While Miles instinctively, nobly, foolishly, rushes forward to help me, only to get caught in Haven's snare as she grips the shirt in one hand and her best childhood friend in the other.

Her fingers squeezing tightly around his neck as Miles kicks and gasps and struggles to free himself.

And one look in her eyes is all it takes to see that she means it.

To see just how dark and evil she's become.

Everything they've shared means nothing to her.

She has every intention of killing him if for no other reason than to hurt me.

To force me into choosing, whether I like it or not.

Flashing me one last, horrible grin as she squeezes Miles so hard his eyes are about to burst from his head—simultaneously shrieking with delight as she drops the shirt into the blazing fire where it's greedily met by the flames.

All of it happening so quickly, in less than a fraction of a second, though it seems to play out in slow motion before me.

Her face looming, hateful and obscene, gleaming with the victory, the absolute thrill—of getting to me.

So while Damen untangles himself from Jude, I draw back

my fist, recalling the manifested version of this scene I re-hearsed all those months ago, and noting how it's nothing like the all-too-real version that plays out before me.

Mostly because I have no regrets.

No reason to apologize.

No choice but to kill her before she kills Miles.

I slam my knuckles straight into her chest, feeling it connect smack into the sweet spot.

Seeing the flash of shock in her gaze, as Damen snatches Miles from her grasp, and I leap into the flames.

My flesh scorching, burning, bubbling, peeling—the pain white hot and agonizingly searing.

Though I pay it no notice.

I just keep going, reaching, grasping, seeking.

All of my focus narrowed down to this one single thing—trying to save the shirt—even though it's clearly too late.

Even though it's been swallowed whole, consumed by the flames, leaving no trace that it ever existed.

Vaguely aware of the sound of Miles's and Jude's frantic cries coming from somewhere behind me.

Vaguely aware of Damen's arms grasping, holding, soothing, pulling me out of the fire and smothering the raging inferno that's consuming my clothes, my hair, my flesh.

Pulling me tightly to his chest, whispering into my ear over and over again that it'll all be okay. That he'll find a way. That the shirt doesn't matter. The important thing is that Miles and Jude are safe and we still have each other.

Begging me to close my eyes, to look the other way, to avoid the hideous sight of my staggering, gasping, dying, former best friend.

But I don't listen.

I allow my eyes to meet hers.

Taking in her snarl of hair, her blazing red gaze, her sunken cheeks, her emaciated body, her crazed expression, and her voice filled with absolute, all-consuming hatred when she screams, "This is *your* fault, Ever. *You're* the one who made me this way! And now you're gonna pay for this—I swear you're gonna—"

Unable to stop looking even after she crumbles, and breaks, and swiftly slips away.

thirty-nine

"You had to do it." Damen looks at me, mouth grim, brow creased with concern. "You did the right thing, you had no choice."

"Oh, there's always a choice." I sigh, meeting his gaze. "But the only thing I feel badly about is who she became, the way she chose to handle her power, her immortality. I don't feel badly about the choice that I made. I *know* I did the right thing."

I drop my head on Damen's shoulder and allow his arm to slip around me. Thinking how even though I know I made the only real choice that I could under the circumstances, that doesn't make it any easier. Though I choose not to voice that, not wanting to worry Damen any further.

"You know, one of my acting coaches used to say that you can tell a lot about a person from how they handle times of great stress." Miles glances between us, his neck still roughed up and red, his voice hoarse and scratchy, but thankfully, he's well on the mend. "He said true character is revealed by the way people react to the bigger challenges in life. And while I definitely agree with that, I also think the same can be said of how people handle power. I mean, I hate to say it, but I'm really not all that surprised by the way Haven reacted. I think we all know she had it in her. We went all the way back to elementary school, and as far as I can remember, she always had this really dark side. She was always driven by her jealousies and insecurities, and, I guess what I'm trying to say is, *you* didn't make her that way, Ever." He looks at me, his bloodshot eyes and pale face bearing his distress at losing his friend—at almost being killed by his friend—but still desperate for me to believe it. "She just was who she was. And once she realized her power, once she started thinking she was invincible, well, she just became *even more* of who she was."

I look at Miles, silently nodding my thanks.

Then I sneak a quick peek at Jude, who's off in the corner searching through the large stack of oil paintings propped up against the wall, determined to keep quiet, keep to himself, feeling responsible for everything that just happened, and mentally kicking himself for yet again messing with my plans in a pretty big way.

And yet, even though I wish he hadn't done what he did, even though it definitely resulted in disaster on a colossal scale, I also know he didn't do it on purpose. Despite his tendency to interfere in my life, always managing to come between me and the one thing I want most in this world, it's not like he's *trying* to get in the way. It's not like it's the least bit intentional. In fact, it almost seems as though he's *driven* to do it.

As though he's being guided by some higher force—even though I'm not even sure what that means.

"So, anyway, what should we do with all of the rest of it?" Miles asks, having already helped Damen and me collect Roman's journals, or at least all the ones we could find.

The last thing we need is for someone else to stumble upon them, and read the firsthand account of one very flamboyant person's very flamboyant (and flamboyantly long!) flamboyant life—even if they probably would just assume it was a work of over-the-top fiction.

"We box it up and give it to charity, I guess," Damen says, smoothing his hand over my back as he gazes around a house that's completely jammed with all manner of antiques from all different periods. Basically everything that was once kept in storage or at the store has been moved here. Though it's anyone's guess what Haven planned to do with it. "Or we have an estate sale and donate the money to charity." He shrugs, seeming a little overwhelmed by the task.

Unlike Roman, Damen was never a hoarder. He managed to exist for centuries with only the items he needed at the time, while saving only those that truly meant something to him. But then, Damen knows how to manifest. He knows just how plentiful the universe really is. While Roman never mastered that gift, probably didn't even know it was possible, and instead became greedy, believing there was never enough, and that if he didn't snatch something up, then someone else would, so he'd better get to it first. And the only time he was ever willing to release or let go of anything was when it resulted in great profit for him.

"Then again, if you see anything you really want, feel free to take it," he adds. "Otherwise, I see no reason to keep it, I have no interest in any of it."

"You sure about that?" Jude asks, speaking up for the first

time since it all happened. Since I killed my former best friend and sent her straight to the Shadowland. "No interest in *anything*? Not even *this*?"

I turn, we all turn, only to find Jude standing before us, spliced brow raised, dimples on full display, as he holds up a canvas revealing a glorious, vibrant oil painting of a beautiful titian-haired girl twirling in a never-ending field of red tulips.

I gasp. Swallowing a huge mouthful of air, instantly recognizing the girl as *me*—the *me* of my Amsterdam life—but unsure who the artist could be.

"It's beautiful, isn't it?" Jude gazes between us, though his eyes land on me. "In case you're wondering, it's signed by Damen." He motions toward the hand-scrawled scribble in the lower right corner. Shaking his head as he adds, "I was good in my former life, no doubt about that. From what I've seen in Summerland, Bastiaan de Kool certainly had his share of talent—he lived a pretty good life too." He smiles. "But still, as hard as I tried, I could never quite *capture* you in the way Damen did." He shrugs. "I just couldn't seem to master that—*technique*."

He hands me the painting as my eyes continue to graze over it. Seeing how it's all there—me, the tulips, and even though Damen's not pictured, I can still *feel* his presence.

Can *see* the love he held for me in every last brushstroke.

"I wouldn't be so quick to just box it all up without taking a really good look at least," Jude says. "Who knows what other treasures can be found here?"

"You mean, like *this*?" Miles slips into the black silk smoking jacket Roman wore on the night of my seventeenth birthday—the night that came so close to going so tragically wrong—until I finally found the courage, the strength in my heart, to push him right off me. "Should I keep it?" he asks, tying the sash tightly around his waist and striking a series of fashion-model–type poses. "I mean, if I'm ever asked to audition for a role as Hugh Hefner, I'll have the perfect thing to wear!"

And I start to say *no*.

Start to ask him to please just take it off and put it away.

Start to explain how it holds far too many bad memories for me.

But then I remember what Damen once said about memories—that they're haunting things.

And because I refuse to be haunted by mine—I just take a deep breath and smile when I say, "You know, I think it looks really good on you. You should definitely keep it."

forty

"Do you think anyone's ever done this here before?"

I kneel down, my knees sinking into the leftover dirt from the hole I just dug, as I glance up at Damen beside me. The rich, moist soil providing a nice cushion as I lean forward and place the velvet-lined box containing all that remains of Haven—her jewelry and clothing—into the space I just made, as Damen looks on.

"Summerland is a very old place." He sighs, his voice tight, filled with unease and concern. "I'm sure most things have been tried at least once."

He places his hand on my shoulder, and I can *feel* the worry streaming off him. He's worried that I'm only pretending to be fine with my choice. Convinced that deep down inside I'm not nearly as okay as I claim.

But even though I'm left incredibly saddened by my actions, I don't doubt them or question them for a second.

I'm no longer that girl.

I've finally learned to place my trust in my *self*, to listen to my *gut,* to heed my own overwhelming *instincts,* and, be-cause of it, I'm at peace with what I now know I had to do. Even if it means one more lost soul has been sent to the Shadowland, Haven was far too dangerous to be allowed to continue.

But that doesn't mean I don't want to honor her.

That doesn't mean I can't still hold out a bit of hope for her.

Having recently been there myself (thanks to her), I know exactly what she's going through. Falling—floating—forced to watch the mistakes of her past, over and over again. And if I was ready to learn from it and better myself, well, maybe she can do so as well.

Maybe the Shadowland only *feels* like an eternity spent alone in the abyss.

Maybe there really is a second chance at some point—a shot at redemption for a newly rehabbed soul?

I lift the lid off the box, wanting to take one last glimpse at the sky-high boots, the skintight minidress, the tangle of jewels—all of them blue—the dangling earrings, and the pile of rings, including the silver skull ring she wore back on the day we first met.

Back when neither one of us could've ever imagined our friendship ending like this.

Then, just before I close it, I manifest a single red-velvet cupcake with pink sprinkles that I place right on top. Remembering how it was her favorite, one of the earlier, more harmless addictions she so happily indulged.

Damen kneels down beside me, squinting between the cupcake and me when he says, "What's that for?"

I take a deep breath, take one last look, then close the lid again. Scooping up heaping handfuls of loose dirt that I let fall through my fingers and onto the top when I say, "Just a little reminder of the old Haven, the way she was back when we first met."

Damen hesitates, studying me carefully. "And who's this reminder for—her or you?" he asks.

I turn, eyes grazing over his jaw, his cheekbones, his nose, his lips, saving the eyes for last, I say, "The universe. It's silly, I know, but I'm just hoping a sweet little reminder will convince it to go easy on her."

forty-one

"Where to now?" Damen wipes the dirt from his jeans, as I shrug, and gaze all around. Knowing the pavilion's out, it would be grossly inappropriate after everything that just went down, and it's not like I want to go home anytime soon . . .

He looks at me, having just heard the thought, so I decide to fess up and say, "It's not like I don't know I have to go home eventually, but trust me, there will be *major* hell to pay when I do."

I shake my head, allowing the whole ugly scene with Sabine to stream from my mind to his, including the part just after I stormed out of the house, when I manifested a bouquet of daffodils and a BMW right in Munoz's view, and seeing Damen wince at the sight of it.

Suddenly getting a whole new idea though not quite sure how to approach it, I glance all around us and say, "But maybe—" I pause, knowing he's not going to like it, but resolved to broach it anyway. "I mean, it's just a thought, but what do you say we go visit that dark side again?"

I peer at him, seeing him reply with an *are you crazy?* look, and, yeah, maybe I am. But I also have a theory, and I'm eager to see if I'm right.

"I just . . . there's something I want to see," I tell him, knowing he's still a long way from convinced.

"So let me get this straight." He rakes his hand through his hair. "You want us to go visit that creepy part of Summerland, where there's no magick, no manifesting, nothing much of anything other than a steady supply of rain, a bunch of burnt-out foliage, miles and miles of deep, swampy mud that practically doubles as quicksand, and, oh yeah, some creepy old lady who's obviously gone completely mad, and who, as it just so happens, is totally fixated on *you*?"

I nod. That about sums it up.

"You'd rather do *that* than deal with Sabine?"

I nod again and this time I lift my shoulders too.

"Can I ask why?"

"Sure." I smile. "But I probably won't answer 'til we get there, so just trust me, okay? There's something I need to see first."

He looks at me, obviously reluctant to go through with it but even more reluctant to deny me, he quickly manifests a horse for us to ride as I close my eyes and urge him to take us to the darkest, dreariest part of this place.

And the next thing I know, we're there. Our mount coming to a crashing halt as Damen and I fight to stay on his back. Rearing and bucking and pawing the earth, forcing Damen to coo softly into his ear, assuring him he need go no farther, and calming him down enough for us to slide off his back and have a good look around.

"So, just like we remembered it," Damen says, eager to ditch this place for somewhere warmer, brighter, better.

"But is it?" I venture toward the spot where the mud begins, tapping my foot softly against it. Testing its softness, its deepness, trying to determine if it's changed in some way.

"I don't know what you're getting at." He peers at me. "But as far as I can see, it's just as wet, barren, muddy, and depressing as the last time we were here."

I nod. "That's all true, but does it somehow seem . . . *bigger* to you? Like, I don't know, like it's . . . *growing* or *expanding* in some way?"

He squints, not quite following where I'm going with this, and knowing I'll risk sounding crazy or, at the very worst, completely paranoid, I still choose to go ahead with it anyway, since I could really use a second opinion.

"I've got this theory—"

He looks at me.

"Well—" I take a deep breath and gaze all around. "I can't help but think that I might somehow be the cause of all this."

"*You?*" Damen squints, brows merged with concern.

But I look right past it and quickly continue. Desperate to finish, to get the words out before I have enough time to really stop and listen to myself, before I lose all my nerve. "Look," I say, voice tense and hurried. "I mean, I know it sounds stupid, but please hear me out first."

He nods and flashes his palms, showing he has no plans to stop me.

"I'm thinking that maybe . . . well, maybe this place started growing when all the bad things started happening."

"Bad things?"

"Yeah, you know, like when I killed Drina."

"Ever—" he starts, eager to dispel it, to erase all the blame.

But before he can finish, I'm talking again. "I mean, you've been coming here for a really long time now, right?"

"Since the sixties." He shrugs.

"Okay, right, and so, I'm sure that during all this time you've looked around a good bit, did your fair share of exploring, especially back in the beginning."

He nods.

"And during those times, you said you'd never seen anything like this, right?"

He nods and sighs, though he's also quick to add, "But then again, Summerland is a *very big* place. It's quite possibly infinite for all I know. It's not like I've ever come across any kinds of walls or borders, so it's quite possible it's been here all along and I missed it."

I look away, trying to act as though I'm more than willing to drop it if he is, but I'm not the least bit convinced.

I can't help feeling there's something here that's either *caused* by me or that I'm *meant* to see, or *both*. I mean, that's what got me here in the first place. I simply asked the Summerland what it wanted me to know about it and it landed me here. But what I don't know is *why*.

Is it somehow connected to all of those souls that, because of me, have ended up in the Shadowland?

Are they somehow making it grow?

Like adding fertilizer to a batch of weeds?

And if so, does that mean it will continue to encroach and maybe even take over the rest of Summerland?

"Ever," Damen says. "We can explore if you want, but

there's really not much to see, is there? It seems like it's just more and more of the same, doesn't it?"

I gaze all around, reluctant to give up so easily, and yet not really knowing what I'm looking for, or even how to go about proving my theory. So I start to turn away. Start to move toward him again when I hear it.

The song.

Drifting from behind me, as though carried by a long and distant breeze, but still there's no mistaking it.

No mistaking the voice—the words—the eerily haunting tune.

And I know without looking it's *her*.

Turning to find her pointing finger, her crooked, gnarled hand, raised high as she sings:

> *From the mud it shall rise*
> *Lifting upward toward vast dreamy skies*
> *Just as you-you-you shall rise too . . .*

Only this time, she continues, adding more lines she definitely didn't sing the last time we were here:

> *From the deep and dark depths*
> *It struggles toward the light*
> *Desiring only one thing*
> *The truth!*
> *The truth of its being*
> *But will you let it?*
> *Will you let it rise and blossom and grow?*
> *Or will you damn it to the depths?*
> *Will you banish its worn and weary soul?*

And just when I'm thinking it's over, she does the weirdest thing.

She holds her hands up before her, cupping them as though anticipating some kind of offering, as Misa and Marco suddenly step out from behind her and stand on either side.

The two of them flanking her, gazing intently upon me, as the old woman closes her eyes in deep concentration as though trying to manifest something spectacular.

But all she gets for her efforts is a spray of gray ash that emanates from the center of her palms and falls gently to her feet.

And when she lifts her gaze to meet mine, her face appears stricken, as her eyes stare accusingly.

Damen grasps my arm and quickly pulls me away. Away from her. Away from *them*. Desperate to escape this creepy scene.

Both of us clueless as to who she is, where she came from, or what the song could possibly mean.

Both of us having no idea what her connection to Misa and Marco might be.

Only one thing is clear—the song is a warning.

The words intended for *me* to heed.

To hear.

She continues to sing, her voice soft, melodic, her words chasing behind us as we run back to our horse.

Back to the place of magick and manifesting and everything good.

Back to the relative safety of the earth plane, where we land side by side on a stark empty beach.

Our hands loosely clasped as we lie back on the sand and

fight to catch our breath. Trying to make sense of the words, the disturbing scene we just witnessed.

Gazing up at a black, moonless sky bearing not one single star.

My night star is gone.

And for a moment, I'm overcome by this horrible, foreboding feeling that it'll never return.

But then Damen whispers my name, his voice piercing the silence, piercing my thoughts.

And when I turn on my side to face him, seeing the way his face looms before me, his gaze filled with such reverence, so loving and kind—my mind floods with relief.

My night star is no longer here because I'm no longer in need of it.

The two of us shine in its place.

"That song is for me," I tell him, voicing the words I know in my heart to be true. "Haven's death, losing the shirt . . ." I pause and take a deep breath, feeling the assuring warmth of his finger as it gently traces my cheek. "It's all part of my karma. And now, apparently, there's something more I'm meant to do."

Damen starts to speak, eager to comfort, to refute it, to erase the concern from my face.

But I'm quick to stop him, bringing my finger to his lips.

I've no need for those words.

Whatever the old woman sings about, I'm ready to face it.

Only later, not now.

"We'll deal with it," I say, my words at his cheek as I pull Damen to me. "Together, we'll deal with everything. But for now . . ." My lips meet his, lingering as I savor the soft, sweet, *almost* feel of them. "For now let's just be grateful for *this*."

Destiny is within reach . . .

Don't miss the final book
in the Immortals series

Everlasting

Coming Summer 2011